THE GINZA GHOST

Paul Halter books from Locked Room International:
The Lord of Misrule (2010)
The Fourth Door (2011)
The Seven Wonders of Crime (2011)
The Demon of Dartmoor (2012)
The Seventh Hypothesis (2012)
The Tiger's Head (2013)
The Crimson Fog (2013)
(Publisher's Weekly Top Mystery 2013 List)
The Night of the Wolf (2013)*
The Invisible Circle (2014)
The Picture from the Past (2014)
The Phantom Passage (2015)
Death Invites You (2016)
The Vampire Tree (2016)
(Publisher's Weekly Top Mystery 2016 List)

Original short story collection published by Wildside Press (2006)

Other impossible crime novels from Locked Room International:
The Riddle of Monte Verita (Jean-Paul Torok) 2012
The Killing Needle (Henry Cauvin) 2014
The Derek Smith Omnibus (Derek Smith) 2014
(Washington Post Top Fiction Books 2014)
The House That Kills (Noel Vindry) 2015
The Decagon House Murders (Yukito Ayatsuji) 2015
(Publisher's Weekly Top Mystery 2015 List)
Hard Cheese (Ulf Durling) 2015
(Crime Fiction Lovers Top 10 Nordic Noir 2016 List)
The Moai Island Puzzle (Alice Arisugawa) 2016
(Washington Post Summer Book List 2016)
The Howling Beast (Noel Vindry) 2016
Death in the Dark (Stacey Bishop) 2017

Visit our website at www.mylri.com or
www.lockedroominternational.com

THE GINZA GHOST

Keikichi Osaka

Translated by Ho-Ling Wong

The Ginza Ghost

This book is a work of fiction. The characters, incidents, and dialogue are drawn from the author's imagination and are not to be construed as real. Any resemblance to actual events or persons, living or dead, is entirely coincidental.

First published in Japanese in *Kaizō, Kitan, Profile, Shinseinen, Shin Tantei Shōsetsu and Teishin Kyōkai Zasshi*, between 1932 and 1947.
THE GINZA GHOST

For information, contact: pugmire1@yahoo.com

FIRST AMERICAN EDITION
Library of Congress Cataloguing-in-Publication Data
Osaka, Keikichi
[Twelve short stories]
The Ginza Ghost / Keikichi Ōsaka
Translated from the Japanese by Ho-Ling Wong

Contents

INTRODUCTION

Taku Ashibe

"Is there any other Japanese writer who has shown such pure, such persistent love and understanding of the orthodox detective short story? Is there any other Japanese writer who has shown such profound mastery of the intelligent detective story?" - Rampo Edogawa (1936)

"And I was shocked. Were there any other writers who could write such pure, *honkaku* short stories as he had done? I even felt enraged at the fact his works had been ignored." - Tetsuya Ayukawa (1975)

"He had a dream. His dreams were made out of tricks and logic. He poured all the unique experiences he had come across inside this fantastic mould he had of his dreams, and with that he gave life to his flawless creations." - Masa'aki Tatsumi (2001)

Keikichi Ōsaka was by no means a fortunate writer. He was too short-lived for that, and most of his career overlapped with the period in history when detective novels were ostracised. However, his works, which had been presumed forgotten, were then dug up by *honkaku*[1] mystery fiction aficionados, such as the writer Tetsuya Ayukawa. Now Ōsaka's stories are received warmly by a whole new generation of readers, as if they had been written only yesterday. From a certain point of view, one could even say that there are no writers as fortunate as he.

Keikichi Ōsaka (real name: Fukutarō Suzuki) was born on March 20th, 1912, in the city of Araki in Aichi Prefecture. After graduating from a commercial school, he published *The Hangman of the Department Store* in the magazine *Shinseinen* (*The New Youth*) in

---

[1] Translator's Note: *Honkaku* (orthodox) mystery fiction refers to a form of detective fiction that is as much literature as it is an intelligent game, where fair play and logic are deemed its greatest qualities. The term was first coined by Saburō Kōga in the 1920s.

1932 on the recommendation of mystery writer Saburō Kōga. It is said his pen name was derived from the way his younger brother signed his letters, "From Ōsaka. Keiji," which made an impression on him.

After his debut, he published short stories prolifically in the few detective story magazines that existed at the time, and his first book *Shi no Kaisōsen* (*Yacht of Death*) was published in 1936. In the same year, he published one story after another in *Shinseinen* for six months straight starting with *The Three Madmen*. This was an opportunity offered only to the most promising of writers. His deep, intellectual style and his penchant for coming up with the strangest incidents from commonplace settings like modern city life or worksites in the mountains or near the sea, were not, however, met with much support from his own generation.

In addition, with the start of the Sino-Japanese War in 1937, people started to consider the western-style fictional detective story as an undesirable element in society. Ignorant concerns were raised, claiming that the detective story constituted a danger, as tales about Japanese people wounding and killing each other would suggest that public order in the country was in disarray.

For this reason, Ōsaka had no choice but make the switch to comedy and spy stories. He kept on writing, but was finally drafted in 1943, and sent as a soldier to China, and afterwards to the Philippines.

He died on Luzon Island on July 2nd, 1945 (some sources say September), having succumbed to a disease under the very harsh circumstances. If he had survived, he would have been witness to the revival of the detective story in Japan after World War II. And the style most coveted in that revival period was the *honkaku* mystery story he had mastered.

Sadly, the Japanese detective story moved on after the war without Ōsaka, and in time his name was forgotten. But, more than thirty years after his death, his works started to be rediscovered and included in new anthologies, introducing him to a new generation. And, once the internet generation started, Keikichi Ōsaka fan sites sprang up, where information about him and his works was exchanged. This development led to several new publications of his work.

The stories in this collection are a selection from Ōsaka's *oeuvre* focusing mainly on his impossible crime stories, but also including two of his best whodunits. I will give a short introduction to each story below in order of appearance.

The Hangman of the Department Store (1932) is Ōsaka's debut work, and also the first story in his Great Detective Kyōsuke Aoyama series. The setting is the department store, a facility which had made its appearance in the modern cities of Japan, serving as a brand new space for consumers and entertainment. A person strangled to death is thrown off a department store roof in the middle of night, his body covered in mysterious wounds. It would have been impossible for anyone to enter the store from outside, but it doesn't appear as though any of the persons inside the store could have been responsible for the crime, either. What Aoyama deduces with the help of his magnifying glass is a truly ironic and grotesque truth.

The Phantasm of the Stone Wall (1935) is the fifth work in the Kyōsuke Aoyama series. A woman is murdered in front of her home on an incredibly hot and stuffy summer day, and two men dressed in white kimonos are seen running away from the scene of the crime. But another witness coming from the other side of the road says he did not see them. Twin brothers are arrested, based on the footprints at the crime scene and the testimonies of witnesses. However, neither of them actually committed the murder: another, single individual was responsible. What made the midsummer illusion possible?

In *The Mourning Locomotive* (1934), we are introduced to the workers in a railway locomotive depot. Cleaning away the remains after a deadly accident is just part of the daily routine for these people, but even they are surprised when one pig after another gets run over. And it's always the same locomotive and the same operators which are involved. Meanwhile, we are introduced to a mysterious girl in a shop in a nearby town who is always looking outside through one of the windows.... The ending of the story is truly tragic and explains how this harrowing and puzzling case is due to the indescribable feelings of human beings. Many people consider this "crimeless tale of mystery" to be Ōsaka's masterpiece.

In *The Monster of the Lighthouse* (1935), a baffling series of events occurs in a lighthouse standing on a lonely cape in an isolated part of the sea. The top of the lighthouse is partially destroyed by a gigantic rock, and a monster, similar to a red octopus, is seen diving into the sea. It does not seem as though the monstrous destruction could have been the work of any human being, but Saburō Azumaya, the director of a nearby marine laboratory, manages to propose a perfectly logical explanation of the seemingly supernatural happenings, which also have a painful human side to them.

The Phantom Wife (1947) was published posthumously. In order to fully appreciate the story, it's important to understand the form of many Japanese ghost stories. Often, poor, weak women are cruelly tortured and killed by their despotic husbands, and only after their demise do they finally get the opportunity for revenge. Once they become ghosts, they leave their belongings around, together with their typically female footprints, scaring their enemies and the people around them. Also keep in mind that, in the time period when the story takes place, many traditional objects which had once been used and worn by both men and women had become mostly associated with women alone, as men had been faster at adapting to Western clothing styles.

The Mesmerising Light (1936) starts off with the exciting, impossible phenomenon of a car disappearing from a mountain road which had been sealed off at both ends. The explanation for the car's disappearance is still itself within the bounds of normal common sense, but the explanation of how the situation arose and the explanation of the midnight illusion are truly unique. We are presented with our third great detective after Aoyama and Azumaya: the attorney Taiji Ōtsuki who manages to solve the mystery of the murder which lies behind the accident from a simple glance at the murder weapon.

The Cold Night's Clearing (1936) is an eerie tale which occurs on a winter's night. A set of ski tracks leads away from a chaotic murder scene into an empty field covered by snow. The tracks become shallower and shallower and eventually disappear, as if the murderer and the child they had kidnapped had flown off into the sky.... However, the truth of the case is beyond imagination. Let me add also that the fate of the child in this story is not unheard of, even in modern Japanese society.

The Three Madmen (1936) is one of Keikichi Ōsaka's best known short stories and the critical reception at the time of publication was exceptional, even though it is, in a sense, a very orthodox whodunit. In it, the logic of both sane and insane people vie for contention, and once these two kinds of logic switch position, a very surprising culprit is revealed. The idea of drawing parallels between reality and fantasy throughout the tale of a crime and its solution was unknown at the time the story was published. There is a reason why people in later generations grew appreciative of Keikichi Ōsaka.

The Guardian of the Lighthouse (1936) was published several months after *The Monster of the Lighthouse*, in a magazine for organisations related to the Ministry of Communications, which controlled the mail, telephone, telegraph and lighthouses, and also uses the structure of the lighthouse in the plot. Perhaps Ōsaka tried his hand at this variation because the intended readers of this story were different from the people who usually read literary magazines like *Shinseinen*, where *The Monster of the Lighthouse* had been published. The horrible truth behind the disappearance of a person here is a simpler take on a theme often examined in Ōsaka's stories: the relation between human beings and machinery, nature and other phenomena.

The Demon in the Mine (1937) is the final story Ōsaka contributed as a *honkaku* mystery writer. A single miner is sacrificed in the name of safety inside a coal mine with extremely harsh working conditions. But then one death after another occurs, suggesting that the spirit of this miner is killing off the people who sealed him up inside a tunnel. And what does the line 'We hit the sea!' mean? This "locked room" story with human greed and Mother Nature as its background is of a scale not previously seen when the story was first released.

The Hungry Letter-Box (1939) was written as a spy story, but one can also clearly recognise Ōsaka's other side as a comedy author. What makes the story interesting is how Ōsaka uses the character of a spy as the person planning a unique crime and creating an impossible situation. I think it proves how good a detective writer Ōsaka really was.

The Ginza Ghost (1936) starts with a murder in the backstreets of Ginza, the number one amusement area in Tōkyō, both in the present and the past. The crime happens on the first floor of a tobacco shop, witnessed by the waitresses of the bar directly opposite on the other side of the street. Two bodies are soon discovered, but while it appears to be clear who must have killed whom, medical examination concludes that the murderer had died much earlier than her victim! How could that be possible? Yet it is, simply by looking at things in a slightly different manner—a magic trick that only Keikichi Ōsaka could have pulled off.

Keikichi Ōsaka wrote many other detective story masterpieces in addition to those collected here. Their settings vary from the brilliant setting of the modern city, with locations such as department stores, amusement areas and newly developed scenic driveways, to the Spartan worksites of the period, such as lighthouses, mines and whaling ships. While there are no gothic mansions or village communities cursed by some peculiar tradition in his stories, the incidents which do occur in his unremarkable settings are all unique and brimming with imagination.

What is singularly unique in the world of Keikichi Ōsaka is that humans aren't the only entities which can commit impossible crimes and create baffling mysteries. It is not unusual for even inhuman things to lay a trap for humans, or for humans to become one with machinery.

What makes this all so surprising is that all of these ideas and themes of Ōsaka have been turned into true *honkaku* detective stories, and that a young man in this twenties accomplished all of that in just a couple of years. It is nothing short of a miracle.

As previously mentioned, Keikichi Ōsaka was ill-starred enough to have been forced to turn away from his chosen path of detective fiction, after which the cruel hand of Fate struck him down at the tender age of thirty-three. Rumour has it that he visited Saburō Kōga before he was drafted into military service, and that he entrusted Kōga with the manuscript of a novel-length detective story he had written in secret. Unfortunately, Kōga passed away suddenly shortly afterwards, and to this day the manuscript has not been discovered.

Could that manuscript have been a *honkaku* mystery story, the genre he had given his heart to, but had been forced to abandon? If so, can you begin to imagine the kinds of tricks and logic he would have used, and the miracles and illusions he would have showcased? All we can do is to read the works collected in this book and his other works, and fantasise about the contents of that lost novel.

And so I sincerely hope that people in the English-speaking world will learn about Japanese *honkaku* mystery and one of its greatest pioneers.

Taku Ashibe Tokyo 2016

Taku Ashibe is the author of more than twenty mystery novels and was the first recipient of the Ayukawa Tetsuya Award (western name Tetsuya Ayukawa).

The English-language version of his novel *Kōrōmu no Satsujin: Murder in the Red Chamber* was published in 2012 by Kurodahan Press.

PUBLISHER'S NOTE:

Ōsaka's stories were written in a period when various measurement standards were used in Japan, depending on the industry. The Japanese government was encouraging the use of the metric system, but this was not uniformly followed. It was not unusual to see metres and kilograms mixed with traditional Japanese measures in the same text, as happens in several of these stories.

Nevertheless, to avoid excessive interruptions and footnotes, the most frequently mentioned Japanese units are listed below, together with their approximate western equivalents:

1 *chō*	120 yards	109 m.
1 *jō*	10 feet	3.03 m.
1 *ken*	6 feet	1.818m.
1 *shaku*	1 foot	30.3 cm.
1 *sun*	1.2 inches	3.03 cm.
1 tsubo	36 square feet	3.3 sq. metres
1 *tatami* mat	3ft x 6ft (18 sf.)	1.65 sq. metres
1 *kan*	8 1/4 lbs	3.75 kg.
1 *monme*	1/8 oz.	3.75 gm.

THE HANGMAN OF THE DEPARTMENT STORE

The incident happened approximately two months after I'd first made the acquaintance of Kyōsuke Aoyama at a film preview. I think it was a German film.

I'd received a phone call from my company at five-thirty in the morning, and Kyōsuke and I had hurriedly taken a taxi to the R Department Store, in order to gather the news about an apparent suicide of somebody who had leapt off the building earlier that morning.

Kyōsuke was three years my senior and had once been renowned as a highly original film director, but he'd been unable to accommodate the interests of the common film-viewing public or the crass commercialism of the industry, so he'd retired and now spent a quiet life studying whatever interested him. He was of steadfast character, yet often surprised me with his highly-developed sensitivity and great powers of imagination. But he also possessed an extraordinary analytical mind and had developed a wealth of knowledge in many fields of science.

In the early days of our friendship, I'd planned to use his amazing knowledge for my own benefit, to assist me in my work. But, as the months passed, my designs soon turned into feelings of admiration and respect, so I decided to leave my hometown lodgings for the apartment building where he lived and move into the room next to his. That goes to show how fascinated I was by the man called Kyōsuke Aoyama.

It was only ten past six when we arrived at our destination. The victim had fallen to his death at the rear of the department store and his body lay in an alley facing northeast. The alley was already full of nearby merchants, workers and early-rising passers-by, who were gazing up towards the roof of the store and chattering amongst themselves.

The blood on the asphalt had already started drying and the body had been placed temporarily in a storeroom of the Purchasing Department. The medical examination was already over by the time we entered the room. My cousin, who had been promoted to the position of senior police detective of the XX Police Station, welcomed us. He explained that it wasn't actually a suicide case but a homicide case, because the victim, a twenty-eight year old single man called Tatsuichi Noguchi, had been strangled. He'd worked as a cashier in the jewellery department, and a valuable pearl necklace, decorated with a number of diamonds, had been lying near where the body had landed. The necklace had been one of two items which had disappeared two days ago from that department, and the body and the necklace had been discovered at four o'clock in the morning by a guard making his rounds. My cousin announced—not without some self-satisfaction—that he himself was leading the investigation, and we were given permission to approach the body and study it for ourselves.

The sight reminded me of a poppy flower. The skull had been pulverised and the face was distorted and coloured in a ghastly manner by the dried-up red-black blood. Violent strangulation marks could be seen on the neck, the ashen skin had ripped open in several places, and blood had seeped into the collar of the victim's terry cloth pyjamas. The clothes had been opened for the medical examination, and there were welts running crisscross over the pale chest. A rib on the left side of the chest, following the line of one of the welts, had been cruelly broken. Furthermore, countless painful-looking abrasions and grazes had been left on the exposed parts of the body: both palms, the shoulders, the lower chin, the elbows and more. The terrycloth pyjamas had also been torn in several places.

While I was taking down notes about the horrible sight, Kyōsuke boldly touched the body's palms and made careful observations of the grazes and the strangulation marks on the neck.

'How much time has passed since his death?' asked Kyōsuke, straightening up. The medical examiner, who had been observing him with curiosity, replied:

'Probably six or seven hours.'

'So that means he was murdered between ten and eleven o'clock last night. And when was he thrown off the building?'

'Based on the coagulation of the bloodstains in the alley and on the head of the victim, I'd say it was no later than three o'clock in the morning. Pedestrians were using that alley until at least midnight, so I think we can limit it to sometime between midnight and three o'clock.'

'I agree. Another question: why is the victim wearing pyjamas? He wasn't working here as the night guard, was he?'

The medical examiner couldn't answer Kyōsuke's question. One of the six store clerks—now dressed in pyjamas—who had been questioned by my cousin the senior police detective, replied instead:

'Noguchi was indeed on night duty last night. Our department store has a special rule, whereby people from each department must also take shifts as night guards. Of the people working in the store, Noguchi and I were on duty last night, as well as the five over there, making seven in all. We were joined by the three caretakers over there, making ten in total. The seven of us all stayed in the same night guard's office. But we don't really know each other that well. You want to know about last night? As you may know, we're open until nine o'clock every evening. We close at nine o'clock, and it takes a good forty minutes after that before everything goes quiet in the store. By the time we had locked everything up, switched off all the lights and gone to bed, it was already almost ten o'clock. After he'd changed into his pyjamas, Noguchi went out again alone, but I assumed he was going to the bathroom, so I didn't think anything of it. I slept soundly until four o'clock in the morning, when a policeman woke me up. Oh, by the way, the night guard's office for the caretakers is in a different place from ours. They're on the ground floor and we're at the rear of the second floor. The door that leads from the fifth floor to the roof? No, it's not locked.'

After the clerk had finished his testimony, Kyōsuke asked the eight other persons on night watch whether they had anything to add, but none of them had anything of significance. One person, who worked at the children's clothing department, said he'd had a toothache last night and hadn't fallen asleep until one o'clock. He hadn't noticed that Tatsuichi Noguchi's bed had been empty all the time, nor had he heard anything suspicious.

Kyōsuke continued with a question about the necklace, and this time it was the head of the jewellery department who answered, wiping his face with a handkerchief to mop up the perspiration.

'I was surprised by the news and hurried here immediately. Noguchi was a good man. It's a terrible thing that's happened. He wasn't someone who got on the wrong side of people. The theft of the necklace? No, I can't believe Noguchi could have had anything to do with it. The necklace disappeared from the shop the night before last, you see, around closing time. The necklace and another item, two in total. Together, they're worth precisely twenty thousand *yen*. Based on the circumstances, I suspect the thief was one of our customers, because we searched not only the people who work in the jewellery department, but every employee in the building, from head to toe. It's been a very busy two days. And now it has ended like this. I'm utterly perplexed.'

Transportation for the body arrived just as he finished. The three caretakers who had been on night watch lifted the heavy-looking body up and, with unsteady steps and anxious expressions on their faces, carried it out of the room. Kyōsuke stared at the sight for a while, as if he had things left undone. Eventually he turned around, slapped me on the shoulder and cried out energetically: 'Let's go up to the roof.'

It was almost opening time. A crowd of sales clerks was busy folding up the white cotton sheets which had covered the products and carrying in new products for every sales counter. I watched them from the elevator, which quickly took us up to the roof. I took a deep breath, as if to shake away the gloomy atmosphere, as I gazed out over the roofs of the city that sprawled into the distance beneath the early autumn skies.

Kyōsuke walked over to the northeast side of the roof, from where the victim Noguchi had presumably been pushed. He crouched down and looked at the tiled floor, stuck his hand in the shrubbery, about three *shaku* wide, which had been planted inside the iron railing encircling the roof, and even dug around the roots of some of the plants. A curious gleam appeared in his eyes as he called out to me in a quiet voice. Meanwhile, I'd been captivated by the sight of a caretaker feeding a tiger on the west side of the roof, and by a man repairing an advertising balloon on the east side[i].

'Admiring the tiger? But I think we've come upon the trail of our prey too… This is turning out to be quite an interesting case.'

As Kyōsuke walked away I realised that he'd really taken a keen interest in the case and, full of curiosity, I followed him down to the fifth floor. There I found a telephone booth, performed my journalistic duties by reporting back to my newspaper, and accompanied Kyōsuke to the food hall.

The hall was quiet, as it was still early in the morning. But in a corner, at a table near the window, my cousin the senior police detective and one of his subordinates were chewing on some very thick sandwiches. When he spotted us, he got up and brought more chairs to his table. We happily sat down with him and the waitress came over to take our orders. Kyōsuke, who had been looking at the gorgeous window grates, grabbed her arm before she could walk off and confirmed with her that the windows on all the floors were similarly protected.

We tucked into our breakfast, and my cousin started talking as he sipped on his hot tea:

'The case is complex, but the solution is simple. I'm a firm believer in investigation at the crime scene itself, you see. And, as you've heard, the murder happened between ten and eleven o'clock last night and the victim was thrown off the roof between midnight and three in the morning. Considering those times, and the fact that all the doors and windows were securely locked and nobody could have come from outside, we can assume the murderer was someone from inside the department store. Yes, to be clear: it was somebody who was inside this very store last night. You're the only ones I've told so far, but I intend to perform a very rigorous interrogation of each of the men who were on night watch. There is one thing that poses a slight problem, however, and that's the necklace. If Noguchi's killer was also the person who stole the necklace, why did he leave it behind afterwards? And if the thief was in fact the victim Noguchi himself, what could the murderer's motive have been? To get to the bottom of those questions I shall first have the fingerprints on the necklace examined. Well, enjoy your meal.'

So saying, my cousin left us with a cheerful farewell and his subordinate followed him out of the food hall.

Kyōsuke, who had been eating in silence, now grinned faintly and began to speak:

'You said he was your cousin, didn't you? Well, there's nothing you can do about that. The police here in Japan like to concentrate on the motive behind a crime right from the start. Unfortunately, that means that whenever they come across a case where motive is just a superficial element, or—as in the present case—appears to be incomprehensible, things start to get difficult. There is, of course, logic behind wanting to look for the motive. But it leads to over-simple, stereotypical thinking which assumes that motive is the *only* basis for investigating a crime. So, for what it's worth, I believe it's much more important to focus on the three characteristics of the victim's wounds, rather than the necklace. They are, firstly: the strangulation marks on the neck and the welts and abrasions on the chest, which were obviously made by an exceptionally strong force.

At first I assumed they were made by some weapon used like a whip, but I was wrong. Secondly, the large number of grazes running across the victim's palms. There were also calluses there. Thirdly: the many abrasions left on the exposed parts of the body: shoulder, chin, elbows, *et cetera*.

'Let's take each of them in turn. From the first characteristic I infer that the murder was either the work of multiple culprits, or one person of exceptional strength. The second characteristic, the grazes on the palms, suggests clearly that the victim had been holding something which had caused his palms to be chafed. As for the third, the abrasions all over the victim's body, the wounds are superficial yet wide and rough and were clearly not made by a knife or any metal object. They were made by some dull, heavy, rough object, and we can assume it was a similar object to the one that made the wounds on the palms. From which we can deduce that the object which made such wounds was present at the crime scene at the time of the murder. Which means that either this object was already close to hand as the victim and murderer were struggling, or else the murderer brought the weapon along himself. I suspect it was the latter. Now let's go back to the strangulation marks and the abrasion marks on the chest. You'll note that there were no clear ligature marks, only areas where the lifeless skin had ripped and bled. This makes me think that the same rough, thick object which made the grazes and abrasions was also responsible for the marks on the neck and chest.

'Now I have to rethink what I said at the beginning: the countless abrasions on the victim's body were not caused by coming into contact with some strange object lying around at the crime scene as the victim was struggling with the murderer. The wounds were in fact caused by a snake-like weapon, with which the murderer attacked him persistently. But what will prove most interesting for further deductions are those singular grazes on the victim's palms. Surely you are not going to suggest the deceased played tug-of-war with somebody?

'Now we've established that the wounds were made during a struggle, the next question is where the struggle and the murder took place. Given that all the clues pointing to murder have been left intact, it seems ludicrous to suggest that the murder was committed outside the department store, and that the murderer had gone to all the trouble of carrying the body inside and all the way up to the roof for the sole purpose of making it appear as if the victim had fallen from the building on his own. Not to mention that the entire building was locked up tight at night. How about the hypothesis the murder was committed inside the department store? The surprising fact that the victim did not cry for help during his struggle in the moments before his murder helps contradict this theory. Ergo, the murder took place at the last remaining location: the department store roof. This is a fairly obvious conclusion and the police will probably agree with it. Even though I think that theory is correct, however, I must point out one or two obvious problems with that conclusion. For example, I first suggested that the murderer was either an exceptionally strong man, or that there were multiple men, based on the characteristics of the strangulation marks. But the theory of multiple murderers has been disproven by my foregoing analysis. People thrown together on night watch in an organisation like this do not plot together. So we arrive at the conclusion that the murderer is one, very powerful, man. Who could that person be?'

'The case is beginning to become quite complicated.'

I had been listening intently to Kyōsuke's theories and my excitement had reach boiling point. Kyōsuke lit a cigarette, took a deep drag and then continued as a flicker appeared in his eyes.

'Complicated? You're wrong, it's become simple. If I were to pretend I was Sherlock Holmes, I'd say: "When you eliminate the impossible, whatever remains, however improbable, must be the truth." So the crime took place on the roof. And don't forget that there were no footprints left in the shrubbery. We have the many curious grazes on the victim's palms, an exceptionally powerful murderer and a ubiquitous murder weapon. With these clues as our basis, let's proceed to a thorough examination of the premises. Let us procure a magnifying glass and go up to the roof again.'

We stood up and left the food hall. The sound of ordinary daytime activity had returned to the building as customers were starting to arrive. I could hear a cheerful jazz tune from the music department one floor below flowing over the streams of people on the gallery.

We purchased a medium-sized magnifying glass at the optical department on the third floor and made our way through the waves of people to go up on the roof again. It had been closed to the general public because of the incident, and a couple of officers stared at us inquisitively as we entered the scene.

Deep furrows of concentration appeared on Kyōsuke's brow as he cocked his head and took a long look at every corner of the roof. Then he took me across to the northeast corner, from where the body was thought to have fallen. He then brandished his magnifying glass and started investigating the railing and the shrubbery even more intently than before. He soon straightened up and started mumbling to himself, as if he'd remembered something, and walked over to the tiger's cage on the west side of the roof. He seemed lost in thought as he stared for a while at the large African male tiger having a relaxed nap. But then he suddenly turned round and looked straight up into the clear, open sky. A gleam appeared in his eyes and he strode quickly to the balcony on the east side.

The large grey advertising balloon floating slowly in the clear blue sky above the balcony was a wondrous sight to behold, and I held my breath in awe.

To my surprise, Kyōsuke grabbed the man in charge of the balloon and started questioning him aggressively.

'What time did you arrive here this morning?'

'Err, the weather last night was bad, so I became worried and came earlier than usual this morning, at half past six.' The man answered in a polite manner as he turned the handle of the winch to release more rope.

'So you were here on this balcony at half past six?'

'No, I arrived at the store at half past six, but then I heard about what had happened and went outside to take a look at the body, so I didn't get up here until seven.'

'Was there anything unusual about the balcony when you finally got here?'

'Not that I noticed. But the gas hose had become tangled up and the balloon had lost a lot of buoyancy. It was just drifting along and had dropped so much in height it looked as if it could drop down at any moment. But that happens often after bad weather.'

'You always keep the balloon afloat, even at night?'

'Usually we bring it down and moor it here, but sometimes we underestimate the weather and keep it up, as we did yesterday.'

'And you mentioned the balloon lost buoyancy?'

'There was a hole in the envelope which I had actually fixed a month ago.'

'Aha, so that's why you were repairing it just now. By the way, how much buoyancy does this balloon have?'

'At normal pressure it can take 600 kilograms easily.'

'600 kilograms is certainly an impressive number. Thank you.'

After he had finished his questioning, Kyōsuke gazed up at the advertising sign that was attached to the rope connected to the balloon.

At the precise moment the balloon had reached its maximum height and the rope had been pulled tight, the senior police detective arrived.

'So you were all taking a nice breather up here? Splendid, splendid. By the way, we found out that the fingerprints on the necklace did indeed belong to the victim, Noguchi. Look at this, they came up as clean as a whistle.'

So saying, he pulled out the beautiful, glimmering necklace and held it in front of us. And, sure enough, two big fingerprints were clearly visible on the large jewels. 'That is indeed great news,' said Kyōsuke with a smile. 'Oh, if it isn't too much trouble, I'd like to borrow a little of that mercury-chalk powder, or whatever it is.'

My cousin looked perplexed as Kyōsuke took the analysis equipment and made his way to the winch, where he skilfully dusted some of the grey powder on the handle and swept the excess away with the camel-hair brush.

'Now I come to think of it,' said the man in charge of the balloon, who had been looking thoughtful, 'when I pulled the balloon in this morning to repair it, the valve of the gas injection port was still open.'

'So the valve was open?' Kyōsuke looked up in surprise and started to think. 'Hmm, that will be very useful evidence,' he mumbled to himself and then returned to the work at hand. He peered at the surface of the handle through his magnifying glass and turned to the balloon engineer.

'When you touched the handle this morning, you weren't wearing your gloves, I assume.'

'That's right. I was in a hurry to lower the balloon for repairs....'

Kyōsuke borrowed the necklace from the senior police officer and compared the fingerprints with those on the handle. I crouched down next to him. It was clear that the two sets of prints were completely different.

'So, here are this gentleman's prints on the handle, but the victim's prints—the ones on the necklace—are nowhere to be seen. That's good. Now could you please carefully lower the balloon for us?'

The engineer looked suspicious when he heard Kyōsuke's request, but he donned his worker's gloves nonetheless and began turning the handle of the winch.

One foot. Two feet. The advertising balloon slowly started its descent.

Magnifying glass in hand, Kyōsuke walked over to the rope as it was being reeled in and watched it carefully. After some thirty-five feet had been reeled in, he ordered the man to halt the balloon's descent and called the senior police detective over.

'I've found your killer.'

We were all taken aback by Kyōsuke's remark. He was pointing to a section of the thick hemp rope where clearly visible bloodstains had seeped in.

'These are the bloodstains from the wounds on the victim's neck. Our business with the balloon is done, and you may raise it again. Oh, wait. Wind the whole rope in. There's something I forgot. I need to check if I was right.'

The balloon engineer, perplexed, started turning the handle once more.

My cousin was gnashing his teeth, looking in turn at the slowly descending balloon, the movements of the balloon engineer and the silhouette of Kyōsuke's face. After a while, the balloon was completely reeled in and the envelope was bobbing above our heads. Kyōsuke opened the valve of the gas injection port and inserted his hand. He searched around inside the envelope and it wasn't long before he was holding a second beautiful necklace in his hand.

'Of all the nerve!'

The senior police detective was about to jump on the balloon engineer.

'Please hold it. You're mistaken. Your murderer is the balloon. This advertising balloon here. Take a look.'

Kyōsuke used some of the grey powder on the gas injection port's metal fittings, the valve and the newly discovered necklace, brushing the powder away with the camel-hair brush. We could see what appeared to be the same fingerprints on all three objects.

'Please check them. I assume they're the same.'

'Hmm. Yes, as you say, these are the fingerprints of the victim, Tatsuichi Noguchi.'

My cousin looked as if he had seen a ghost. Kyōsuke turned to me.

'Can you do something for me? Make a phone call to the Central Meteorological Observatory and ask them for the weather conditions in the Tōkyō area last night.'

I went down to the fifth floor phone booth as requested, and wrote down the information received. I returned to the roof again and passed the note to Kyōsuke.

'Thanks. I see, I see, low pressure at 753 millibar and heavy wind from the southwest. Alright, we're done here, so you can raise the balloon again. And I will now explain my conclusions.'

He lit a cigarette, watched the balloon take flight again, and quietly started his tale.

'First of all, I formulated the following basic assumptions. One: the murderer was an exceptionally powerful individual who was not one of the night guards. Also include the fact here that the doors and windows were all locked tightly. Two: the murder took place on the roof. Also make note of the passive clue that there were no marks left anywhere here, not in the shrubbery, not on the railing, not on the tiled floor, not anywhere. Three: the one weapon which was used for the crime was a long object with a rough surface which could twist at will. Or, simply put, a rope. Four: there was no clear motive for the murder. Starting with these assumptions, I let my imagination run as freely as possible. It didn't take long for me to arrive at the admittedly tentative conclusion that the rope attached to the balloon was the murder weapon, and I came up here to burnish my theory and collect new evidence.'

Kyōsuke paused to turn to the balloon. He continued in a louder voice.

'Two days ago, Tatsuichi Noguchi, who was working the evening shift, stole two necklaces. He naturally assumed that everyone in the building would be subject to a rigorous search, so he hid the necklaces in the safest place he could think of: inside the balloon.'

Kyōsuke turned to the balloon engineer.

'I assume you don't keep watch over the balloon all night? Of course not. So, last night, the victim had been assigned to watch. Hiding the necklaces must have been the only thing on his mind. So it was that, around ten o'clock, before the guards went to bed, he went up to the roof to check up on the balloon. There he discovered to his dismay that the balloon had a hole in it and was slowly losing buoyancy and height. He hurriedly began pulling on the rope to pull it down to the roof. But, although the balloon had lost some buoyancy, it was still a balloon capable of carrying 600 kilograms when completely filled with gas. As the thief desperately tried to reel the balloon in, the rope chafed the palms of his hands. He opened the valve of the gas injection port to check whether his loot was still safe. As things had not yet cooled down, he decided he couldn't risk taking the stolen goods out of their hiding place, so he got the gas hose out and started refilling the balloon with gas. And, as gas started pouring in, the balloon's buoyancy started to increase again, needless to say. It was here that the victim made his biggest mistake. When he had first discovered the balloon's state, he had used his bare hands, not the winch, to reel it in. The proof for that is that his fingerprints aren't anywhere to be found on the handle of the winch. The only fingerprints on the handle are those of the balloon engineer, when he also was in a hurry to pull the balloon in. So, as he was filling the balloon with gas, the thief was holding the fitting of the gas injection port and the rope. He only realised his mistake of not using the winch when the balloon started to regain buoyancy. In a panic, he probably tried to secure the rope somewhere on the winch to prevent the balloon from rising further. But the balloon, now able to float on its own again, detached itself from the gas hose and, with the valve still open, headed for the sky. The victim was desperate to prevent it. While being careful not to be pulled along, he tried to tug on the rope with both hands. But the only result was that the thick, rough rope, still rising, left a host of grazes on his hands. By the time the advertising sign was airborne too, the victim's hideous fate was sealed. As he struggled, his body became entangled in the rope which was unreeling from a coiled pile at his feet. That led to a horrible conclusion. That is, as the victim struggled, his body started to get entangled in the rope, which had been rolled up near his feet. Try as he might to fight back, the inexorable rope left countless abrasions all over the exposed places on his body: on his shoulders, his chin, his elbows and more, and even made tears in his pyjamas. Eventually the rope twisted itself around his neck and chest. Unable to move any more, he was lifted into the sky. The balloon rose higher and higher, pulling the rope tight. The victim couldn't breathe any more, his rib was broken, and he started to bleed from the chafing wounds on his neck. Tatsuichi Noguchi literally left for the heavens.'

Kyōsuke then looked at the note I had passed him.

'From midnight until two-thirty, a low pressure area of 753 millibar passed by the Tōkyō area, as well as a violent wind from the southwest. The combination pushed the balloon in a north-easterly direction. There was a hole in the balloon, and that, accompanied by the low pressure area, made the balloon lose buoyancy. When the rope consequently lost tension, the victim's body was released and thrown down. But not onto the roof of the department store. He fell on the asphalt of the alleyway to the northeast of the building. The shock of the body being thrown away by the rope was what caused one of the necklaces inside the envelope to pass through the open gas injection port and follow the dead man down to the ground. Although death occurred several hours before the rope released the victim, the blood inside bodies of people who have been strangled remains fluid for a relatively long period, so the destroyed head still managed to bleed profusely after hitting the asphalt.'

Having finished his explanation, Kyōsuke turned his face to the sky.

Up in the beautiful blue heavens, the advertising balloon—the mysterious hangman of the department store—drifted peacefully as gentle breezes caressed it.

First published in *Shinseinen*, October Issue, Shōwa 7 (1932).

---

[i] Japan has a long tradition of small entertainment parks on the roofs of department stores, which thrived especially in the period after World War II. The first one was opened in 1903, featuring children's games like see-saws and rocking horses. Other department stores soon followed with facilities like fountains, lakes, gardens, mirror houses and more. In 1923, Matsuzakaya's department store in Ginza, Tōkyō opened a rooftop zoo with a lion and a panther.

THE PHANTASM OF THE STONE WALL

1

Immediately to the west of the apartment building where Yūtarō Yoshida lived in the town of N— stood the Akimori residence. It was a large south-facing mansion whose grey tiled roof, covered here and there with lichen, was barely visible from his window because of the chestnut and evergreen oaks which surrounded it. The grounds of the old mansion were also encircled by a sturdy wall unusually high for the neighbourhood, which had only been repaired the previous winter. A six *ken* wide road ran peacefully from east to west in front of both buildings, separating the main gate of the mansion from a lengthy but narrow 300 *tsubo* lot. To the south of the vacant, weed-covered lot stood a cliff several *jō* high, cutting cleanly through the white rock.

Ever since Yūtarō Yoshida had moved here he'd been curious about the Akimori residence. His interest was not so much in the old mansion's appearance, but more about the household members who resided inside. It had been almost six months since he'd moved in, and while he'd occasionally caught sight of a young woman, presumably a maid, at the back entrance—which faced a path at the western corner of the stone wall—never once had he spotted anyone looking like a member of the Akimori family, nor had he ever seen the large, old wooden front gate actually open. The family was obviously reclusive, shunning all contact with the outside world: to Yūtarō's eyes, it was as if the Akimoris had been left behind on this small hill at the foot of the mountain, forgotten by society.

According to rumours he'd heard, there were only three in the family: the father—a man in his late sixties—and his two unmarried sons. Also living in the sizeable mansion were a middle-aged house manager and his wife, who worked as the housekeeper, and two maid-servants. Even the people who told him these rumours had never seen the old master or his two sons for themselves. But, unsuspected by Yūtarō, and without warning, the Akimori residence would become the stage for a mysterious and utterly inexplicable case, with him in the middle.

It happened on a steaming-hot midsummer Sunday. At half-past two in the afternoon, having just finished writing a letter home, Yūtarō suddenly remembered that the postman was due to arrive at any moment for the second pick-up of the day, so he hurriedly left his room. Customs are an unrelenting practice and, sure enough, the reliable old postman was already crouching in front of the letter-box in front of the apartment building, just about to insert his key. Yūtarō went over to the man, greeted him, and handed him his letter. As he studied the old postman, wrinkled and covered with perspiration, he thought about how hot and how silent it was. This was an especially quiet neighbourhood, even for one at the foot of the hills. Almost nobody ever passed by and, this being a particularly hot day, there was not even a cat loafing around on the six *ken* wide road in front of the building. There was only tranquillity, bathing in the sunlight. It was during this moment of silence that tragedy struck....

Yūtarō and the postman suddenly heard a muffled shriek coming from the direction of the Akimori residence. They turned in surprise to see, about thirty *ken* down the road, two men dressed in simple white *yukata* kimonos[i], standing beside a large, dark lump lying on the ground by the front gate. The two figures started to run alongside the high stone wall, away from where Yūtarō was standing. They were running so close to each other it looked as though they might bump into one another. A moment later they had disappeared around the corner where the road turned in a northerly direction. It had happened very suddenly, and they had been thirty *ken* away, so Yūtarō was not able to make out who the two figures were, but he was sure that they were of identical build and each was wearing a white *yukata* with a black waist band. Yūtarō suddenly felt slightly light-headed and leant back against the letter-box. The red-hot skin of the iron box brought him quickly back to his senses and, realising that the old postman had already started running towards the Akimori residence, Yūtarō immediately followed in his footsteps. By the time they reached the gate there was no sign of the two suspicious men. The large, dark lump was, as they had feared, the figure of the assailants' victim, who had fallen over with her face to the ground, but was still breathing faintly. She was a middle-aged woman with a pale neck. A red liquid was already oozing onto the pavement. Anxiously, the postman crouched down and tried to help the woman, while pointing with his chin to the stone wall. He was telling Yūtarō to chase after the two men!

The six *ken* wide road first started its gentle curve to the north in front of the Akimori main gate, but both road and wall then made a sharp turn to the north at the western corner of the wall. When Yūtarō turned the corner and took in the long path to the north in front of him, he could see the long stone wall of the Akimori residence to his right and a similarly long, but not quite so high, brick wall to his left, protecting the mansion of some baron. There was absolutely no place to hide along the lengthy path, yet there was no sign of the culprits!

Instead of the two assailants, Yūtarō saw a man dressed in a Western suit carrying a black leather suitcase. He looked to be a salesman.

Yūtarō asked: 'Have you seen two men dressed in white *yukata* coming down this path?'

The man seemed surprised and shook his head vigorously.

'I have seen no such men. Has something happened?'

'Something awful,' exclaimed Yūtarō, showing his agitation. 'Someone was just murdered in front of the Akimori residence....'

'What!' The man paled visibly. 'A murder! Who was killed?'

Yūtarō had already turned back to return to the crime scene and the man ran alongside. Between breaths he introduced himself: 'I am... the Akimoris' house manager... My name is Yaichi Togawa.'

Once they turned the corner and the front gate came in sight, the two continued running without exchanging a word. The postman had turned the woman over and was pressing a handkerchief against the wound on her chest. As soon as the man in the suit saw the woman lying lifelessly on the ground, he cried out: 'Ah! Someko!'

He looked around like one possessed.

'...It's my wife...!'

He sat down next to her.

From around the corner of the wall, Yūtarō could hear the raucous noise of *chindon'ya* street musicians[ii].

2

Several minutes later, at the police box[iii] of N—.

Rookie constable Hachisuka had been dozing off, fighting with the sandman in the oppressive heat.

A *chindon'ya* musician arrived at the box, completely out of breath. He had a sign saying "Café Lupin" on his back, and bells and *taiko* drums hanging in front. He quickly explained that, as his group was passing in front of the Akimori residence, they had learnt that a horrible murder had happened there, with three bewildered men attending to the victim. He had come running here to inform the police.

A murder! Constable Hachisuka jumped up as if he'd been stung. He looked up at the clock. It was ten to three. He made a quick phone call to the police station and hurried out to follow the *chindon'ya* musician.

At the crime scene, the three men had been joined by the maids of the Akimori household and a couple of onlookers. Yūtarō had been shooing the onlookers away, but once he caught sight of Constable Hachisuka, he stepped towards him and handed over a bloody knife. He explained he had picked it up about five *ken* to the west of where the victim had been lying, on the road next to the stone wall.

Constable Hachisuka immediately started to question the witnesses.

'...So what you're saying is that... young Yoshida here started chasing after those two men dressed in *yukata* from this side. And at the same time, Mr. Togawa was walking down the path around the corner. Hmm, a sort of pincer movement... Yet there was no sign of the murderers. That means....'

Constable Hachisuka went over to take a look at the narrow path for himself. He bit his lip and frowned as his eyes slowly scanned the length of the path. His gaze fell on the little wooden back entrance just north of the western corner of the Akimoris' wall. He turned to look at the witnesses and smiled grimly. Both Yūtarō and house manager Togawa knew exactly what was on Constable Hachisuka's mind and both nodded.

'This is terrible,' said Togawa with a troubled expression on his face. 'It appears that is the only way they could have escaped.'

Constable Hachisuka strode determinedly to the little door, opened it and went inside the grounds of the mansion. He returned quickly, looking triumphant.

'I knew it. There are footprints here!'

At that moment, a group of police officers arrived, led by a senior police detective. Constable Hachisuka handed over the evidence that Yūtarō had given him and proudly reported on his preliminary investigation. Further questioning of the witnesses quickly followed. The victim was Someko, the housekeeper of the Akimori household, and wife of the house manager Yaichi Togawa. As for the crime, both Yūtarō and the postman had witnessed the deed, and because it was beyond any doubt that cause of death had been a single stab wound, the body of the woman was soon released. Based on the testimonies of Yūtarō, the postman and house manager Togawa, the detective decided to proceed with the examination of the footprints Constable Hachisuka had discovered.

They first opened the back entrance and stepped inside the grounds. Right opposite them, about five *ken* away, stood the entrance to the kitchen. To their left was the inside of the stone wall. To the right, beyond the planting in the wide garden, stood the main mansion. The *engawa* veranda[iv] that gave access to the house was also visible from their spot. The ground was slightly moist, probably because the plants had been given water during this heat. Footprints of shoes and felt *zori* sandals were overlapping each other on the ground between the back entrance and the kitchen, presumably made by the household's servants and tradesmen making their rounds. The footprints Constable Hachisuka had found, however, were immediately to the right of the back entrance and continued from there, through the planting of the front garden, all the way round to the front of the main mansion. They were footprints made by garden *geta* sandals and there were a lot of them.

Examination showed that the footprints could be grouped into four sets, which meant that two persons with garden *geta* sandals had walked up and down in the area. Had they come here from outside, and gone out again? Or had they come from inside and then returned to the mansion? This question was later answered because with *geta* sandals you can clearly tell which way is the front. Two pairs of such sandals which perfectly matched the tracks on the ground were quickly discovered in front of the *engawa* veranda, at the place where people take their shoes off at the garden doors of the main mansion.

This meant suspicion fell on the people of the Akimori household. The police officers became more excited. The senior police detective left Constable Hachisuka behind to guard the footprints, and entered the main building through the *engawa* veranda. Under the watchful eyes of Yūtarō, the postman and house manager Togawa, the investigation of the Akimori household began.

The old master of the house, Tatsuzō Akimori, declined to answer any questions as he suffered from an illness which prevented him from moving around. The house manager and the maids all confirmed the existence of the illness, so the detective called for the two sons. When Yūtarō and the postman saw the two men, they turned pale.

The two sons looked exactly the same in both build and appearance, and both were wearing white *yukata* with a *kagasuri*[v] pattern and a black silk crepe waist band. They were called Hiroshi and Minoru, and they were both twenty-eight years old.

They were obviously identical twins.

For a moment there was an eerie silence. But the postman appeared to have had enough, and in a trembling voice he exclaimed: 'These were the ones!'

The senior police detective started questioning the two thoroughly. But the Akimori twins both claimed they had been taking an afternoon nap in the wisteria arbour in the back garden until moments ago, and knew nothing about what had happened. They both denied having anything to do with the crime, and both claimed they had not come out into the front garden.

The two maids were called for again. Natsu, the older maid, however said that she was the one in care of the old master, so she hardly left the annex building in the back and knew nothing about what was going on in the main mansion. Kimi, the younger maid, said that the two young masters had indeed been sleeping in the wisteria arbour, but that she herself had also had an afternoon nap for about an hour after that, and that shortly before the incident had happened, there had been a phone call and the housekeeper Someko had asked her to watch the house during her absence. Kimi felt sorry she had fallen asleep again, as she was still drowsy at the time.

The testimony of the maids showed the alibi of the twins was very shaky, but what really made things worse for them was that, every time Someko Togawa's name came up during the questioning, the twins would look scared and start stammering, conveying a very bad impression to the officers in charge. The senior police detective sent one of his subordinates to the forensic department of the Metropolitan Police Department, in order to get a comparison of the twins' fingerprints with those on the grip of the murder weapon they had retrieved.

3

Meanwhile, rookie constable Hachisuka, who had been given the task of guarding the footprints, was secretly feeling quite pleased with himself for having been of such tremendous help with his very first murder case since joining the police force. With everything going so smoothly, his job almost seemed like nothing more than a game. He locked his hands behind his back and strolled up and down along the footprints, nodding to himself.

As he took a closer look at the footprints, he noted that they were quite interesting. That thought was still in Constable Hachisuka's mind as he crouched down near the door of the back entrance and picked up a pink-coloured advertising flyer which had been stepped on by the footprints left by the garden *geta* sandals, in this case prints heading for the back entrance—which meant that the person who made the tracks had come from the garden planting and stepped on the flyer as they went out through the small door. Let's see. Appears to be an advertisement for a café. Lupin… Lupin? Hadn't he heard that name before somewhere?

Constable Hachisuka stood up with a thoughtful expression on his face. Just at that moment, he spotted the maid Kimi exit the kitchen after her questioning, and walked over to her. 'I've got a little question,' he said. 'Where do you receive the newspaper and advertising flyers in this place?'

'Er, the newspaper?' The maid wiped her hands on her apron. 'The newspaper is always brought in through the back entrance and delivered here at the kitchen. The mail, too. But, as to the advertising flyers, they just open the small door slightly and throw them inside the garden from the back entrance.'

'I see. Thank you.'

Constable Hachisuka nodded his thanks, but his face turned paler and he began to look distressed. The lively spirit he had shown previously had disappeared, and he started to bite his lip and poke his temple with a trembling finger.

That's odd. So someone had stepped on the flyers thrown into the garden from the back exit. Could that be right? Is that really what happened? No, no. It didn't make any sense! Constable Hachisuka started contemplating the matter more deeply, standing there as if rooted to the spot.

At that moment, the senior police detective and his men, having finished their investigation, came out of the house in high spirits, bringing with them the twins Hiroshi and Minoru. Constable Hachisuka suddenly became alarmed. In a fluster, he walked up to the senior police detective and said: 'Please wait. I still have some doubts.'

'What?' The detective leant towards him. 'Doubts? This is no time for jokes. It's all clear. Forensics called. The fingerprints on the handle of the murder weapon were an exact match with those of Hiroshi Akimori!'

With no way to refute that, Constable Hachisuka bit his tongue.

The party left the grounds shortly thereafter. The Akimori twins were basically treated as the murderers and would be detained at the local police station. With that, the case appeared to have come to an end.

Constable Hachisuka, however, was far from satisfied. When his shift ended that evening, he started racking his brains again over the problem and decided to return to the Akimori residence. The constable had the maid he had talked to earlier watch him as he once again crouched down near the spot at the back entrance, where the flyer which had been stepped on by the garden *geta* sandals had been found, and he started thinking it all over.

This was a flyer for Café Lupin, and there could be little doubt it had been scattered there by the *chindon'ya* musicians. So had the *chindon'ya* musicians thrown the flyer inside first? Or had the two murderers passed by this spot first? The only possible interpretation of the facts in front of him was that the flyer had been left behind first, and that afterwards the two murderers had passed by and unknowingly stepped upon the flyer with their garden *geta* sandals. Exactly. That was an undeniable fact. And that meant the *chindon'ya* musicians must have passed by here before the murderers had gone out through the back entrance—and therefore before the tragedy had occurred. Wait a second. Was that right? That couldn't be right: the *chindon'ya* musicians had only arrived after the murder had happened. It didn't add up at all!

Perplexed, Constable Hachisuka stood up.

That's it. He had to question the *chindon'ya* musicians. Perhaps they did pass by before the crime had happened. It didn't seem likely, but he had to confirm whether it was true or not.

Constable Hachisuka left the Akimori residence and turned to walk alongside the stone wall towards the east.

What if, as he suspected, the *chindon'ya* musicians had thrown the flyer inside after the crime had happened? That would mean the footprints of the murderers...yes. It would mean it had been a horrible trap.

Constable Hachisuka continued with his reflection on the facts. Little did he know that he was about to run into another impossible problem.

He had just arrived at the crime scene, in front of the main gate of the Akimori residence, when he suddenly stopped in his tracks. He stared in front of him and cocked his head. He clicked his tongue in annoyance and continued on his way. On arriving at the apartment building next door, he went inside and said to the person behind the counter: 'Please call Yūtarō Yoshida down.'

Yūtarō was dead tired from the questioning and had been dozing off in his room, but he got up in surprise and descended the staircase. Once he saw Constable Hachisuka's face, he asked: 'Has something else happened?'

'No, but I do have something I need to ask you. Please follow me,' the constable replied as he walked off.

'What's the matter?' Yūtarō asked as he followed the constable. But the policeman continued walking without uttering a word. When they arrived at the spot where he had been just before, on the pavement in front of the main gate of the Akimori residence, he turned and said: 'The place we're standing now is the crime scene, where the victim was lying, correct?'

Yūtarō was surprised by this unexpected, yet very obvious question. He trembled as he nodded. Constable Hachisuka looked intently at young Yūtarō, as if he were fishing for something.

'I believe you're an honest witness, but I recall you said you were standing right next to the letter-box in front of your apartment building when you saw the victim lying here, did you not?'

'Yes, that's right,' replied Yūtarō, then quickly added: 'If you think I'm lying, ask the postman.'

'Hmm, I see. Furthermore, since we're standing here, we should naturally also be able to see the letter-box in front of your building, is that right? Well, can you see it?'

Yūtarō suddenly turned pale. For there was no letter-box at the place where he was looking! The street lamp which was supposed to be standing a few *ken* before the letter-box was casting its dim light in the darkness of the early evening, but there was no sign of the letter-box, as if it had been swallowed up by the stone wall.

Police Constable Hachisuka put his hand on Yūtarō's shoulder and asked, with emotion in his voice: 'How do you explain that?!'

4

Yūtarō had been caught completely off guard by the revelation, and had spent the whole night thinking it over, getting hardly any sleep. The next morning, Yūtarō was awakened early by the constable. He was in a very bad mood as he dressed and left his room.

'I need your help with something,' the rookie police constable said in a surprisingly friendly manner as they descended the staircase. 'I didn't sleep a wink last night, either. I spent all night looking for those *chindon'ya* musicians, you see. And you have to keep this a secret, but I discovered something very startling. You see, some time after the crime, those *chindon'ya* musicians left a flyer, and the two murderers apparently stepped on it with those garden *geta* sandals. But the *geta* footprints weren't made during the crime: they were made afterwards, on purpose, to incriminate the twins. It's a horrifying trick. I don't know who the real murderers are, but they're certainly not the Akimori twins!'

They were leaving the apartment building. The constable, paying no attention to Yūtarō's surprise, suddenly looked angry.

'But nobody at the station will listen to what I have to say. They have witnesses, they have evidence, and what's worse, during the questioning held later at the station, they discovered those twins and the housekeeper were having a liaison. Can you believe it? I don't know whether the woman was given money for her "services," or whether it was something that came out of that woman's own curious desires, but in any case, their relationship is a very powerful motive for murder. And then there's that fact we talked about last night. It's all going bad now. But I'm not going to be defeated.'

When they arrived in front of the main gate of the Akimori residence, Constable Hachisuka took a large tape measure out of his pocket and, with Yūtarō's help, started to make very accurate measurements concerning the miracle that had occurred there at the stone wall. But no matter what they tried, it was impossible to see the spot where the victim was lying from the location of the letter-box, as the spot was hidden by the gentle curve of the stone wall. Similarly, one couldn't see the letter-box from the spot where the victim had been lying, either. Constable Hachisuka stopped taking measurements and said: 'Yoshida, I'll ask you for the last time, so please help me out and answer honestly. Did you and the postman really see the crime scene while standing next to this letter-box?'

Yūtarō was getting angry at the constable's persistent questioning, but he remained calm and answered in the same manner as the previous night.

'So you are sure. I'm sorry for doubting you,' said the constable as he put the measure away. 'That means that this long stone wall has moved closer to the road by at least three *shaku* compared to when you two saw the crime. That's obviously impossible, but thanks anyway.'

As he thanked Yūtarō, the constable added: 'But do note that this might become a matter of questioning the reliability of the witnesses, so beware: you might get asked about this again.'

So saying, Constable Hachisuka went home, looking very downcast.

'This has become a rather troublesome matter,' thought Yūtarō. Could he perhaps have been mistaken? No, no, he was absolutely not mistaken. But still, it was very curious. And Constable Hachisuka had said the Akimori twins weren't the murderers. But who could they be, then? Who was the murderer, and who was the accomplice? Was there another set of twins around? Or perhaps...?

He remembered the parting words of Constable Hachisuka. A matter of questioning the reliability of the witnesses? Bah, that was something he really didn't appreciate. Yūtarō kept on turning the problem over in his mind. But no matter how he looked at it, he couldn't solve it. When Yūtarō finally realised he would never solve the case on his own, he started searching his mind for someone who could help him, someone he could trust.

Ah! Kyōsuke Aoyama!

Yūtarō recalled the curious man who of late had occasionally appeared at lectures at his school.

That was it! That man claimed he had experience with criminal cases. If Yūtarō could explain the case to Aoyama, surely he would give him some advice.

After school, Yūtarō went to visit Kyōsuke Aoyama.

'Wasn't that case already closed?' asked Kyōsuke as he offered Yūtarō a chair. But once Yūtarō had confided the facts he himself had seen and heard as a witness, the new hypothesis of Constable Hachisuka that proved the twins to be innocent, the strange happening at the stone wall and the troublesome position he himself was now in as a witness, Kyōsuke Aoyama started to show more interest. He asked two or three questions during Yūtarō's account of the events and closed his eyes to think, but at last he stood up.

'I understand your concerns. I will help you out. But like that fellow Hachisuka said, the Akimori twins are not the murderers. Who are, then? You'll have to wait until tomorrow night for that.'

5

It goes without saying how long the following day felt for Yūtarō. Time went by excruciatingly slowly. As soon it became dark, the impatient Yūtarō finished his supper and flew out of his apartment building.

Kyōsuke Aoyama had been waiting for Yūtarō in his armchair. 'I met with your Constable Hachisuka today. He is a very intelligent young man,' said Kyōsuke. 'I've no doubt he'll get promoted for his work on this case.'

'So you know the identity of the real murderers?'

'Of course. I'd already grasped most of the case while you were telling me the story last night. You shouldn't be surprised. Don't you realise it's a very simple case? You and the postman were on that road and chased after those two men. The house manager came from the other side. But there was no sign of the murderers. You looked at the only way out of that path: the back entrance of the Akimori residence. There you discovered the footprints of the murderers. However, those footprints were made long after the crime happened. So what does it mean…?'

'…It means the murderers didn't go inside through the back entrance at that time?'

'Precisely. And at that time, the three of you were the only people outside the stone wall. Now you understand, don't you?'

'I think I get it… No, actually I don't think I do.'

'How vexing. The murderer was standing outside the stone wall at the time. The murderer was one of the three of you!'

Yūtarō was about to cry out that it couldn't be true. But Kyōsuke calmed him down.

'Among the three of you, there was one man who went through the back entrance inside the grounds between the time the *chindon'ya* musicians passed by and left that flyer, and the time that Constable

Hachisuka arrived after being called by those same musicians. That person is the murderer.'

'So you mean house manager Togawa is the murderer?'

'Yes. By the way, how much time did Togawa spend inside?'

'About five minutes? But he only went in to leave his bag and inform the people of the household....'

'Ah, yes, that bag. That was what Constable Hachisuka and I examined today. Inside the bag was one white *yukata* set and a black waist band! Here's what happened. While everyone was having an afternoon nap, Togawa made a phone call to his wife and called her outside. And in front of you witnesses, wearing the *yukata,* he stabbed his wife with the murder weapon, on which he had previously left the fingerprints of one of the twins. He then went around the corner where you couldn't see him, took the *yukata* off—revealing the suit he was wearing beneath it—and put the *yukata* in his bag. Later on, he'd leave his bag back inside the house, quickly do the trick with the garden *geta* sandals footprints and then go and wake the maid.

'It's really simple. The police said the twins had a motive for a *crime passionnel* because the woman and the twins had a liaison, but I did the reverse and realised that her husband Yaichi Togawa also had a motive.'

'But who was his accomplice, then?'

'Accomplice? There was never such a person.'

'Wait. Are you just going to ignore my powers of sight? I clearly saw two murderers....'

'I guess you're justified in getting angry at me. The accomplice you're talking about has a very intimate connection with the miracle which occurred at the stone wall. The murderer had figured out the truth behind the so-called miracle. Committing the murder in front of you as witnesses, especially in front of the postman who always arrives in the neighbourhood at the same time every day, was part of his crafty plan. Oh, what's the matter? Does your head hurt? No, that's only normal. The miracle of the stone wall is indeed a mystifying problem. I have my own thoughts about it, but I don't think you'd believe me if I'd simply explain it briefly to you. Please be patient for another few days. Anyway, I have to go to the police now.'

It was three days later when Kyōsuke Aoyama finally expelled the source of Yūtarō's headache.

It was incredibly stuffy and hot that day, just as on the day of the murder. Kyōsuke, Yūtarō and police constable Hachisuka, were walking down the path to the western side of Akimori residence, while being roasted by the scorching heat of the two-thirty afternoon sun. When they arrived at the famous corner, Kyōsuke announced: 'Our experiment will start now. I think it will succeed. We'll be walking back alongside this stone wall in the direction of the front gate of the Akimori residence, to the spot where the victim was lying. If we can see the letter-box in front of us—the letter-box we shouldn't be able to see—then I'll have solved the truth behind this miracle. Okay? Let's go.'

Yūtarō and police constable Hachisuka felt as if they were being bewitched by something as they walked on. Five *ken*. Ten *ken*. Fifteen *ken*. It was only another five *ken* until they reached the front gate of the Akimori residence, but still nothing. Four *ken*. Three *ken*. And, there, the miracle finally occurred!

There were still about three *ken* away from where the victim had been lying, but there the bright figure of the red letter-box appeared from behind the stone wall, the same red letter-box that was standing thirty *ken* down the road in front of the apartment building. As they proceeded, the image became clearer and clearer, and eventually, the image of the letter-box separated itself from the stone wall. But how curious! They could make out another letter-box—the exact same letter-box—overlapping with the first one. Once they stood right in front of the front porch, they saw two red letter-boxes standing next to each other thirty *ken* in front of them. Yūtarō felt slightly dizzy in his head and had to close his eyes. But then Kyōsuke said: 'Look, there's the twin brother of the postman!' And yes, there was the grotesque sight of twin postmen, both wearing black-and-white uniforms and carrying large, black sacks as they walked down the pavement this way from the letter-box. But as the twin brothers approached the three men, the figures of the twins started to overlap and eventually merged into one single person. And moments later, that honest-looking postman opened his eyes wide in surprise, and stood still looking at us.

'Ah! It was a mirage!' Yūtarō exclaimed suddenly.

'Hm, you're not completely wrong, but also not completely right,' said Kyōsuke. 'Basically, it's a form of air reflection. When there's a local change in air density through a difference in temperature, it's possible to see projections of things from very extraordinary angles because of the way the light bends. And we do indeed call that a mirage. What just happened is scale-down version of a mirage. Today is an extremely hot day, just like the day of the murder. This recently repaired, large stone wall facing south has been bathing in the heat reflected from the empty lot on the other side of the road and the heat that results from other smaller conditions like the length and height of this wall, resulting in a local change in the density of the air, precisely along this wall. So from where we are standing now, the light that passes by the letter-box over there is reflected off the air and bent in an incredible manner: thus the miracle of the stone wall was born.'

Kyōsuke pointed to the postman with his chin and laughed. 'Haha. Look. The postman, too, has approached us closer than we had agreed, and has now ceased being a twin. He must have seen us appear in a similar way, that's why he standing there in surprise. In another thirty minutes the temperature of the stone wall will drop, and once any of the complex conditions necessary to bring forth this miracle are gone, we won't be able to see that letter-box over there. Well, well, it appears your headache is over now.'

First published in *Shinseinen*, July Issue, Shōwa 10 (1935).

---

[i] *Yukata* are simple, informal kimono.

[ii] *Chindon'ya* are street musicians in eccentric dress who go around in the streets advertising and announcing events. The practice started in the late 19th century, but they disappeared almost completely after television became widespread.

[iii] A *kōban*, commonly known in English as a police box, is a small neighbourhood police station, usually only housing only a small number of police officers.

[iv] An *engawa* is a veranda outside traditional Japanese homes leading directly into the garden.

[v] *Kagasuri*, or "mosquito pattern," consists of a cluster of very fine crosses, somewhat similar to mosquitoes.

THE MOURNING LOCOMOTIVE

Why yes, you're absolutely right. When the weather clears up like this, travelling by train is really comfortable. By the way, where are you headed? Oh, Tōkyō? So your university is in Tōkyō? Yes, I see. Splendid… Oh, you mean me? Ah, I'll get off right before that, at H City. Yes, there. Where they have that locomotive depot.

Perhaps you can't tell from the way I look, but I actually used to work there until two years ago. I worked there for an eternity, but something happened and I quit the job.

But every year on this day—on the eighteenth of March—I go back to H City, for a tragic task I have to perform for a poor woman. Eh? Why did I quit my job at the railway? Hmm, the world is a curious place. You see, exactly one year ago, on the eighteenth of March, I was travelling by train to H City, and I was accompanied by a fine-looking university student, just as I am now. Like you, he was kind enough to ask me about what had happened. It must be the Buddha's will…. Ah, but I will gladly tell you about it. You students are really so open-hearted….

The reason I quit my job and why I head out to H City every year is rather peculiar and some might call it fateful. My story might not be quite to your taste if you study the latest sciences, but it will help pass the time until you reach your destination.

My story goes back several years, to that fan-shaped locomotive depot at H Station where I worked. You might call it a roundhouse…. There was a large old locomotive there, all covered in soot which the workers had dubbed The Mourning Locomotive. It was once a splendid-looking freight train tender locomotive, model number D50-444. Above the four powerful coupled driving wheels, each as hard as a millstone, stood the steam dome—round and clean like the forehead of old Fukusuke[i]—as well as a big boiler—round as the belly of a pregnant woman—and on top of that was a pipe, shaped like a tea kettle.

For some strange reason it was also the most accident-prone of all the locomotives in the depot, having been involved in the most run-over incidents. It had been constructed at Kawasaki in the year of

Taishō 12 (1923) and had immediately been put into operation pulling freight trains on the Tōkaidō Line, but subsequently became a very troublesome machine. From the time of its introduction until it was taken out of service, it was involved in over twenty run-over incidents, a record for H Depot.

Furthermore—and I don't know whether it was just sheer bad luck that clung to this ill-fated tender locomotive, or whether it was fate—but over that long period, almost a decade, it was always the same two unfortunate men operating the locomotive whenever an accident occurred.

One of them was the locomotive operator, whose name was Senzō Osada. He was one of the older graduates of the N Railway Training Centre. He was a large man, thirty-seven at the time of the first incident. If he'd shaved off that fake-looking short moustache, he'd have looked much younger, like that actor Kikugorō[ii]. He was usually called "Osa-Sen" by most of the people at the depot, which sounded like an actor's stage name. The other was the assistant-operator, Fukutarō Sugimoto. He was a small man, not yet thirty, with a fair complexion and a lean build. He always had a smudge of soot smeared under his nose, almost like Osa-Sen's moustache.

Both of them were easygoing and friendly and liked to chase women when they'd had a few drinks, but each started to become uneasy as the horrible accidents involving D50-444 started to pile up. Initially, they didn't mention the fact to each other, but it was taking a toll on their minds. Things came to a head one autumn night, three years before the incident I'm going to tell you about. A cold rain shower so typical of the season had fallen and the cursed locomotive had run over a forty-year old mad-woman beneath a bridge near H Station. At Osa-Sen's suggestion, they decided to perform a novel ritual to comfort their minds. As a sort of memorial service to the spirit of the victim, they hung a cheap wreath of flowers from the ceiling of the cab during the forty-nine days of the mourning period.

It didn't take long for their little ritual to gain the widespread approval of their colleagues. People came to respect and admire the thoughtfulness of the two men. From that moment on, Osa-Sen and his assistant Sugimoto realised that their little act had been in fact a very meaningful one, so each time they had an accident they would hang a fresh wreath in their cab for forty-nine days. Over time, D50-444 became known as "The Mourning Locomotive."

Now pay close attention, Mr. Student. In the winter of two years ago, D50-444 got involved in not one, but a whole series of bizarre incidents.

It started early in February, on a morning with severe frost. At the time, D50-444 was working day and night between Y and N as a freight train. It was puffing exhaust smoke whiter than the frost when it arrived at the freight platform of H Station, exactly on time at five-thirty in the morning.

Under the supervision of the conductor and the freight manager, they started loading the cargo off the train, and the assistant stationmaster went around checking the train with a lamp in his hand. Meanwhile, assistant-operator Sugimoto lit a Golden Bat cigarette with the fire from the boiler, stuck it between his lips and hummed a tune as he went down the iron ladder with an oil-can in one hand.

But Sugimoto quickly returned to the cab with a changed expression on his face. Without uttering a word, he sat next to Osa-Sen, who was staring at the pressure gauge. In a strangely calm manner, Sugimoto removed his hat and gloves, breathed on the palms of his lean hands, and rubbed the soot away from beneath his nose. This was a sort of tic of Sugimoto's whenever he discovered parts of a victim clinging to the wheels of the locomotive. By the way, D50-444 was such a gigantic locomotive, it was not unusual for the operators not to notice if they ran over one or two persons in the night.

Osa-Sen's mood changed when he learnt the news. In a shrill voice he called for the station workers. The assistant stationmaster quickly ordered a temporary change of locomotive, and D50-444 was admitted inside the depot together with the two engineers.

With the help of several other depot workers, they started cleaning the locomotive. For a depot worker, there are few jobs more horrible than having to clean up after an accident. Some victims are killed in a relatively clean way, as if they'd been cut by some sharp instrument. Their arms would be cut in pieces, for example, or their legs would be sliced clean off, or the head and the body split apart. In such cases, you'd only have a couple pieces of ground flesh sticking to the wheels of locomotive, accompanied by some vague black smears. Any man with strong nerves could work on that without much trouble: it was no different from cleaning the cutting board in a butcher's shop. But if the victim had been pulled inside all the way to the centre of the chassis, their body parts would get ripped apart by the tremendous force. You'd end up with necks around the axle, or arms and legs caught by the wheel centre or the coupling rod. In cases like these, the lower body of the locomotive would be painted with a black-reddish substance and would reek tremendously of blood. The clothes of the victim—whether those of a man or a woman—would be ripped apart and get stuck here and there below the locomotive. Cleaning a locomotive of such a mess is a really sickening task.

So D50-444 was turned around on the turntable and brought into the roundhouse and once they took a good look, they could see the mush so typical of when someone had been run over and ground to pulp.

Sugimoto grimaced as he sprinkled some cheap perfume on a towel, which he put on like a mask and tied to the back of his head. Holding a rubber water hose in front of him, he went inside the three *shaku* opening inside the gauge right beneath the locomotive.

There he made a bizarre discovery. Usually, Sugimoto would spray water over the lower part of the locomotive, keeping his eyes open for things caught up there, such as the clothes of a young girl. But this time, he couldn't spot any signs of the clothes of the victim, not even a trouser leg. What he did discover, however, was a small, hairy lump of flesh instead. He picked the piece up with a pair of tongs—as if he were carefully constructing a jigsaw puzzle—and took it out. It was passed around for everyone to try to determine what it was. Hirata, the vehicle inspector, pointed out that the hairs on the flesh were too thick and hard for a human. This caused quite a stir, and several of the older people at the depot were called in to re-examine the piece of flesh. And what do you think their conclusion was? To their surprise, they determined it was the skin from the belly of a black pig!

Confirmation of this surprising find occurred a couple of hours later by a railway track workman who discovered the horrible remains of a large, fully grown black pig ripped to pieces at a curve about six miles to the west of H Station—in B Town, an area housing the prefectural agricultural school, where many local farmers raised pigs as a side-business. It had somehow managed to get over the fence around a pigsty and met its unfortunate fate while walking along the tracks at the curve. Thus was the incident cleared up relatively easily. Osa-Sen, friendly and thoughtful as ever, bought a new wreath of flowers to hang in his cab and returned to work.

But one morning several days later, fresh lumps of flesh from a black pig were once again discovered under the wheels of D50-444 when it arrived at H Station at five-thirty. Investigation showed that the incident had occurred at the exact same location as the previous one. This was very odd, but nothing you couldn't ascribe to mere coincidence. They hadn't finished their first forty-nine days of mourning, but Osa-Sen and his assistant Sugimoto hung a new wreath of flowers in their cab next to the one for the first pig.

And would you believe it, Mr. Student? A few days later, the wheels of D50-444 were covered by what was probably the soft flesh of a white pig, and assistant Sugimoto was obliged to wipe the soot away from beneath his nose again. It was the third time, at the identical time and place as the previous two occurrences. Mr. Iwase, the head supervisor of the depot, decided to contact the police box in B Town.

According to the report from Constable Andō of the police box, the three pigs had come from three different owners in the outskirts of B Town, and they had each been stolen on the day of the accident. But they had no idea who was behind the horrible prank. All anyone knew was that The Mourning Locomotive, D50-444, had been as busy as monks during *Higan* week[iii].

And then it happened again.... No, Mr. Student, I am absolutely not pulling your leg. The same accident really occurred again. The circumstances were all identical to the previous three times. It was a white pig that was run over. Its nose had been caught on the crank of the main driving wheel, so it turned around and around like a pinwheel as the locomotive advanced.

Supervisor Iwase of the depot and Supervisor Nanahara of Vehicle Inspection were absolutely furious. If it was a prank, it had gone too far. A team of three, led by Mr. Katayama, the assistant-supervisor of the depot, was sent to B Town to investigate.

And what follows is basically a tale of detection, as told to me afterwards by one of the investigators. It's a pretty interesting one, and I'll tell you what I know about it....

Katayama, the assistant-supervisor of the locomotive depot, was exactly what you'd expect from someone who graduated from the Imperial University. He was still new to railway work, but was an intelligent and resourceful man who knew how to get things done. He's moved on in his career since then, and is now in a high position at the Home Ministry. Anyway, he took a clerk from the depot with him—his subordinate at the time—and, led by a clerk from the

Railway Maintenance Section, he made his way to B Town the following day on the two o'clock train.

The curve in the tracks where it all happened was not even one mile away from B Station, in the direction of H Station. The inner track of the curve was the up-track, which ran alongside a pine forest, while the outer track was the down-track, running next to a mulberry field. The group arrived at the concrete mile post, which had some numbers written on it. The Railway Maintenance clerk pointed out that everything had been cleaned up after the fourth accident, which had occurred the day before. According to him, all four accidents had occurred at this very same spot; each time, the ends of a plain straw rope had been found on both the mile post and a large nail sticking out of the sleeper. It was a sturdy nail, driven into the sleeper to prevent the curving rails from moving around, and this particular nail, like all the other nails, was sticking halfway out of the sleeper.

At the end of his explanation the Railway Maintenance clerk added one last comment: '...So in short, we suspect that the person behind these incidents fastened a rope between the nail in the sleeper on the outside rail and the mile post next to the inside rail, and then tied a pig down in the middle of the rails so it would get run over by the train.'

Mr. Kayatama pointed out that all the piggy victims would have been alive and asked why the pigs, who had to have been terrified, did not run away, given that they were only tied down by a rope which would have been relatively easy to break. The culprit probably used the curve to prevent the locomotive operators from seeing the pigs and stopping the train, but the pigs must have been able to hear the rumbling of the oncoming train.

After he decided there was nothing more to discover at the site, Mr. Katayama told his guide he wanted to visit the farmers from whom the pigs had been stolen.

The group took a short-cut which ran across a mulberry field, and did not take long to arrive at the B Town police box. They asked the imposing Constable Andō, with his fine moustache, to show them the way, and he led them to the farm where the fourth victim had come from.

The owner was a well-built farmer in his fifties, with a pockmarked face. He welcomed the party and, timidly bowing his head countless times, he showed them the unpleasantly dirty pigsty made of cedar bark. There he started to whine about how the stolen white pig was the pig he had treasured most, that it was a Yorkshire Large White sow of at least sixty *kan,* and that he couldn't stop crying because it had been cruelly devoured by the locomotive.

Assistant-supervisor Katayama turned to Constable Andō.

'I heard the pig was stolen in the middle of the night and was run over in the early hours of the morning?' he asked.

'That's what happened to all four of them,' replied the constable.

'And how were they stolen?'

'If you open the door in the low fence, they'll wake up right away and then it's simply a question of luring them with some dried confectionery. They'll follow you just like that,' Constable Andō explained.

'Your conclusion after your investigation is that, in all four cases, the pigs were taken away like that?'

'Yes. The stories of all four victims basically match up.'

Mr. Katayama continued with his questions.

'It might be a bit bothersome, but could you tell me the exact dates when each of the four thefts occurred?'

'The exact dates? Wait....' Constable Andō took a notepad from his pocket. 'Let's see, the first happened on the eleventh of February. The next was err... the eighteenth of February. And then the twenty-fifth of February. And yesterday was the fourth of March. All of them happened in the middle of the night, before five o'clock in the morning.'

'...Exactly what I thought. There's always a seven-day period between the thefts. Today is Monday, so that means that they're always stolen on the early hours of Sunday.'

Mr. Katayama thought deeply for a while.

'Can you think of anything which always happens here on Sundays? In fact, it doesn't even matter which day of the week. Something that happens once a week, as part of a routine. Anything at all, it doesn't matter how trivial it might be. For example, businesses or schools that are closed on Sunday, or a barber or public bath that's closed on a certain day in the week. In other words, tell me about everything in this town which happens at a seven-day interval. It doesn't matter what it is, I want to know everything you can think of.'

Constable Andō was, of course, very surprised by this question, but he thought for a while as he frowned, and then looked up again.

'...As for businesses, well, the H Bank branch office, town hall, the office of the credit cooperative, the agricultural school and the elementary schools are all closed on Sunday. I'm sure the spinning factory is closed on the first and fifteenth. The barber closes twice a month, only on days with a 7 in the date. The public bath also closes twice a month, only on days with a 5 in the date. But those are regular days off, and they don't close each week. The silk market hasn't started yet, but the egg market is held every fifth day. And what else is there… Ah, yes, the agricultural school has a sort of bazaar every Saturday afternoon.'

'Aha, what do they sell there?'

Constable Andō answered: 'They're learning agriculture, so it's mostly stuff the students themselves have cultivated. Vegetables, fruit, flowers and things like that. They're doing quite well, actually.'

Mr. Katayama appeared to be very pleased by the answer and changed the subject.

'As you still haven't found the culprit, what are your plans for further investigation, and how are you going to prepare against further developments?'

Constable Andō replied in an agitated manner: 'We've taken precautions, of course. But we simply don't have enough manpower.'

'Well, do what you can do, but don't attempt too much. I'll take my leave now,' said Mr. Katayama, and he ushered his subordinate and the clerk who was acting as his guide outside. The party then left silent B Town that evening.

His subordinates had spent quite some time together with this assistant-supervisor of the locomotive depot, but they always thought it regrettable that Mr. Katayama could sometimes act very strangely, raising suspicions with other people. After they'd left B Town and returned to H Locomotive Depot, Mr. Katayama started on his usual work routine the following day, as if he'd completely forgotten about the bizarre case of the Mourning Locomotive. For the next few days he conducted business as usual. One of his subordinates couldn't take it any longer and questioned Mr. Katayama about it on the morning of the fifth day. He was given a very surprising reply.

'But what else is there for me to do at this moment?'

However, the attitude of the assistant-supervisor changed completely that night.

It happened at around three in the morning. Mr. Katayama woke up one of his subordinates—a man called Yoshioka. They went outside and into a car.

Yoshioka had no idea where they were heading, but after a high-speed drive through the darkness for about half an hour, Mr. Katayama stopped the car and stepped out on to a field. Signalling with his eyes to Yoshioka to follow him in silence, they left the car and entered a nearby pine forest. Yoshioka slowly awakened as they crossed the forest. When they crouched among some shrubs, he realised that the pine forest ended about ten *ken* in front of them, and that beyond that lay the curve in the tracks near B Station. As it became colder due to the night frost, it finally dawned on Yoshioka what Mr. Katayama was planning. The watch around Mr. Katayama's wrist—with an illuminated dial—showed the time: four-thirty. Of course! It was now the eleventh of March: the early Sunday morning. Mr. Katayama naturally anticipated that the pig thief would show up there. Yoshioka could feel a shudder run down his spine at the thought. He buried his face in the collar of his coat and made himself smaller, crouching beside Mr. Katayama.

At exactly forty-two minutes past four, a night train roared past on the up-track, immediately followed by silence. Not even five minutes had lapsed when Mr. Katayama suddenly stiffened and silently shook Yoshioka's shoulder.

Yoshioka held his breath.

Yes, from the path across the mulberry field, far, far away, he could just make out the low, but somehow satisfied-sounding squeal of a pig. It was almost like a dream.

The squealing got closer in the following two minutes, and they soon heard the sound of footsteps on the pebbled path. A dark figure appeared on the railway. Beneath the pale light of the stars, they could make out a sleeved figure, probably wearing a coat and a pair of long trousers. The feet he was pulling along with some kind of rope belonged to a white pig. Who knows from where it had been stolen? The man would occasionally bend over and give it some food, but then he stepped over the down-track and stood on the up-track—slightly west of the centre. There he gave the pig some more food as he looked around and scanned his surroundings. It was too dark for them to make out the man's face.

The pig thief then started with his task. The theory the clerk from the Railway Maintenance Section had expounded about five days ago at this very same spot turned out to be correct. The dark figure tied the pig down and scattered plenty of food in front of his poor victim.

Mr. Katayama and Yoshioka got up silently and cautiously started to approach the figure.

But how unfortunate! They hadn't even advanced twenty steps before a dead branch made a loud crack from beneath Yoshioka's feet. Yoshioka jumped, and sprinted towards the rails.

At the same moment, the pig thief turned around towards the pine forest and screamed out in a strange manner, like the cry of a bird. It quickly hid its face in its clothes and darted off along the rails. Yoshioka sprinted along the rails after the dark figure, but he soon lost sight of it. In the distance he could hear Mr. Katayama crying out to him.

Yoshioka felt it was his fault the figure had escaped, but as there was nothing he could do about it now, he returned back to the curve.

There, Mr. Katayama told him there was absolutely nothing he should feel bad about. 'There's no need to get impatient. But look at this cute pig here. As I suspected from the start, there was no way that any pig would allow itself to get run over like that just by tying it down.'

A closer examination showed that there was indeed something unusual going on. The pig was standing very tensely on its four legs, moving its head back and forth, and spitting out something while it cried out in pain.

'The poor beast has been poisoned.'

Mr. Katayama untied the rope and the two of them pulled the poor pig along through the pine forest in the direction of where they had left their car. The pig, however, had vomited heavily several times on the way, and by the time they arrived at the car, it couldn't walk any more. It started to convulse. They had no choice but to tie it to a tree nearby and order the driver of the car to take them to the police box in B Town. The moment they stepped inside the car, they could hear the noise of a train passing by on the other side of the pine forest.

'That's the freight train pulled by D50-444,' said Mr. Katayama. They headed towards B Town and asked Constable Andō to take care of the pig. Then they sped back across the outskirts of the town in the early, bright morning, back to H Station.

'Will you have that pig killed and dissected?' asked Yoshioka.

'No, no. I don't have any business with that pig any more. I'm already in possession of the food and poison administered to the pig,' said the assistant-supervisor, and he produced three or four *senbei* rice crackers—shaped like flowers—from the pocket of his coat.

They were coloured with red and blue spots, and the surfaces of the rice crackers were all covered with what appeared to be small berries, half the size of an *adzuki* bean[iv].

'This was the main objective of our adventure from the start,' explained Mr. Katayama. 'I had, of course, not expected to actually get my hands on these rice crackers. You see, this is what I suspected right away. It would have been impossible for someone to kill the pig right after they'd stolen it, and then carry it on their own to that place. So the thief had to bring the pig alive to the tracks. And it's inconceivable the thief could have succeeded so many times with this scheme of running the pigs over by the train, if all he'd done was to fasten a rope between the nail and the mile post on the other side of the tracks and tie the pig down in the centre. So the thief had to either kill the pig after he had tied the pig down, or at least make it impossible for the beast to move. Suppose the thief had either beaten it to death, or stabbed it to death with some sharp instrument, or killed it with a strong poison? That would mean he had some means of killing the animals instantly, and that in turn would mean he wouldn't have needed to tie them down. He could have just killed the pigs and left them behind on the rails. But that was something the culprit had not done. So I concluded that the poison in the dry confectionery didn't cause any acute reaction, so the culprit slowly lured the pig to the tracks with the poisoned food. There he'd tie the pig up and give it some more. The poison would start to work, and then D50-444 would arrive.... Anyway, that is the gist of what I imagined. But what could this dry confectionery be? I have never seen such colourful *senbei* rice crackers[v]. Have you ever seen any like these?'

Yoshioka shook his head. The two arrived at H Station soon after, and they started examining the curious clues they had gained from their adventure, with the locomotive depot offices as their base of operations.

The next day, Mr. Katayama remained inside the entire time, thinking about the confectionery in question, but on the day after he finally got out and continued his investigation. He returned in the evening and, after finishing the meal which had been delivered there, he called in Yoshioka and another investigating clerk and gave them their instructions:

'Tomorrow morning I want you to go to B Town. What I need you to do is... well, let me explain this first.' He placed the confectionery in front of the two men. 'Thanks to my investigations so far, I now know what these confections are. They're very strange, shaped like a toy windmill, and look too horrible to eat. And indeed, they're not usually made for consumption. They belong amongst the lowest grade of confectionery, and are called *kazarigashi*, or "decorative confectionery," but around here it seems they're usually called *harigashi*, "display confectionery." You must have seen them before? They're used at funeral services. And I also looked into the berries pasted on the surface of these *senbei* rice crackers. They're the fruit of a small evergreen plant of the magnolia family. Its academic name is *illicium anisatum*, or Japanese anise, but we usually call it *shikimi* or *hanashiba*. The fruit of the plant contains a poison called Shikimic acid. It belongs to the picrotoxins and causes convulsions. Now it starts to become a bit technical, but the physiological reaction to the acid is stimulation of the nerves in the hindbrain, causing convulsions similar to those of epilepsy attacks, which in turn cause a temporary loss of consciousness during those same convulsions. It's possible to die from ingesting Shikimic acid in some cases, but it's not considered a strong poison. You can find the plants growing naturally in the mountains south of central Japan. But there's another use to this plant. And now it gets really interesting. You see, they've been planting them around graveyards as an offering to the deceased for a very long time, and in some areas they also place the branches and leaves of the plant inside the coffin, beside the deceased. However in most regions, people dry the leaves or crumble up the stem, and use it as a raw material in the incense burnt for the deceased, or at their gravestones. So, now do you see the connection? Please take note that both the *senbei* rice crackers and the berries are two very unique clues. Let me turn back to our poor pig. If I'd been in the culprit's shoes, I wouldn't have used such unusual items. I'd have used some regular food to lure the pig, such as carrots, and I wouldn't have gone to all the trouble of tying it down. I'd have just killed the animal with one good whack with a hammer, and then I'd have placed the dead beast on the rails. But as we've seen, our culprit chose to do something very unnatural, with an almost theatrical selection of props. So where does that lead us? The fact that our culprit uses these decidedly unique objects each time means that they are convenient items for him to lay his hands on. In other words, these objects are related to our culprit's daily life. So what I want you to do is to go out to B Town and its surroundings, and see if there is a store there selling funeral accessories that has both these display confectioneries and self-made incense sticks.'

And well, Mr. Student, that is why those two went out to B Town the following day.

It's a very small rural town, so asking around at the police box, town hall and other places quickly led to the conclusion that there was no shop handling funeral accessories around there that answered to Mr. Katayama's description.

The two dispirited subordinates returned to H Station, and reported their findings to the assistant-supervisor. To their surprise, he replied in a surprisingly pleasant manner: 'I rather suspected it'd turn out like that. That's perfect. While you were gone, I went to the depot and asked around to see where Osa-Sen of the Mourning Locomotive gets his wreaths, and I learnt that he always gets them from Jippōsha, a shop selling funeral accessories in the backstreet market area of H City, right behind this very depot. I also learnt that the shop not only sells display confectionery, but makes and sells its own incense. I'm going there right now. If we can go there ourselves and confirm that there is some sort of connection between Jippōsha and B Town that occurs once a week, that would mean the case would be well on its way to its logical conclusion.'

And so the three of them left the office and went out round the back of the depot. It didn't take long for them to find a shabby-looking two-storey funeral shop: Jippōsha.

Mr. Katayama entered first and, in a seemingly experienced manner, ordered a small wreath. A man in his fifties with a ruddy face and a broad forehead—bald and pointy—was busy crushing some dried plants inside a mortar with an incredibly gloomy expression. As soon as Mr. Katayama placed his order, the man—probably the owner of the business—started to arrange white imitation flowers on a small, round wreath of straw which had been wrapped with green tape. Meanwhile, Mr. Katayama looked around the store.

There was a big glass cabinet behind the counter with what appeared to be display confectionery. The sliding paper door next to the cabinet, which led to the back of the building, was slightly ajar. Through the gap they could see a young woman—probably the daughter of the owner. Her posture was a curious one, with only her face visible from a strange angle. The woman had been gingerly peeking through the sliding paper door—revealing only her face—ever since the men had entered the shop. Never before had Mr.

Katayama seen such a charming face. Her hair was done in a simple manner, with a bun at the back of her head, but with her round, chubby face, her skin as fair as candle wax, her small nose and mouth and her round eyes that looked as gentle as if silk had been laid out there… it was almost frightening how alluring this woman looked. As she stared at the group, she forced a weird smile on her face and shrieked out a 'Welcome' to them.

I was told about this visit over and over again after the incident was over. Anyway, the moment Mr. Katayama laid eyes on this girl, he felt he would never be able to forget her. He himself didn't know how to describe the odd feeling, but it was as if her image had been burned right into his eyes. So there we had this strange daughter, and her fearsome looking father…. Yes, there was definitely some deep secret hidden within this household…. You know, just a feeling… Oh, I seem to have been talking quite a lot about the girl.

Up to that point, Mr. Katayama had been looking around the shop in silence, but then a satisfied gleam appeared in his eyes. He turned to the father, who was busy working on the wreath and asked him as he pointed to the various beautiful plants kept in a pail:

'Those are beautiful flowers. Do they grow even in this cold weather?'

The man raised his head.

'Of course, but only in the greenhouses of the agricultural school in B Town. You can buy them there on Saturday evenings. Here, it's finished. That'll be sixty *sen*[vi]. Thank you.'

Mr. Katayama took the wreath, paid the price and exited the shop. Yoshioka followed closely behind, but as he looked back he could see the bewitching, gloomy woman still staring out of the door, showing only her face.

Once outside, Yoshioka caught up with his boss and asked him in bewilderment:

'Mr. Katayama, that man confessed he went to B Town every Saturday afternoon, so why didn't we nab him right away?'

'Because we're not the authorities,' answered the assistant-supervisor. 'And there's no need to rush things. Suppose we had detained him, what conclusive evidence do we have at this stage? Granted, I'm more than sure that the culprit you chased last night was indeed that man. However, wouldn't it be best if we waited a few days and caught him right in the act on Saturday night, so he can't deny the accusation? So, stay calm, at least until Saturday, and let's devote our attention to the remaining mysteries we have.'

And so the group obediently returned to the depot.

The following day, Mr. Katayama started an investigation into the gloomy father and daughter of Jippōsha, by asking around in the neighbourhood.

Over the next two days, they learnt one new fact after another. The father and daughter led a lonely life, with just the two of them to keep each other company. They were not well-off by any means, and had little contact with their neighbours. The daughter's name was Toyo and she was a demanding woman. Curiously, she hadn't gone out of the house at all during the last few years, but spent day after day peering out of the backroom through the half-open paper door at the people passing by on the street, as if waiting for someone. The father, on the other hand, was very fond of his daughter and would do anything for his Toyo. Whenever his daughter had a tantrum, he became so anxious to placate her—even breaking into tears—that it was embarrassing to behold. The daughter's hysterical behaviour had worsened over the previous six months, but had become strangely calmer this last month, when she'd started singing old-fashioned popular songs like *Katyusha* or *The Sunken Bell* in a cheerful, childlike voice and talking loudly to her father in a happy manner. Then, suddenly, for no apparent reason, she'd become hysterical again in the last few days.

I myself was extremely surprised by how thorough Mr. Katayama's investigation had been. You see, I myself had often visited that shop for purchases. And each time I'd see the daughter's face peeking from beyond the paper sliding door. She'd laugh in—how can I put it?—a seductive manner, and with her wide-open soft, silky round eyes aimed at me, her gentle but intense look would penetrate right into my mind.... After each visit, my only recollection was how seductive she looked. And her father was just as Mr. Katayama's investigations had described. Even when he was busy working he would take the time to look back at his daughter with loving eyes, and say things like: 'You'll catch a cold if you leave that sliding door open,' or 'Why won't you have a chat about the trains with this customer here?' I was witness more than once to his loving care of his daughter, handling her as if she could break with just a touch.

Anyway, once Mr. Katayama appeared satisfied with his investigations, he summoned his subordinates and a constable of H

Police Station to the pine forest near the curve in the tracks the following Saturday night—early Sunday morning, to be exact—to catch the father. And so, on the eighteenth of March, at four-thirty in the morning, the four of them were to be found silently crouching in the darkness.

It was shortly after that, however, that Mr. Katayama's plans started to go wrong. Five minutes went by after the night train passed at forty-two minutes past four, but to their surprise, the pig thief did not make an appearance.

Ten minutes. Twenty minutes. The group kept holding their breath, but their target did not present himself. Had he become cautious because of what had happened last time? Eventually, the freight train pulled by D50-444 thundered past.

'…Hmm. He must have noticed our stakeout. We'll just have to go straight to Jippōsha then,' said Mr. Katayama as he stood up in a foul mood.

The group caught the next train back to H Station, and it was already morning when they crossed the station grounds towards the locomotive depot on their way to Jippōsha. But there they saw Osa-Sen of the Mourning Locomotive and his assistant Sugimoto plodding slowly towards them. And the soot beneath Sugimoto's nose had been wiped clean!

'It happened again.'

'What happened?' exclaimed Mr. Katayama.

'I definitely felt it this time. It was beneath the bridge about one block away from the station. It was a woman's hair that was clinging to the wheels of the locomotive. It wasn't a pig….'

The group left the task of arresting the owner of Jippōsha to the police officer, and turned back. It didn't take long for them to arrive at the scene where the train had run over the victim, slightly west of H Station.

It was already morning, so onlookers were already crawling all over the freezing bridge and around tracks wet from frost. When the group managed to push their way through the crowds, the very first sensation that reached them was the reeking smell of flesh and blood. The next thing was the gruesome sight of a woman's head almost beneath their feet, the upper half of which was missing, her brains and both her eyeballs having flown off somewhere. Through her eye sockets and the hole in her head they could see the railway track covered in black bloodstains. As they stared at this horrific sight, it slowly dawned on them that it was the daughter of the funeral shop owner.

Mr. Katayama led the trembling group further down the track. The sight of what was lying on the rails caused widespread vomiting.

There appeared to be two woman's legs, severed at the tops of the thighs, but about eight or nine *sun* in diameter, as thick as logs. The skin was ashen-grey, deprived of the colour of life. Mr. Katayama crouched down beside them with a pale face, but didn't hesitate to poke the skin. A number of creases appeared at the spot, but the skin didn't give. Mr. Katayama wore a troubled expression as he said gravely:

'...These are not swellings caused by the cut. Have you ever heard of how the parasite *filariasis*, which closes the lymphatic system, can cause lymph accumulation, or how *streptococcus* can infect your body through just a small wound, causing swellings? Sometimes, those symptoms are followed by *elephantiasis,* which is what we have here. A friend of mine at university suffered from it, too. The disease affects mostly the legs, with the skin swelling up due to the inflammation, making the patient lose their mobility. I haven't heard of any cases of *elephantiasis* leading to death, but apparently it's quite hopeless to expect recovery....'

He stood up.

'Now we must draw a veil over the case. Who would have guessed that a few incidents of pigs getting run over would end up in a tragedy like this? I've been careless. The girl almost certainly committed suicide. Let's discuss it further while we make our way to Jippōsha. If that man sees his beloved daughter dead like this, he'll go mad....'

And as the group walked on, Mr. Katayama briefly explained the last remaining mystery of this bizarre case: how his intuition had led him to the motive behind the thefts of the pigs by Jippōsha's owner.

Mr. Student, I don't know whether I was happy that Mr. Katayama's intuition was on the mark, but the fact he was correct was soon borne out by a farewell letter found by the medical examiner on the body of the girl, addressed to Osa-Sen of the Mourning Locomotive.

The girl's letter... look, I have it with me right now. Rather than repeating Mr. Katayama's explanation, you'd better read through it yourself. To be honest, it is impossible for me to repeat that self-satisfied explanation of Mr. Katayama's. It's too heartbreaking.

This tale… it's a terribly painful memory to me. It hit me very hard so many years ago. Please read the letter yourself….

Dear Osa-Sen,

I am Toyo, the daughter of the owner of Jippōsha. By the time you read this letter, I will have left for a place where I won't feel embarrassed again. That is why I am able to write everything down here. Please heed what I have to say.

I have lived an unfortunate life ever since I was a child. My family does not have much money, so my father and mother were not able to give their daughter as much happiness as other children. So, four years ago, when I got a small wound on my right leg because of a little accident at the age of nineteen, I was not able to go to the doctor often enough. My wound got infected, and I caught a disease called St. Anthony's Fire. I went to the doctor, who cured it, but about six months later I caught a similar disease and it took me a lot longer to recover. Finally, I caught a terrible disease called elephantiasis, and both my legs became too horrible to look at. According to the doctor, it is not a fatal disease, but I will never recover from it. And as spring and autumn passed by each year, my legs became worse.

Oh, Dear Osa-Sen.

What an unfortunate woman I am. I wanted to curse my father and mother for giving me this fate. But from that time on, my parents started to treat me differently.

My father became desperate and started to treat me lovingly. My mother begged me to forgive her each day like a madwoman. And in the end, she did become crazy.

And exactly three years ago, on an autumn night when a cold rain was falling, my mother went mad and ran out of our home in her bare feet, and was run over by a train beneath a bridge.

Dear Osa-Sen.

The operator driving that locomotive at that time was you. And you were so kind. You offered a wreath of flowers to the spirit of my mother. And you would come to my home to buy wreaths whenever you had run over a person. What a pure heart you must have.

Oh, my dear, dear Osa-Sen.

From the time I first saw you at our shop, I fell deeply in love with you. I could not stop thinking about you. My father eventually found out about my feelings. By that time, I was all he had on his mind, so whenever you'd come to buy wreaths, he'd always take as much time as possible to make them.

But heed what I have to say, my beloved Osa-Sen.

My body is too horrible to look at, so I could not get any closer to you. But as time went by, I felt more frustrated, and I became more hysterical and demanding with each passing day. How often did I not cry out to my father about how much I wanted to see you, even though you only came to us two or three times a year? My father couldn't stand to watch my suffering any more, passing each and every day peeking from the backroom in the hopes you would come. So about one month ago, my father promised that each week, whenever he'd go to B Town to purchase flowers, he'd pray to a very effective god for me. And what do you think happened? That very effective god looked down at poor me, and made it so I could see you each Sunday. Oh, can you just believe how blessed I was? I'd sing each day, and have pleasant chats with my father....

But that only lasted for a short time, and you did not come last Sunday. And my father said heaven would get angry, so he couldn't pray any more, so that night he only planned to buy flowers. I wasn't able to control myself any more, and had a big row with my father.

Oh, my beloved Osa-Sen.

I had hold of a drill used to make coffins at the time, and with it I accidently killed my own father.

There is no reason for me to live any more. Embracing this letter, I will depart for the place where my mother is by your hand. I will leave a wreath of flowers at my home after I finish this letter. Please hang it in your locomotive for this wretched girl.

The seventeenth of March (Evening).

Toyo of Jippōsha

...You've finished reading the letter? As written here, by the time the group led by Mr. Katayama arrived at Jippōsha, the father was already cold, leaning over a half-built coffin, with a large drill plunged through his stomach up in the direction of his heart.

Mr. Student, I think you now understand why I quit my job at the railway, and why I return each eighteenth of March—on the day that woman of Jippōsha died—to visit the public cemetery in H City. What? Ah, yes, you're right.... You probably already guessed some time ago, but I am Senzō Osada, also known as Osa-Sen of the Mourning Locomotive. Oh, I seem to have spoken for quite some time. It appears we're near H Station now. Well then, I bid you farewell.

First published in *Profile*, September Issue, Shōwa 9 (1934).

---

[i] Fukusuke is a god of merchant prosperity, recognizable by his large, bald forehead.

[ii] Kikugorō Onoe is a stage name dating from the eighteenth century used by a group of actors of *kabuki*, a classical form of dance-theatre. Actors can succeed to the prestigious title. Kikugorō VI (1885-1949) held the name during the time *The Mourning Locomotive* was published. He was regarded as one of the greatest *kabuki* actors of the first half of the twentieth century.

[iii] *Higan* week is the week of the spring equinox, in which many Buddhist memorial services are performed.

[iv] The *adzuki* bean (occasionally spelled *azuki* or *aduki*) is an important element in Japanese cuisine, especially as an ingredient for red bean paste, which is often used as a filling for Japanese sweets.

[v] *Senbei* (occasionally spelled *sembei*) are rice crackers made from glutinous rice. There are various shapes and flavours available.

[vi] One *sen* is 1/100 of one *yen*. It is no longer in use.

THE MONSTER OF THE LIGHTHOUSE

1

The murky sky was covered by a veil of sea fog so typical of the North Pacific Ocean on that fateful night when, without any warning, the light of the Shiomaki Lighthouse suddenly disappeared. We were working in the marine laboratory on the other side of the bay.

Fishery laboratories and lighthouses don't fall under the same jurisdiction, but our work had the sea in common, so we were on friendly terms with our neighbours in the lighthouse, in this region faraway removed from human society. In fact, as we were always peering into our microscopes to stare at fish eggs and assess the quality of *kompu* kelp, the reassuring sight of Shiomaki Lighthouse, which projected a gently shining ray of light over the wild seas at night, always comforted us. We had fostered a sense of admiration for our neighbours within. So when the night guard got laboratory director Azumaya and me out of our beds to tell us about the strange disappearance of the light, we set out along the dark beach path towards Cape Shiomaki with a sinking feeling in our stomachs.

Cape Shiomaki jutted out into the sea for about half a nautical mile, surrounded by many reefs. At a point several miles north of the cape, a cold current moving south from the Kuril Islands along the Sanriku coast comes into contact with a warm current moving in a northerly direction. At that location, those currents are transformed into a ferocious undercurrent flowing into the reef area of Cape Shiomaki. Blocked by countless projections on the sea floor, the undercurrent breaks up and suddenly rises to the surface. If you were to take a look at the sea surface, you'd see multiple streams silently racing against each other. That was why there were disproportionately many accidents here on densely foggy nights and sailors feared the place, calling it the Demon's Cape.

Several months earlier, reports had started spreading, originating with the crew of a freight ship which had barely avoided running aground on the reefs. The reports claimed that the light of the Shiomaki Lighthouse would sometimes act erratically, especially on nights with dense fog. Normally, the lighthouse sent out a beam of bright light every fifteen seconds, but on such occasions, it would sometimes only send out a light every thirty seconds. Now, it is the Inubō Lighthouse, several hundred miles further south, which sends out a light every thirty seconds, so steamships making the troublesome trip back from the northern seas through persistent fog could be fooled by this eerily erratic light. If they'd move starboard in their joy at having reached Cape Inubō, they'd immediately run into the underwater rocks and reefs and get sucked into the maelstrom. Sailors are a superstitious lot. Whether the terrible rumour was true or false, it started getting into the heads of sailors and it wasn't long after that—about one month ago—that on one particularly foggy night a freight ship did indeed hit the underground rocks. It had sent out dozens of distress calls, repeating its report on the anomaly going on at Shiomaki Lighthouse, but the ship eventually disappeared completely. The incident had become public, and the Shiomaki Lighthouse had been given a serious warning by the authorities.

Shiomaki Lighthouse was a third class lighthouse under the direct control of the Ministry of Communications. It had two keepers, and—including their families and others—six people altogether were living there. One of the two keepers in particular was an extremely trustworthy employee, reliability personified. Jōroku Kazama was almost sixty and lived there together with his daughter Midori. His serious nature, which reminded people of an old warrior, attracted much respect. And what made the old keeper even more reliable was the fact that he was a fervent believer in science, and unlike many of his age, did not believe in the supernatural. Even when the warning from the authorities came, he only answered curtly:

'We have a rotation shift to guard the lighthouse each and every night, so there is no way a thing like that could have happened here. It was probably an unfortunate trick of the light caused by a flow of thick sea fog, or a large flock of migratory birds inside the fog that reflected the light. But now it has grown into a larger story, making everyone suspicious of us.'

Yet, despite the stern old keeper's declaration, a distinctly bizarre incident had just occurred at Shiomaki Lighthouse.

The light had at first been sent far out into the grey fog every fifteen seconds, as normal, but then it suddenly turned into an eerie continuous beam of light for about two seconds, then vanished into the ominous darkness. All we could make out was the occasional low, heavy boom of the fog horn through the relentless roar of the sea.

We made our way quickly as possible to the tip of Cape Shiomaki and, just as the outline of the gigantic, thirty-metre high white tower loomed out of the fog, we suddenly saw two men appearing silently in front of us out of the darkness. They were Mitamura, the wireless radio operator, and Sano, the attendant.

'Oh, it's you….' The small attendant called out and ran towards us as soon as he recognised us.

'I'm so glad you came.' Radio engineer Mitamura immediately started speaking. 'Our radio has broken down, so I couldn't contact anyone. We were about to come over to the laboratory.'

From the strangely nervous behaviour of these two men, I imagined that something out of the ordinary had happened. As we walked together towards the lighthouse, Mitamura started to explain.

'It's Mr. Tomida, the lighthouse keeper who was on night watch tonight… something horrible has happened to him. It's really unbelievable. Mr. Kazama will explain it in detail to you.'

The attendant, who had been trailing behind us, suddenly muttered unexpectedly.

'It finally appeared….'

'What appeared?' asked Director Azumaya. The attendant shook his head several times, as if to disavow his own words.

'A-a… ghost appeared…'

2

We passed through the concrete gate and entered the well-lit grounds of the lighthouse. The three small living quarters to the right and the wireless radio cabin to the left were all brightly illuminated, but darkness had enveloped the top of the lighthouse, which stood in the centre of the grounds, facing the sea. Reflecting the light of its surroundings, the white figure of the lighthouse appeared to be floating faintly in the darkness, resembling the lines of a female *sumō* wrestler. At the foot of the lighthouse stood the old lighthouse keeper Kazama, reminiscent of General Nogi[i] with his greying beard, who was trying to calm down a pale, middle-aged woman. When he saw us, he had the attendant Sano take the woman to the living quarters and then turned to us.

'That's Tomida's wife Aki. She is in a terrible mental state, so I can't show her the place where it happened until she has calmed down. I really can hardly believe it.'

As he was speaking, old Kazama tried to light a candle, but because of his trembling hands, he had to strike several matches to get a flame.

I had met with him a couple of times before, but this was the first time I had seen him shaken like that. There was no hint of the unbending old warrior to be seen. He stepped out in front of us, the flame on the candle still flickering, and as he quietly opened the entrance of the lighthouse, he turned to us again.

'…A-anyway, please come see what has happened.'

Director Azumaya, radio engineer Mitamura and I followed him into the gloomy stairwell. As soon as we were all inside and the door had closed behind us, the lighthouse keeper suddenly came closer and whispered:

'…This is the first time in my long life I have seen a ghost….'

I felt my whole body freeze to hear the usually sanguine Kazama talk like that.

'…I'll explain everything right from the beginning,' said the old man, as he led us up the dark, steep spiral staircase. His voice reverberated against the high inner wall and an indescribably creepy whisper of an echo repeated after him.

'…I wasn't on watch tonight but Tomida had been helping out with the wireless radio during the day, and tired as he was, he'd sometimes doze off. And then there are the rumours, and my insolent daughter has not been in a good mood tonight, so with all that on my mind, I just couldn't fall asleep. Then, about an hour ago, I was finally about to doze off when I suddenly heard the loud noise of glass breaking from high up. And at almost the same moment, I heard a powerful, metallic noise, as if a machine were breaking down. I sat up in dazed shock for a moment, but then I realised that if the noise had come from above, it could only have come from the lighthouse, and I hurried anxiously out of my living quarters. I gazed up, and all I could see was total darkness: the light from the lantern room on the top of the tower was out. Before I knew it I had cried out at the top of my voice to Tomida, who should have been up there in the lantern room. There was no answer, but I could feel the earth rumble from the foot of the lighthouse. I realised something terrible must have happened so I made my way over to the lighthouse, where I met up with Mitamura, who like me had quickly left his wireless radio cabin.'

Here, the old lighthouse keeper stopped to take a breath. The spiral staircase was starting to seem almost like an optical illusion and was getting on my nerves. Mitamura, who was standing behind us on the spiral staircase, added:

'Yes, both Mr. Kazama and I heard that creepy noise. And when we arrived at the lighthouse entrance, we heard a low, but absolutely hair-raising groaning voice—it must have been Mr. Tomita—and the groan wasn't even over when we heard that indescribable voice of a ghost….'

'The voice of a ghost?' asked Director Azumaya, very intrigued.

'Yes, it was definitely a ghost. There's no way it could have been the voice of a human being! …It sounded as if it was laughing and crying at the same time… Yes, yes, like one of those toy balloon flutes.'

'There are migrating birds which have a similar cry,' observed the old lighthouse keeper.

'They might be similar, but they were still quite different. It's more accurate to say it resembled the cry of a rutting cat.'

'Oh, yes, yes, you're right.' Kazama dropped the topic. 'Anyway, I had Mitamura go back to the wireless whilst I continued up the staircase with the candlestick in my hand. And when I finally arrived in the lantern room at the top—which also serves as the night watchman's room— I witnessed the most terrifying sight….'

'A ghost?' asked the director.

'Yes. It had made its way inside by breaking those thick glass panes surrounding the lantern room with a gigantic rock.'

At that moment, Mitamura cried out and pointed to the steps of the staircase up ahead of us. Illuminated by the weak light of the candle, I could see a pool of dark blood which had flowed down the steps. I held my breath. Without exchanging a word, we entered the lantern room, where we saw for ourselves the violent traces left by the monster.

Large glass panes enclosed the room all round, but there was a big hole in one of the panes facing the dark sea. Cracks had spread out from the hole in all directions like a spider's web. A chilly sea wind caused fog to flow in through the hole, causing the candle flame to flicker. A gigantic triangular lamp holding a large Fresnel lens stood right in the centre of the small, cylindrical room. Part of it had been heavily damaged, and it appeared that petroleum gas was leaking out of the dark mouth of the burner, because I could hear a faint hiss. Large gears—a characteristic of these revolving lighthouses—were set in the frame of the massive lens, which rested on top of a cup-shaped mercury bath. The gears were connected in turn to a sophisticated rotation device, but that had been smashed to pieces. A weight should normally have been suspended down the shaft located right in the centre of the lighthouse—to provide the rotating force for the lens—but the rope had broken.

But the truly atrocious image which caused me to avert my eyes was that of lighthouse keeper Tomida's body, which was lying beside the broken machinery. Blood had spewed out in all directions, the eyeballs looked about to pop out of the head and it resembled nothing so much as a flattened meatloaf on which rested a wet rock.

'…It's horrible… that's a very large rock,' said Director Azumaya.

'I'd say it probably weighs forty or fifty *kan*,' said Mitamura. 'I doubt that even two big men could have carried it all the way up here. And to be able to throw it thirty metres up, through the glass pane, from the edge of the sea… only a monster could have done that.'

'So what about that ghost you saw?' The laboratory director turned to old Kazama. The lighthouse keeper grimaced.

'…As I explained, just at the very moment I entered this room, I saw that horrendous fiend dive into the sea from that platform outside, on the other side of those broken glass panes. It looked like a terribly large boiled octopus, wet all over, red and squashy….'

'An octopus?' Director Azumaya cocked his head.

'An octopus has suckers, so it could have climbed up here,' I said, half-joking. But the director shook his head.

'No, in waters such as we have here, where there's a cold current, you might find some giant Pacific octopuses with sizes starting at two, three metres, but you'd hardly call them red.'

I turned my gaze to the linoleum floor, where I could see the traces made by the monster. Besides the many fragments of glass and the sea of blood, I could also make out some slimy fluid substance which had been spilt here and there on the floor, from which came an indescribably foetid smell which was pervading the room.

3

'I just don't understand.' After a while, Director Azumaya gave up. 'I have no idea what happened. But we at least have these facts.' He unfolded his arms. 'If we combine the report of the night guard at our lab with your story…. First, this rock smashed the pane of glass and landed inside the lantern room, destroying the lens and the rotation machinery and crushing Mr. Tomida. At that moment, the rotation of the lens ceased, stopping the movement of the beam of light, but the light soon went out anyway because of a problem with the gas pipe. Next, the rope attached to the rotation machinery snapped, and the weight—which provided the rotating force—fell all thirty metres down the central shaft, causing the ground to tremble on impact, after which Mr. Tomida cried out for the last time. And then, to cap it all, at that moment, a monster appeared, making that terrifying cry and excreting the creepy fluid here… I confess I have no idea what to make of it all.'

'I've never in my life experienced anything like it!' exclaimed Kazama.

The director turned to address him. 'So what did you do when you came upon this horror?'

'I was shocked of course, but I decided to go back down, and on my way I met Mitamura here coming up.'

'The wireless radio wasn't working,' explained the radio engineer.

Kazama continued: 'The antenna set between that iron pole over there and the railing in front of the glass pane here had been broken by the rock. So we split up again. I went downstairs to wake up Sano, while Mitamura went up to the lantern room. But we had to do something, so after some deliberation, I sent Mitamura and Sano to your laboratory to get help.'

'I see. I'm afraid we haven't been of much help,' said the director, starting to become practical again. 'But we can't leave things as they are. Mr. Kazama, could you prepare the back-up lens right away, without touching the evidence in the room? It's pitch-dark outside at sea now. Mr. Mitamura, can you repair the antenna and restore communications as quickly as possible? We'll help too.'

The two men hesitated for a moment, but, as if lured by the sound of the waves, they started descending the lighthouse stairs. Director Azumaya and I took another look at the disorderly room, while we tried to keep calm.

Nothing had prepared us for the important discovery we made. In a shadowy corner of the room, we found a dull hatchet with dark blood on the blunt blade.

The expression on the director's face changed and he crouched down to take a closer look at Tomida's body. It didn't take long for him to discover a fatal wound above the right ear, which appeared to have been freshly made by the hatchet. He stood up.

'From the way the blood from this wound has set, I'd say it was made first and therefore it's the true fatal wound. So, by the time the rock crashed through the glass, lighthouse keeper Tomida was already dead. But that means that the cry heard after the noise made by the crashing rock was not made by the deceased. This changes everything.'

'Then what was the source of the ghostly cry?' I blurted out.

He didn't respond and seemed lost in thought. Then he started to talk again.

'Listen, I think that first of all we need to work out where this huge rock came from. I don't see any barnacles or sea snails clinging to it anywhere, though there are plenty of those creatures in the seas around here. That means that the rock was lying somewhere above the high water line. But judging from how damp it is, it obviously didn't come here from the mountains, either. Why don't we take a little walk outside, to look at the area of high tide?'

And so we went down to the water's edge at the base of the lighthouse.

There, the sharp wind blowing from the dark, foggy ocean showered us with spray from the waves. At a spot just beyond where the waves were at their most violent, we came upon several similar rocks, all wet from the spray.

Between two of the rocks I unexpectedly discovered a length of thick rope going down to the sea. When I reached for it and pulled, the rope gave, so I started rolling it in. It was pretty long. After a while, I reached the end, only to find that a thin piece of cord had been tied to the end of the rope. I pulled on the cord, which also turned out to be quite long. When I had finally rolled the whole thing up, I remarked to the laboratory director in wonder: 'How odd.'

He had been staring at my peculiar catch the whole time, and now declared: 'Things are becoming very interesting. We'll have to consider this new discovery very carefully! Let's ask them what they were using it for.'

So saying, he took the rope from me and started walking back to the lighthouse grounds, which we reached just as Mitamura was exiting the storage cabin in front with a bundle of wires. Director Azumaya asked him point blank:

'Is this rope yours?'

'Yes. We have several of them in the storage cabin. Oh, but there's a thin cord attached here… Where did you find it?'

The director didn't answer. Instead, he looked up at the dark sky above us, and asked: 'The height of the lighthouse up to the floor of the lantern room is thirty metres, I think? Could you please check the length of the rope?'

Mitamura used a tape measure and announced:

'…The rope and the cord are twenty-six metres, each.'

'Twenty-six, you say? Wait….' Director Azumaya stared up at the dark sky again. 'Mr. Mitamura, what is the weight of the rotating lens?'

'I'd guess it's easily one ton?'

'One ton. One ton equals slightly more than 266 *kan*. Then the weight that's lowered into the thirty metre shaft at the centre of the lighthouse—the weight that serves as the force which rotates the lens—that thing must be quite heavy too.'

'Yes, it's at least eighty *kan*. It's like a gigantic stone mortar. It descends the shaft slowly, and once it reaches its lowest point, we wind it up again.'

'I see. When did you last wind it up?'

'Yesterday afternoon.'

'So the weight should still have been high up in the shaft tonight.'

'Yes.'

'Thank you very much. Oh, do you mind if I smoke a cigarette there in the wireless radio cabin?' asked the director. He dragged me inside the cabin and closed the door. 'Listen, I think I'm on to something. But first I want to test my theory out on you.'

4

Director Azumaya sat down on a nearby chair, lit up a cigarette and started to talk.

'First of all, whether it was a monster or a human being, our violent being pushed one end of the thick piece of rope through the small air vent below the glass panes of the lantern room, thus suspending it above the rocks outside. Then they descended from the lighthouse, went outside and tied the thick rope to the rock we later found in the lantern room. Returning to the top of the lighthouse, they took the other end of the rope, which they had left in the lantern room, and opened the cover of the rotation machinery. They tied the rope to the handle of the weight—which had been hanging near the top of the closed-off shaft—with a slip knot, which can be untied by simply pulling on one end. They then tied one end of the thin cord to the end of the slip knot, making sure to keep the other end of the cord in the lantern room. When all the preparation was complete, they used the hatchet to cut the rope which attached the weight to the winch on the rotation device. And….'

'Oh, it'd be like a well bucket, with a pulley!' I cried out. 'The rock would be pulled up from outside the lighthouse into the lantern room by the terrible force of a weight of eighty *kan* falling down the shaft. But if it had happened like that, the quake made by the weight hitting the ground should have happened at practically the same time as the sound of the glass pane and machinery breaking.'

'I have, naturally, considered that point,' the director continued. 'But, you see, by accident or by design, while the shaft is thirty metres *deep*, the rope is only twenty-six metres *long*. We're supposed to believe that a monster from the sea threw a large rock into the lantern room, destroying the rotation device, after which the rope holding the weight eventually broke, allowing the weight to drop down and cause a quake, but that's not what happened at all. In fact, our "monster" first killed the lighthouse keeper Tomida, then tied a thick rope to the handle of the weight, and then a cord to the end of the knot. So, after the "monster" destroyed the machinery, it pulled on the end of the cord, which loosened the knot tied to the handle, dropping the weight completely down to the bottom of the shaft. That's why our two witnesses first heard the glass pane and machinery being broken, and only felt the quake later, after a short pause.'

'I see.' I nodded.

'As for our "monster" or fiendish human being, they pulled the rope up from inside the shaft—it was no longer tied to the weight—and also loosened the end of the rope tied around the rock now lying on top of Tomida. They couldn't go down the staircase, as people startled by all the noise had started climbing up, so they tied the rope to the railing on the platform outside the lantern room—again with a slip knot with cord attached—and climbed down the rope to one of the higher boulders, one lying five or six metres higher than the base of the lighthouse. There they undid the knot again in the same way, by pulling on one end, and threw the rope and the cord into the sea….'

'Marvellous!' I cried out, greatly impressed. 'Even the feeblest of men could have pulled that feat off with a little effort. But was this the work of a ghost or a human being?'

'That is the question,' said Director Azumaya, getting up. 'Now we have identified the trick behind the rock, it does appear as though it could only have been the work of a human being. However, that reliable, earnest Mr. Kazama insists he saw a monster, and we still have that liquid smeared all over the floor of the lantern room, and that strange groan and the cry.... Anyway, let's go up to the top of the lighthouse once again.'

And so we made our way up to the dark lantern room once more. Mitamura was there already, together with some of his equipment. As soon as he saw us, he said he was going to repair the antenna and would appreciate it if we could assist him. So I went out onto the dangerous-looking platform on the other side of one of the other windows, holding a bunch of wires and playing the local electrician.

The wind had become quite a bit stronger, which had dispersed the fog slightly but made the waves rougher, with the result that ferocious waves were crashing into the rocks precisely thirty metres below the platform we were standing on.

'We're quite high up,' said the director. 'It'd be quite difficult for anyone to climb down a rope here.' He suddenly brightened and posed a peculiar question to Mitamura, who was working next to him.

'Could you please show me your palms for a second?'

Aha, he was planning to find the monster by looking for calluses on the palms. What a brilliant idea!

There were no calluses on Mitamura's palms, however. The director suddenly looked embarrassed and, not without some shame, decided to leave us. He hurried down the lighthouse stairs.

While I was assisting with the antenna repairs, I was able to peer down and see him appear at the base of the lighthouse, and also just make out what he said to old Kazama, who had just come out of his living quarters.

'Haven't you prepared the back-up light yet?' he shouted.

'I was about to work on that. I have to clean the mess up first.' For some reason, the voice of old Kazama seemed to have lost all spirit.

'Excuse me, but could you show me your palms for a second?' There it was, the same question, as expected. I thought things were about to get interesting, but my excitement was short-lived. There were no calluses on old Kazama's palms either. Then the old lighthouse keeper went into the storage cabin, while the director headed for the living quarters and disappeared from sight.

Repairing the antenna turned out to be quite a difficult job. Both my hands hurt so much I thought they'd break. It was also terribly cold up there, and high enough to make anyone feel dizzy. Eventually, we managed to finish the troublesome chore but, just at that moment, Director Azumaya burst into the lantern room with a distressed expression on his face.

He was visibly upset and could only speak in intervals between gasps.

'...The victim's wife... she overcame the attendant... said she needed to see her husband's body... I think it might be better if we show her as soon as possible....'

'And her palms?' I couldn't contain my curiosity.

'Her palms? Oh, neither she nor the attendant had any calluses on their palms.'

'That means it was indeed the work of something supernatural....'

'No, just a second. After talking with the victim's wife, I paid a quick visit next door, to Mr. Kazama's living quarters, to meet his daughter.... And there I made a great discovery!'

'A great discovery? You mean you found calluses on the palms of his sleeping daughter Midori?'

'No, not that. Nothing at all like that.'

'No? Was there something wrong with her then?'

'I wish I could say that. But I didn't meet the daughter at all. She wasn't to be found in any of the rooms.'

'You say Midori's gone?' Mitamura pounced on the director's words as the dim flame of the candle cast his shadow on the wall.

'She wasn't there. But instead, I saw what the old man had seen... the red, slimy ghost!'

5

After a moment, Director Azumaya regained his composure, glanced quickly at me and turned to Mitamura.

'By the way, Mr. Mitamura, you said you met Mr. Kazama halfway down the staircase when you came up here, right after it all happened. Was Mr. Kazama holding anything in his hands at the time?'

'...Well, now you mention it, he had taken off his jacket and was holding it in his right arm like this.'

'I see. Thank you. Allow me to ask you one more thing. How old is his daughter?'

'Errr, probably about twenty-eight.'

'And how does she behave?'

'How she behaves? Errr... she appears to be a very sensible, good person....'

'Whatever you say will remain between the three of us, so please speak freely.'

'Very well... she was really nice at first... but then....' Mitamura seemed reluctant to speak. '...I think it happened a year ago, around the same time of year. She became really friendly with the engineer of a freight ship who was staying in Mr. Kazama's home at the time, and they... Well, they really shouldn't have eloped. I heard they went somewhere near Yokohama or thereabouts, but her man was an untrustworthy sailor, and as you might expect, he dumped her after he got her pregnant. She returned here about six months ago, her heart broken.'

'I see. And then...?'

'...She was once a really cheerful girl, but the experience changed her completely. And so, after a while, even Mr. Kazama started to look at his own daughter with cold eyes. The poor thing....'

A conflicted look appeared on Mitamura's face, and he started rubbing his hands, as if he now regretted speaking out of line. The director, however, had been listening to him intently. He raised his head and muttered gloomily:

'...I think I have an idea who might have performed that trick with the rampaging boulder.'

'Who was it?! Was it the daughter, or perhaps...'

'It was the daughter Midori, of course.'

He sat down silently on a nearby chair, placed his elbows on his knees and clasped his fingers together. Turning his head a few times, as if still hesitating, he started slowly with his explanation.

'...I'm afraid it's only conjecture at this point, and I'm no expert on romance, but my imagination can't help but lead me down this path. ... Anyway, please imagine a pure-hearted daughter of a lighthouse keeper. One day, she falls in love with a sailor who's been saved from a ship in distress. Her father, however, is a terribly strict person, and does not approve of his daughter's feelings. The two young lovers leave in search of a sweet dream together. But when the girl starts to bear the fruit of their love, the man goes aboard a ship to sail for faraway lands. The girl, deceived, returns home, harbouring unbearable hate in her heart. Her father's cold behaviour towards her only pushes her further into madness, and the sight of ships passing by like a dream, every single night and day, nurtures the hatred in her heart. Her hatred for that one man turns into hatred for all sailors and her hatred for sailors turns into hatred for ships. Wishing to sink all the ships out there, she decides to break the one absolute rule. On foggy nights, she'd wait for the lighthouse keeper to doze off, and interfere in the most deadly way with the lighthouse, the lifeline for sailors. One night, however, she was interrupted by the lighthouse keeper, and in her shock she picked up a hatchet and brought it down on the man's head. Frightened by the horrendous crime she had committed, she played that trick with the rock to bury the evidence of her crime. She'd probably dreamt up the trick earlier as part of a plan to destroy the lighthouse....'

'But what about that horrible monster?' I had to ask.

'There was no monster.'

'But you say you saw it yourself.'

'Now wait a second. Please don't interrupt my story. Her old father is an incredibly strict and earnest man, with a great sense of responsibility. His attitude to his daughter has been cold and there is no way he would forgive her for committing such terrible sins. Despite that, however, the old man's feelings changed completely the moment he arrived in the lantern room after hearing all the chaos. It was at that moment that, for the first time in his life, he made up a completely false story—one about a monster—to hide his daughter's crime.'

'But if it was all a lie, what about those things done by the monster? That eerie slimy liquid, and the groan Mr. Mitamura here also heard, and that unusual cry?'

'Please allow me to finish. The old lighthouse keeper had lit a candle and made his way up the lighthouse stairs, shaking in fear. What do you think he saw when he reached the lantern room? Not the broken glass panes. Not the destroyed machinery. Not the body of the victim Tomida. Listen carefully. He saw two living persons! His unfortunate daughter, half-mad now she had committed a terrible crime and been discovered by her strict father, was standing on the other side of the window glass and he could not prevent her from jumping down into the sea. But there was another person.... A red, soft, slimy being, like an octopus. Yes. The psychological shock, and the excitement caused by all her exertions had led to a premature birth: it was his healthy first grandchild!'

I could not stop myself from crying out.

So that was it! I was surprised at myself for not realising until this moment. That bizarre groan was caused by the agonizing, convulsive pains of birth; that peculiar cry like that of a balloon flute was the first cry of a newborn baby; and the strange, slimy fluid was the amniotic water that had now fulfilled its task of protecting the fetus. I started to understand how old Kazama must have felt at the moment he saw the cute face of his first grandchild, appealing to the soft spot in his heart.

At that moment, my pleasant mental image was interrupted by the slight creaking of the door. The disheartened old lighthouse keeper, Jōroku Kazama, appeared in the entrance, the dim light reflecting on his swollen eyelids.

First published in *Shinseinen*, December Issue, Shōwa 10 (1935).

---

[i] Count Maresuke Nogi (1849-1912) was a general in the Imperial Japanese Army and a prominent figure in the Russo-Japanese War of 1904-05. He was seen as a national hero in Imperial Japan, dedicating his life to the emperor and the army. One episode has Nogi asking the emperor permission to commit suicide to atone for the soldiers he lost during his capture of Port Arthur. He was denied, but Nogi eventually did commit ritual suicide on the funeral day of the Meiji emperor.

THE PHANTOM WIFE

Well then, allow me to tell you the story right from the beginning. You know, by the time you reach my age, you'll be aware that a lot of curious things happen in this world, but I swear to heaven it was the first time in my life I'd experienced anything so horrendous.

By the way, you already know the name of my master, who met with that tragic fate, don't you? Yes, yes, it was all over the newspapers. Shōjirō Hirata was my master's name, and he was forty-six at the time. The papers got everything else wrong of course, but at least they got those two facts right. He was the headmaster of N Technical School and an outstanding, disciplined teacher. His only shortcoming was perhaps that he was too earnest. Anyway, some time before the incident happened, the master and the mistress divorced, and it's a terrible thing she died like that. His wife—her name was Natsue—she was thirty-four, twelve years younger than the master. The mistress was—just like the papers said—a splendid person: very attractive and kindhearted as well. Maybe I shouldn't mention this, but two years earlier, this old man you're talking to lost his job as janitor at the school, but then got hired as a servant at the residence. I later heard this from the maid, but it was the mistress who arranged all of that for me. How should I say this, the master can be a bit fussy in his ways, but the mistress was precisely what you'd expect from a daughter of a distinguished family: generous and graceful. Because of that, the master and the mistress had never once got into a fight.

I forgot to mention this to you, but unlike the master, the mistress was a pure-bred daughter of the town of Edo[i]. Her family home was in the kimono business in Ningyōchō, and they had a very successful shop there. They had no children, and lived a very peaceful life. Then suddenly their marriage took a turn for the worse, and eventually the master brought up the dreaded topic of divorce.

Now, we of course had no idea why he suddenly began talking about divorce after all that time. The mistress' father also came by two or three times to talk it over with him, but the master obstinately refused to listen and the mistress was taken back to her parents.

And that, yes, that was how the tragedy started. The mistress was weeping terribly as her father took her back—her eyes were all red from crying. And the master himself appeared very upset, and hardly uttered a word through the whole ordeal. We were, of course, very worried about it all, but what could we do? We were just hired staff. And, most important of all, we had no idea of why in heaven's name he had decided on a divorce, so there was nothing we could say. Sumi, the maid, claimed the mistress might've committed an indiscretion, which would've been a good reason for divorce, but I've always known perfectly well for a fact that the mistress was not someone to conduct herself badly. Yes, the mistress was very attractive and, as she was raised in the old downtown *shitamachi* neighbourhood, her interests lay with traditional Japanese culture. She'd often wear a traditional *nihongami* hairstyle—with the hair pulled to the back like *geisha* apprentices—but I can't begin to describe how elegant she looked. I might be speaking out of turn here, but she was without any doubt attractive enough to be the wife of a school principal. And yes, they had no children, so the mistress did often leave the house on her own, but I swear she never once went out alone after sunset. I've come across many different kinds of women in my lifetime, but there are few women like the mistress, who knew precisely how to conduct herself.

Oh, sorry, I've wandered off the story completely, but now I'll talk about the horrible incident. It happened, yes, on the fourth day after they had left each other. The mistress' belongings hadn't been unpacked yet, but the divorce had weighed so heavily on her that she took poison in her family home and passed away. It was a very terrible thing. I heard of this later, but the mistress had left a simple note for the master, where she'd lamented how she'd failed to disperse the clouds of suspicion even though she was innocent. A servant had been sent from Ningyōchō to inform the master of the mistress' sudden death and to bring him the note, and the master's face visibly changed colour.

But listen: it was at that moment that I witnessed first-hand how obstinate scholars can be. The mistress had given up her own life to defend her innocence, and, even supposing she had sinned, one shouldn't be so harsh towards her now she'd gone to heaven, should one? But the master, he said with a pale face that, since they were now divorced, she wasn't family any more, and I don't know whether it was out of pride, or whether he was simply being stubborn, but he didn't even make the effort to attend the funeral. We were of course all anxious about it, but in the end only her own family went to the funeral. And all that tragedy was followed by an indescribably desolate period.

Anyway, if things had just continued like that, nothing would have happened, but to tell you the truth, the tale I told you just now was nothing more than a prologue. Now I'll get to the heart of the subject and, as you all know, a truly terrifying incident happened.

The first time I noticed that the master was behaving peculiarly was on the third day after the funeral of the mistress. As I explained to you just now, the master had obstinately decided not to appear at the funeral and the matter might have ended there, but to us servants, whom the mistress cared for so much, it did not feel right not to pay any respects at all to her. So we asked the master if we could at least visit her grave, and while he initially acted very stubbornly on the surface, I could see he did feel some guilt somewhere inside him.

'Well then, maybe I too should pay a quiet visit to her grave.' Thus he quickly proposed joining us.

I forgot to tell you this, but the mistress' resting place is in the Yanaka Cemetery, which isn't far from our mansion in Tabata, so we went to the grave on foot. We all left together for the grave after the master had finished his work at school, and by the time we'd travelled Dōkanyama Hill and arrived at the cemetery in Yanaka, the sun was about to set. It was a lonesome time of the day.

The master had visited the grave of the mistress' family before, so he knew exactly where it was and walked straight there with the flowers, while I went to the well to scoop up some water[ii]. As a result I arrived a bit later at the grave than he did, but I did nevertheless observe how the master—with his face deathly pale—had turned around in a panic, as if he was fleeing from something.

'I'm not feeling well all of a sudden. We're going back this very instant. Find me a car,' he told me.

I was absolutely stunned, of course. I'd only just arrived there, so I didn't want to turn back without having paid my respects. Nonetheless, I couldn't leave the master alone in that condition, so with regret in my heart, we walked back to a major street in Sakuragichō, and although it was a roundabout route, we did get a car and return to the mansion.

When I looked back afterwards I realised with a shock that—even if it had been difficult—if I'd somehow been able to convince the master to return home on his own, I could've gone to the grave myself and had a chance to see whatever the master had witnessed at that lonely spot. At the time, however, I simply thought it was odd, and I was more worried about the master's condition, so I was not able to make the correct judgment.

So we returned home, and the master's condition quickly recovered, but from that day on, his behaviour started to change. His complexion was always pale, his eyes were always bloodshot, and he always seemed to be on edge. We thought it was because his condition had not fully recovered yet.

Oh, yes, there was even more. The master had always had the habit of reading and writing until late into the night, but that stopped all of a sudden, and he started telling the maid to lay out his bed early so he could go to sleep. And he became obsessed with making sure the doors and windows were securely locked and reminded us all the time. Perhaps we were just imagining things, but it seemed to all of us that he was acting more and more strangely with each passing day. But we couldn't guess as to the reason, and all we could do was worry about the master's health.

Anyway, this ill-starred behaviour—similar to that of Shinzaburō in the classic ghost tale *The Peony Lantern*[iii]—became gradually worse over the course of four days, until that horrible final night.

I tell you, I still shudder simply by thinking back to that ghastly time. That day, the brother of the maid Sumi had arrived from their hometown in Chiba, so she was allowed the night off to go out with him. So this old man here was the only one left to take care of the master. After he'd finished his dinner around six o'clock, he brought out a bundle of documents from his study.

'I am planning to take two or three days off from school starting tomorrow, so please inform Mr. Ueda in Waseda and deliver these to him.'

Mr. Ueda was a teacher at the school who acted as the master's deputy, and as it was still early, I estimated I could be back in two hours, so I quickly left for Tabata Station to head out for Waseda. And, as per my instructions, I locked everything up securely, including the main gate, and left by the back entrance. But now I have to admit that leaving the master all on his own was a terrible mistake.

By the time I'd finished my business and returned, it was already later than I'd originally estimated: eight-thirty. I clicked my tongue, as I was sure the master would complain about that, so I hurried through the hallway to the study. I stood before the door and called out anxiously: 'I have returned.'

But there was no answer. I called out to the master again, opened the door and took one step inside. It was then that I got a shock and stood frozen to the spot. There was no sign of the master inside the room, and I had no idea where he'd gone. But that wasn't what was shocking. The glass door of the window facing the garden had been forced open, and several of the iron bars set in the outer window frame had been wrenched out of their sockets. I could see streaks of darkness pouring into the room like a nightmare. Startled, I stepped towards of the window, but then my eyes wandered off to beyond the open *fusuma* sliding door[iv], inside the *tatami*-floored living room[v], and I could feel myself collapse to the ground.

I had found my master—no longer among the living—lying face-up in front of the alcove pillar. His appearance was so incredibly gruesome I couldn't bear to look at him twice. His eyes were almost popping out of his head, as if he had seen something horrible, and his face had turned ashen. I looked around, and the whole room was in a terrible state, so I knew the master must have put up some resistance, as the *zabuton* sitting cushions and the fire tongs had been thrown all over the place....

And as for what happened next, how I reacted... When I think back, I cannot remember a single thing about what I did then. By the time I'd got a grip of myself, several police officers had already arrived, trampling all over the place as they investigated the case. They had come across some very unusual facts.

According to the police investigation, the monstrous being that had visited my master had obviously been alone, and had been wearing garden *geta* sandals. There was a trail of footprints going over the hedge near the front gate, bypassing the front entrance to the house to go to the rear entrance, and leading to the study window facing the garden, all belonging to the same sandals. As you know, *geta* consist of wooden soles, each raised above the ground by two wooden cross-pieces called "teeth" and held to the foot by a fabric strap passing between the toes. Investigation showed that the knot of the strap—placed on the underside of the base—had also left an impression on the footprints, on the inner side of the marks made by the teeth. This meant the inner side of these *geta* teeth had been worn down heavily enough for the knot to have left an impression as well.

I could feel a shudder run down my spine as I overheard the police officers talking this over between themselves. As I already told you, the deceased mistress loved traditional Japanese culture, so she often wore a traditional *nihongami* haircut, and she also walked with her toes turned inward, even though modern ladies don't walk like that any more. I was startled when she first told me that her footwear would always wear down on the inside very rapidly. As I say, I shuddered when I remembered that, but I made up my mind not to tell the police.

Three of the iron bars, each about as thick as a man's thumb, had been pulled out of the study window facing the garden. Each of the bars had been twisted by some inhuman, violent force, and then been pulled out of the sockets in the window frame. When I saw how the bars had been bent at the centre, and how they had been thrown away under the eaves, I couldn't suppress another shudder.

And as for the poor master's body, it was in truly atrocious shape. Apparently his skull had been smashed, so the master died of a concussion, but his neck had also been snapped. No other wounds were discovered, but the police did find something oh-so blood-curdling clenched firmly in his right hand. I crouched down by his side, and there, can you believe it, between the fingers of his clenched fist, were a few strands of a woman's long hair. And that wasn't all, as I could smell something very nostalgic from those strands: the wax used for a *nihongami* hairstyle....I looked up, my mind a blank. The room was ten *tatami* mats wide, and on the wall opposite the *tokonoma* alcove[vi], stood still the mistress' *tansu* chest of drawers[vii] and dressing table. We hadn't had the time to sort things out yet after the mistress' death, so we had left everything in the room covered with oil cloths. I'd looked up because I'd detected the scent of wax, and my eyes had subconsciously drifted to the dressing table. At that moment I stood up.

I hadn't noticed it before, but the brightly printed silken dressing table cover had been flipped over in an inviting way, and on the floor in front of a half-open drawer lay a comb made of boxwood. I got up instinctively, walked over to the dresser, crouched down and then looked around again. The comb had been thrown down on the *tatami* mat in front of the drawer, and I noticed that three or four strands of hair—just like the ones gripped by the master—had been left on the comb, curled around it in a sinister way....

At that moment, I felt as though I could actually see a ghostly figure seated in front of the dressing table, resetting its disheveled hair before disappearing. My trembling simply wouldn't stop.

And I then came upon yet another sign of ill omen. I'd only noticed it after I'd gone over to the dresser, but fresh incense sticks—the kind used in cemeteries, not in the home—had been dropped all over the *tatami* mat in the corner of the room and been stepped on. Oh, what a terrifying sight! I closed my eyes and started to pray to whomsoever came to mind. I was no longer able to keep my frightful thoughts to myself, so when the police started questioning me, I told them everything: how the mistress was divorced and how she died; about the strange behaviour of the master after we went to the Yanaka Cemetery; and all the eerie happenings that had occurred up to this present time.

A police officer with gold stripes on his epaulette turned to his colleague after listening to my story in silence:

'It appears the old man here thinks that the deceased wife turned into a ghost and came here.'

As he grinned broadly, he turned back to me.

'I see, old man. I guess it's hard to believe that a living person could have caused such a horrible mess. But, depending on how you look at things, even a woman acting alone would be capable of doing all of this. For example, you don't need monstrous strength to pull those iron bars out of the window. There's a trick to it. You first use a towel or some other piece of cloth, loop it around two of the bars, and pull it tight. Then you place a wooden stick inside the loop and turn it around to pull the towel even tighter. It doesn't take long for the bars to bend and fall out of the frame. It's really child's play. And as for the wounds on the deceased, you can make those kinds of wounds with any heavy instrument. As for the *geta* sandals being worn down on the inside, there are plenty of people who walk with their toes pointing inwards besides the wife of the deceased. Got it? One last thing. I need you to direct me to the dead wife's family home in Ningyōchō. We'll need to talk to all the women there.'

So saying, the senior officer started to raise his powerful body out of the seat. But at that moment a young doctor who had been examining the body of the master suddenly appeared.

'Chief Inspector, I'm afraid you're mistaken,' the doctor began. 'For example, your theory about bending the iron bars. Yes, by using your trick, any person can easily bend two bars. But in this case, three bars were bent. Your method only works with an even number of bars. With an odd number you'll always be one bar short to coil the towel around. So those bars weren't pulled out of the window with that old burglar's trick. They were undoubtedly pulled out by someone monstrously strong.

'And as for the *geta* sandals, you appear to assume they were worn by someone in the family in Ningyōchō. But, for the bottom side of a *geta* to be so heavily worn down that the knot of the strap shows on the footprint, means that the person hasn't just worn those garden *geta* sandals once or twice, but must be wearing them all the time. Do you really think that the kind of woman who is elegant enough to sit down in front of a dresser to reset her disheveled hair, would be wearing garden *geta* sandals all the time, in Ningyōchō of all places?'

Having said his piece, the doctor walked over to the corner of the room, picked up some of the incense sticks which were lying on the *tatami* mat, and walked back over to me.

'Do you know where the wife's grave is located in the Yanaka Cemetery?' he asked. I was surprised by the question, but I nodded silently. The shrewd-looking young doctor then asked: 'Could you then please take us there?'

He turned to the police officer. 'Chief Inspector, this bundle of incense sticks is still fresh and was meant to be used after the murder. Let us go to the Yanaka Cemetery now, and show them to the terrifying being who left them here.'

Thus it was that, after a ten-minute ride in a police car, we arrived at Yanaka Cemetery in the middle of the night.

We left the car a good way from the entrance, and, as per the doctor's instructions, did not utter a word as we silently entered the cemetery. The full moon had managed to break through a gap in the clouds, and was casting a pale light on a sea of gravestones as far as the eye could see. It was clear enough to make out the trees surrounding the cemetery, which were swaying gently in the night breeze. I walked in front as the guide, and I shall never, never forget the amazing sight. The impression… was burnt into my eyes.

It didn't take long for us to reach the wife's grave, which sadly had no gravestone yet. We could faintly make out the pale smoke of incense rising in the darkness.

'Oh, but that's smoke,' I said, pointing with a trembling finger. My task as a guide had been accomplished, so the others went in front. The doctor quickly made his way over to the grave and peered intently at it.

'I expected something like this,' he said and he called out to us to come, pointing with his chin. We came over to take look at what was lying in front of the grave. The extraordinary sight had us all frozen to the spot.

In front of the brand new, diagonally standing wooden grave tablet, on top of the pitch-black, damp earth, lay the grotesque figure of someone dressed in flashy *yukata*-cloth night clothing, with long, black hair tied together on the top of his head. It was that of a *sumō* wrestler, lying with his face to the sky. He had bitten his own tongue off.

'We were too late,' said the doctor and he started searching the body. But then his eyes fell on a white piece of paper—a letter. It had been placed next to the incense sticks in front of the grave tablet, which were almost burnt out. The doctor unfolded the letter and, without a word, handed it over to the chief inspector. They showed it to me afterwards. The writing was not refined, but it was written with complete dedication.

Dear Lady, my patron,

I have heard what happened from your father. It was because of me you were falsely accused and I will avenge you. This is the only way I can repay you for your special support.

That was basically the content of the letter.

And yes, after I learned that the letter had been written by a *sumō* wrestler, all that fuss I'd made about large *geta* footprints and garden *geta* seemed so foolish. I was later told by the master of the wife's family home that *geta* sandals of *sumō* wrestlers are often worn out on the inside, because most of the strength of a wrestler comes from the joint of the large toe, when they brace themselves. Everyone in the mistress' family is a great lover of the sport, and the family had been the patron of the *sumō* wrestler who had bitten his own tongue off. His name was Komatsuyama, a promising wrestler of the Ibaraki Stable in the *nidaime* division.

Never would I have guessed that the wife's phantom was in fact a *sumō* wrestler. But I had always believed in the mistress, that she would not have misbehaved herself, and I was proven right, as we know now this all happened because she was a patron of a *sumō* wrestler.

Alas, the scholarly, stubborn master could simply not accept the pure feelings of a *sumō* patron....

Oh, I have been talking on for too long. Well then, I think I will take my leave now….

First published in *Shin Tantei Shōsetsu*, June Issue, Shōwa 22 (1947).

---

[i] Edo is the old name of the city now known as Tōkyō. *Shitamachi*, or 'downtown,' is the old merchant heart of the city.

[ii] In Japan, water is scooped up from a well and splashed over the gravestone during a visit. The tradition originates from Buddhism, where one of the afterworlds, *Gakikai*, is said to be one of eternal thirst and hunger. The water splashed over the gravestone is to quench the thirst of the deceased in case they end up in *Gakikai*. The custom lives on even now, though in modern days it is usually done to clean the grave.

[iii] *Botan Dōrō*, or *The Peony Lantern,* is a classic ghost tale about a man falling in love with a ghost. The man's health becomes worse each time he has sexual relations with his ghostly lover.

[iv] A *fusuma* is a sliding door consisting of a wooden frame and Japanese paper.

[v] *Tatami* are straw mats commonly used as flooring material.

[vi] A *tokonoma* is an alcove in a traditional Japanese room, where usually objects for artistic appreciation are displayed, like scrolls.

[vii] A *tansu* is a mobile Japanese chest of drawers very commonly used in pre-modern Japanese culture.

THE MESMERISING LIGHT

1

It was a dark, stuffy night.

A single phaeton automobile was speeding along the serpentine road towards Jikkoku Pass, heading from Atami to Hakone through the mountains. The car raced dangerously on the zigzagging road with switchbacks as sharp as the teeth on a saw, going left and right as it followed the folding lines of the pitch-black mountainside. It seemed to be in a great hurry, although the vehicle itself was definitely not made for high-speed performance and the road resembled an anatomy chart of the large intestine. By the time someone standing on a spur to one side of the road would have noticed the beam of the headlights, the horn would have honked already and, leaving only the echo of a heavy boom, the light would already be gone on its ascent to the peak. From far away, it might have appeared as if the car were going round in circles, but it was actually slowly climbing the mountain.

The phaeton was a new model, apparently a taxi. A middle-aged gentleman was sitting in the back seat, with the window shade removed. He had placed a black leather bag on his knees, and was dozing off while being violently shaken around. The chauffeur, who wore a Russian hat, would from time to time steal a glance at his passenger through the rear-view mirror as he wearily drove on.

The road would climb all the way to the top to arrive at the automobile toll road leading from Jikkoku Pass to Hakone, which was run by the Gakunan Railway Corporation. It was a typical sightseeing road, and the smart-looking road signs—marked in black on a white background—remained clear in the dark as the car windows flashed past.

The car eventually arrived at an especially dangerous hairpin curve at the ridge of the mountain. The chauffeur leant outside and kept turning the driving wheel to the right. The headlights had until now only been illuminating empty air, but now the two dim headlights hit the part of the mountain on the other side of the dark ravine, shaking like an unstable projector, causing some vertigo. Near the centre of the mountain on that other side was what appeared to be the continuation of the road they themselves were on. A luxurious, cream-coloured coupé was flying along that road like an arrow, making a sharp turn into the darkness.

The chauffeur clicked his tongue in frustration.

Inside the phaeton it was anything but calm. The speedometer was showing the maximum reading, while the radiator was spewing out little clouds of steam. The whole car was shaking tremendously from the great endeavour, which woke the gentleman in the back.

'Are we at the toll road yet?'

'We'll arrive there shortly,' replied the chauffeur without even turning back. At that moment, the speeding coupé could be seen once again for a brief moment on the mountain on the other side of the ravine.

'My word.' The gentleman leant forward. 'Hurrying like that in such a place. And what a stylish car, too. Who could that have been?'

'Probably some drunken gentleman on a drive here from his villa in Hakone,' the chauffeur answered, without giving it much thought.

'Can you pursue him?'

'I can't. I'm doing the best I can, but that car is a completely different machine from this one!'

The gentleman leant back and peered into the darkness outside. From his lowered position, he could see a sudden, fierce flash of white light breaking through the dark mountain shadows, but it was gone in a second. The gentleman felt there was something tragic about it, and repositioned himself on the seat.

Then it happened. Without any warning, the car lost speed and the gentleman was thrown forward and had to place his hands on the chauffeur's shoulders. The car had made a sudden stop.

2

The gentleman looked up and saw a person lying on the road in front of them, illuminated by the headlights. The person raised his head and waved feebly with one arm.

The chauffeur had already jumped out of the car and run out to the prostrate figure. The gentleman followed rapidly. The person lying there was an elderly man, probably a vagrant. He was severely wounded.

'That crazy… car… just now…,' the wounded man groaned. The gentleman immediately bade the chauffeur help him carry the victim into the car.

'… Thank you…,' said the wounded man as he breathed with visible pain. 'As you can see… I'm a traveller of the night… He suddenly appeared behind me… I tried to avoid it… Sir, please, help me….'

It appeared he wasn't able to speak any more, and fell back on the cushions with his mouth open and eyes half-closed.

The gentleman nodded in irritation and moved himself and his bag into the passenger's seat, next to the chauffeur.

'Let's go. And step on it. I don't suppose there are any doctors until we reach Hakone?'

'True enough, unfortunately.'

The chauffeur drove off at full speed.

They finally arrived at the pass.

The road suddenly became level. They were not surrounded by forest up there. It was wave upon wave of grassy mountain fields. From time to time, the revolving light of an aerial lighthouse would make the surroundings as bright as day. A car approached from the opposite direction. The blinding light hit their eyes painfully. Was it the coupé they had glimpsed just now?

No, this car was something completely different: a sedan. A man and woman, presumably newlyweds, wore sleepy faces in the back seats.

'Did you pass a coupé just now?'

As the two cars passed each other, the chauffeur posed the question to his colleague.

'Yes. At the entrance to the toll road!' shouted the other driver with a smile, and the car with the newlyweds drove off again.

After a while the car arrived at the Jikkoku Pass entrance of the toll road. A modern-looking white station building was illuminated by electric lights, and in front of that, a boom barrier—similar to those seen at railway crossings—blocked the road, in the same way as a barrier station.

Two men were standing in the middle of the road, doing something in front of the boom barrier. When the car stopped in front of them, one of the men ran over to the ticket window, which also served as the office.

The gentleman jumped out of the car and went over to the ticket window. While he was taking the toll fee out of his coin purse, he also asked for something else besides a ticket.

'Did a fancy, cream-coloured coupé pass through here just before we arrived?'

'Yes, sir,' the ticket officer replied briskly.

'What kind of man was he? The man in the car....'

'I didn't see him.'

'You didn't see him? But he had to buy a ticket, didn't he?'

'No. That was the car of one of our bosses.'

'What, your boss?' The gentleman pressed further.

'Yes,' said the clerk as he punched the ticket. 'It was the car of Mr. Horimi, an executive of the company, so he doesn't need to buy a ticket.'

'Horimi, you say? Aha, that young executive of Gakunan Railway. So the driver of the coupe was this Mr. Horimi?'

'Well, I'm not sure....'

'There were two men riding the car, perhaps?'

'No, just one person. I'm quite sure of that.'

The clerk seemed to be mistaking the gentleman for a police officer and was answering politely.

'Anyway,' said the gentleman to the clerk, 'there's been an accident. That coupé hit a pedestrian and drove off.'

'A hit-and-run!?' the clerk exclaimed. 'And the victim?'

'We took him in my car.'

'Is he all right?'

'No, he was hit quite severely. I fear he won't make it to Hakone alive.'

The clerk was visibly shocked by what he was told, and his face turned paler by the second.

'How horrible... I thought it was odd.... Actually, we had something strange happen here too.'

'Something strange?' The gentleman leant forward.

'Yes, you see, it was the car of one of our executives, so when I saw it pull up here, I rushed out to raise the boom barrier. But I guess he was in a hurry, because I hadn't raised the barrier completely yet, when the car raced off in a frenzy, hitting the front side of the roof against the bar.'

The clerk pointed to the road in front with his chin. 'The two of us were just busy making emergency repairs.'

Now it was the turn of the gentleman to be surprised.

'Hmmm. Anyway, I will head for Hakone immediately. Oh, do you have a telephone here?'

'Yes.'

'Splendid. Please contact the police in Hakone. Tell them to pick up that coupé right now. Understood? Even if it's your executive or CEO or something, he needs to be caught.'

'We have another way to do that, actually. I can make a call to the other end of the toll road, to the station at the Hakone Pass entrance, to make sure they won't raise the barrier for him.'

'That's a brilliant suggestion. But he might just drive right through it.'

'Don't worry. There's an iron core inside the bar. The car can't pass through it unless it's raised, just like what happened here.'

'I see. That's interesting. So we'll catch him between the exits. Won't that coupé have arrived on the other side already, though?'

'He shouldn't even be halfway yet.'

'Good. Please make that phone call then. Don't let them raise the barrier for any reason.'

The clerk ran back inside the station.

A moment later, the phone rang out loudly, while the half-broken barrier was raised and the gentleman's phaeton—carrying the fatally wounded victim—hurried along the toll road in the middle of the night heading for Hakone Pass.

3

I think that most readers are already familiar with the particulars of the Hakone-Jikkoku automobile toll road, but allow me to explain some simple points here, as they are crucial for a good understanding of the extraordinary incident that will occur in a few minutes.

The mountain range connecting the Jikkoku Pass and Hakone Pass—where this toll road is located—is a main part of the Fuji Volcanic Zone, which runs from north-to-south through the joint where the Izu Peninsula connects to the mainland. The grassy mountains take on the form of an uneven drainage basin, with Sagaminada to the east, and overlooking Suruga Bay on the west. The Gakunan Railway Corporation had purchased this uneven part of the mountain at 2500 feet height, laid a modern, bright automobile road there, and, as in the Edo period, people wanting to make a sightseeing automobile trip had to pay a "border crossing fee" to enjoy the magnificent scenery. The six-mile long toll road which ran from north-to-south was a private road, with stations at both the Jikkoku and Hakone end. It was one single road, with no branch roads. And, as was mentioned, there were boom barriers at both stations, and guards to make sure nobody passes through without paying the fee. It was therefore impossible to sneak onto the toll road midway, nor was it possible to sneak out from the toll road once you had entered it.

However, while it was one single mountain road, it was not a straight road that went on for miles. It was a road of which the main goal was sightseeing, so to make sure travellers wouldn't get bored by the beauty of miles of straight lines, the road also featured many pleasantly smooth curves. The road displayed zigzags, S-curves, C-curves and U-curves as it went past ravines all the way up to the top of the mountain.

But the beautiful scenery of this nice toll road was of course not a match for the darkness. Especially on a muggy, dark night such as the one in question, when the clouds are low, all you can see is the fearful, stretching silhouettes of the bare mountains gradually appearing far away on the horizon, with the last remaining light behind them. It reminds one of a shadow picture of a mountain in the underworld. The car with the gentleman and the wounded man followed the lines of the top of the mountain in the shadow picture. They had reached the midway point of the toll road, hurrying on as if being chased by something.

'I thought I'd seen that car before,' commented the chauffeur as he manoeuvred the steering wheel.

'Do you know this Mr. Horimi?' asked the gentleman, sitting in the seat next to him.

'No, I only know him from pictures in the newspaper. But I know about his villa in Atami. It's on the hilly side of town.'

'Would Mr. Horimi be in residence there now?'

'Well, I wouldn't know. Anyway, the villa has its own garage.'

The gentleman lit a cigarette and smiled contently.

'We haven't passed any cars. That coupé is probably held up at the Hakone Entrance, now the station has closed off the road there.'

To their left, far down below, they could see a group of lights, like sparks of fire in the darkness. It was probably the town of Mishima.

Like a runner nearing the tape, the car started to kick up more dust as it switched into a higher gear. As it entered the last straight stretch, they could see the white-painted station glistening up ahead.

'Oh!' exclaimed the gentleman.

'There's no car there!' The chauffeur raised his voice simultaneously.

The boom barrier was lowered right over the middle of the road, but there was no sign of the coupé anywhere. A swarthy man—probably a clerk—emerged from the station and blocked the road as he waved his arms.

The gentleman stepped out of the car and shouted out as he shut the door with a bang: 'Didn't you get the call?'

'We did get it.'

'Why did you let him pass then!?'

'Eh?'

'Why did you let that car pass?'

'But....'

The clerk appeared to be very surprised. A rattling sound was followed by another man appearing from out of the office. The gentleman looked at both of the men as he said in a grave tone: 'My name is Ōtsuki and I am a criminal lawyer. Even if that coupé is owned by a famous entrepreneur, I will certainly not allow him to run over someone and get away with it. Don't you people have any conscience?'

'Wa-wait a minute,' the second clerk interrupted. He was a serious-looking young man with a broad forehead.

'Please allow me to answer you clearly. Save for your own car, nothing has passed by our station here at the Hakone Entrance, not a coupé, not even a cat!'

4

Several minutes later, Ōtsuki's high-pitched voice on the phone could be heard throughout the station, overwhelming the echoes of the other ringing telephones.

'Yes, hello. The Jikkoku Pass Station? The Hakone Entrance here. I'm the one with the wounded person in my car just now. Did the coupé return to your side? Eh? It didn't? I see, I see. Hmmm. It didn't come here either. It's nowhere. It's gone. On the way? No, of course we didn't see the car. Yes, it is peculiar indeed. Alright, thank you.'

'Yes, hello, is this the Atami Police Station? You're the night watchman? I'm Ōtsuki, the lawyer. Is there someone there I could speak with? Mr. Natsuyama? Yes, please get him on the phone. Lieutenant Natsuyama? Ōtsuki here. No, I'm the one who has to apologise. I am sorry I had to call you so suddenly, but something odd has happened. I'm at the station at the Hakone side of the toll road now. Yes, there was a hit-and-run with a car, but that's what so strange. It doesn't appear to be just a simple hit-and-run. Yes, yes. Of course we chased after it. We closed up both stations and trapped the car on the toll road. But you see, it's disappeared. No, really. Eh? Of course I'll wait. Alright, please hurry then. Oh, and come here in cars, not on motor bikes. Yes, I had my car proceed to Hakone with the victim. He was terribly wounded. Well, I'll see you later.'

'Hello. Hello? Am I speaking with Mr. Horimi in Atami? Yes, I'm sorry for calling at this hour. Excuse me, madam, but you are? Aha, I see. I am Ōtsuki and I'm a lawyer. Some pressing matter has arisen. Is your master at home? Eh? He's not? He's in his home in Tōkyō? Is anyone of his family staying in Atami then? Who? The young miss? She went to Kamakura? Is there anybody else staying in Atami? Er? What? You have one guest. I see, there is a guest there. Well, I am going to ask you something strange, but do you have a car in the garage at your place? Eh? You have? That's odd.... You see, we just spotted your car here near Hakone. I don't know who was driving it, but it was a cream-coloured coupé. If you don't believe me, you should check the garage. Eh? I see, I'm sorry for waking you up. I'll wait while you check.'

'Ah, I'm terribly sorry. Did you check the garage? Ah, so the garage was completely empty? I see, I see. What? Your guest was murdered?'

Ōtsuki dropped the receiver loudly. The office clerks who had run inside the station all looked at each other with pale faces, their bodies frozen to the spot. An ice-cold silence passed by, but Ōtsuki pulled himself together. He picked up the receiver again to make another call.

'Give me the Atami Police Station! Hello, Atami Police Station? Has Mr. Natsuyama left already? He's about to? Quickly, you need to get him on the phone. Oh, Mr. Natsuyama. It's terrible. The car we talked about. That car belongs to Mr. Horimi, you know, of Gakunan Railway. I just made a phone call to his villa, and it appears someone at the villa was killed. Yes, yes, that means the murderer used the car to flee. I don't know who was driving the car, but we will make sure nobody will escape and keep a close eye from both stations, so you head for the villa first and once you've finished your investigation there, you should hurry here. Okay, I'll be waiting....'

5

Horimi's villa was situated in a quiet place even for Atami, on the hilly side of town. The masters of the villa, the Horimi couple, had moved back to their home in Tōkyō at the start of summer. In return, their only daughter, Tomiko, and her private tutor—a foreigner—had come to the villa about ten days earlier. But in the afternoon today, they had been visited by a very unwelcome guest, and the two of them had basically fled to Kamakura. It was this guest who had been murdered. Ei'ichi Oshiyama was his name, and he was an affluent young gentleman.

Ryōzō Horimi had proved himself in many businesses besides Gakunan Railway, but he'd had to incur some painful blows the last few years, and he'd been forced to borrow a fortune from Oshiyama's father. Seemingly aware of this weakness, Ei'ichi had been chasing after Tomiko, who was still too young for marriage.

Tomiko of course detested Oshiyama. So when Ei'ichi arrived at the villa, Tomiko and her tutor Evans left the unsettling place. Evans was an old lady, born in the United States, who had been close to the Horimi family since Tomiko was a little girl. Around the time Tomiko started attending the girls' academy, Evans became her private tutor, teaching her English. Evans loved Tomiko as her own daughter, and as her own granddaughter.

Two maids, mother and daughter, remained at the villa during the master's absence. It was the mother Kiyo who had been awakened from a deep slumber by Ōtsuki's pressing phone call.

Kiyo had picked up the receiver as she rubbed her sleepy eyes, but had hurried outside after being surprised by the strange tale of the person on the other end of the line. When she discovered that the car that should have been in the garage had disappeared, and that the front gate had been left open, she thought it was the guest who had been careless. But when she opened the door of the guest room, she found Oshiyama, dressed in his pyjamas, lying beside his bed in a pool of crimson. Kiyo had run back to the telephone immediately.

After she had answered Ōtsuki, Kiyo quickly called the police. Even after her call, she was not able to move, and stood frozen in the telephone room, trembling.

Lieutenant Natsuyama had been thrown into confusion by all the telephone calls, but he sent some police officers to the toll road, while he himself also took some officers along to Horimi's villa. The medical examiner who had arrived afterwards determined that Oshiyama's cause of death had been the two stabs wounds to the heart made by a knife-like weapon. One of the wounds had not been a clean, straight stab, as it had left a sideways scratch on the victim. Not even an hour had passed since the murder.

Lieutenant Natsuyama took Kiyo to one side and started with some simple questioning. Kiyo was nervous and acted flustered, but did manage to explain how everything had happened.

'And so Mr. Oshiyama went out very late last night, and I think he had some drinks before he returned here. Afterwards, we went to sleep too, so I don't know anything about what happened until Mr. Ōtsuki called us.'

Thus did Kiyo conclude her testimony. Lieutenant Natsuyama went outside through the front entrance, and headed for the garage. With the help of a flashlight, he found several footsteps of a woman made on the ground near a puddle of water, running in the direction of the garage.

The smell of oil hung in the garage, but there was no car.

Lieutenant Natsuyama looked here and there in the empty garage, but then sighed. He crouched down, took out a handkerchief and carefully wrapped it around a shining object lying on the floor.

It was a bloody knife. It was also an impressive-looking knife, the likes of which he had never seen before. It appeared to be a ladies' knife, with a gorgeous shape and a fancy ivory grip with relief. Letters had been engraved in a corner of the grip. The lieutenant brought the light in his hand closer and looked intently at the writing.

Celebrating your seventeenth birthday. February 29th, 1936.

The lieutenant's eyes gleamed. He slid the knife into his pocket and went back to the main building, where he started questioning Kiyo, who was still flustered, again.

'By the way, how old are you? Over fifty?'

'Actually, I'm exactly fifty....'

'Hmm. And your daughter?'

'My Toshiya? She's eighteen....'

'And Ms. Evans?'

'She is well into her sixties.'

'And Miss Tomiko?'

'She's seventeen now.'

'Thank you.' Lieutenant Natsuyama grinned with satisfaction. 'One final question: do all the people in the Horimi household have a key to the villa?'

'Yes.'

'So Miss Tomiko has one too?'

'Yes, probably....'

'Thank you.' The lieutenant turned to a nearby subordinate and told him jubilantly: 'We're finished here. The medical examiner will have to stay until the team from the court of justice arrives. We'll head for the toll road right away.'

6

By the time Lieutenant Natsuyama arrived at the Jikkoku Pass entrance of the toll road, Ōtsuki had already returned there with the police car which had been sent to the Hakone Pass entrance in advance. He had been waiting for Natsuyama's arrival at the Jikkoku Pass station.

The policemen who had arrived first had already split up into two teams, and had been watching the road from both stations. The moment Ōtsuki saw the lieutenant, he called out to him.

'Have you already finished your work at the villa?'

'There was little to do there. We know the murderer escaped here, so I had to come at once. But anyway, I have a good idea of who the murderer is.'

'You already know? Who is the murderer?'

'Well, before we go into that, haven't my men found that car yet?'

Ōtsuki waved his hand in front of him with some annoyance.

'No, that's the problem. It appears that the only possibility left is that it plunged down the ravine.'

'I'm afraid I'll have to agree. We'll have to make a search for it.'

'But you see, searching for that car might be difficult. On my way back here, I kept an eye on one side of the road all the time but considering this darkness, and the fact that this toll road is almost six miles long, well, the ravine by the side of the road is rather deep. The road is also dry, so there are no tracks, and so I have no idea of even the approximate location where the car could have fallen.'

'But we can't just sit here doing nothing.'

'You're right, of course. Anyway, we can first take a look at the ravine on the other side of the road. But to come back to my first question, who could the murderer be?'

'The murderer? It's Mr. Horimi's daughter.'

The lieutenant jumped back inside his car after saying that. The shocked group also got into the car, which backed up and started heading for the Hakone Pass Entrance. Their speed was ten miles per hour.

But they had not even advanced half a mile when the complexity of the investigation started to make the group anxious. They were crawling along the ravine side of the road, but the surface was completely dry and they could not detect any traces of a car having gone off the road. If only a guard rail had been constructed on the side of the road, then they could have guessed where the car had fallen by the broken rail. But this was a road built uniquely for automobiles—not open to pedestrians—so there were only a couple of fancy looking white-painted guard rails placed here and there as decoration, which were useless.

The meaningless and depressing investigation continued for a while, when the car entered an acute, reverse S-curve with no guard rail. The irritated lieutenant clicked his tongue. The car was heading for Hakone Pass, but after taking the first sharp corner, the car was now facing the other way, in the direction back to Jikkoku Pass.

The end of the S-curve resembled a large C-shape with an almost straight bottom. The car passed a traffic sign displaying an upside-down "L"-shape, and had already advanced twenty metres when Ōtsuki suddenly sat bolt upright, as if he had seen something.

'Stop the car!'

The constable immediately stepped on the brakes.

Ōtsuki opened the door, got out onto the footboard and called out to the constable inside the car.

'Please back the car up. Yes, like that. More, more. Okay, stop!'

Nobody knew what was going on.

Ōtsuki sat down in the passenger's seat, taking the same sitting position as before. His voice trembled with tension as he said: 'And now go forward again. But I have to ask you to go as slowly as you can. Oh, and that coupé didn't have its interior light on. The inside of the car has to be dark. Switch the light off.'

The light was switched off and the car started moving again.

'What's the matter?' The lieutenant couldn't take it any more and called out in the dark.

'I think I'm starting to get it. Starting to get to the truth of what has happened. It's almost here.'

'What's almost here?'

'Just wait and you'll see.'

The car slowly made its way back to where it had stopped previously. It was just before the final corner of the C-curve. The road made a sharp corner to the left, and the only thing visible in the headlight was the pitch-black empty space of the ravine.

Ōtsuki had been looking in front of him, but suddenly cried out.

'There it is! Stop the car!'

'Where is what?' the lieutenant asked.

'It's gone already. But it'll be back. You can't see it from there. Come over here.'

The lieutenant leant forward, his head right next to Ōtsuki who had moved to the driver's seat, and looked in front of him.

'There's nothing here.'

'It'll come in a moment. There it was! No, it's not outside the car. It's right in front of you, on the car window!'

'Ah!'

On the surface of the car window in front of him, the lieutenant could clearly see, in close-up, a bright traffic sign displaying an upside-down "L" in mirror-image form, indicating an impossible turn to the right. The sign, however, soon vanished into the surrounding darkness.

The road in front of them turned to the left, but inside the car there had briefly been a traffic sign indicating a turn to the right!

7

'Turning your head back to the rear window when you saw that image projected on the front window was the smart thing to do,' Ōtsuki said, impressed, as he tapped the lieutenant on the shoulder.

Looking through the square glass window behind the back seats, one could see the road close by, glowing faintly red because of the tail light, and the rest was ink-black darkness. But they could see a traffic sign floating clearly in that darkness, illuminated by a bright light coming from somewhere. They had just passed by that traffic sign on the side of the road. This traffic sign had appeared like a mirage in the darkness, but disappeared again immediately. As it kept on appearing and disappearing, it left a bright after-image in the eyes of all the men in the car.

'It was a trick played by Fate,' said Ōtsuki. 'The ray of light is from the aerial lighthouse on the other side of that small hill right next to us, shining here at an angle. The traffic sign in the dark over there warns us of the correct direction, indicating a turn to the left. But when that ray of light reflects off the traffic sign, that image is projected as a mirror image through this back window, onto the front glass window of the car, indicating a right corner. That coupé didn't have its interior light on, the air here in the ravine is clear, and the headlights were shining deep into the darkness. Also, this front glass window is at a slight angle, so this reflection can only be seen by the person in the driver's seat when they are leaning slightly forward. But even so, this false image only appears for a second, and it is unlikely that under normal circumstances, any person would have mistaken it for a real traffic sign and driven off into the ravine.'

'I understand completely now. Let's get down there at once.'

Following the lieutenant's orders, the men all left the car and stood on the edge of the ravine. Crouching down in the light of the car, they didn't take long to find tracks in the grass near the road that appeared to be that of the coupé falling into the ravine.

'We can go down this way, the slope is gentler,' said Lieutenant Natsuyama as he started to climb down, aiming his flashlight at the rocky surface.

'Lieutenant,' Ōtsuki called out as he followed after the detective. 'Did you find any evidence indicating the murderer is the young daughter of Mr. Horimi?'

'I found the murder weapon,' replied the lieutenant. 'It was a fancy ladies' knife, and there was an engraved message saying it was to celebrate her seventeenth birthday. And it was dated spring this year. The daughter Tomiko is seventeen this year.'

Ōtsuki nodded silently and made his way through the grass down the mountain with the help of the scattered light.

'Lieutenant, when you're born, you start out as one year old. When you celebrate your first birthday, you become two years old. When you become three, you celebrate your second birthday. So someone who is seventeen, will celebrate her sixteenth birthday[i].'

'Eh, what?' The lieutenant swung his head around.

'Lieutenant, if the knife said it was to celebrate the seventeenth birthday, it means the owner is eighteen.'

'Eighteen?' The stupefied lieutenant froze in his tracks for a while, but then quickly got a memo from his pocket and unfolded it with trembling hand. 'Oh, I feel terribly ashamed. You are, of course, completely right. But we also have a girl of eighteen.'

'Who would that be?'

'The maid, Toshiya!'

At that moment, the lieutenant's flashlight caught some large collision markings on a flat section of the mountainside.

Ōtsuki exclaimed: 'It must have flipped over there. The car should be nearby. Let's hurry.'

The group started fanning out, without saying a word. Thorny bushes and shrubberies whose names they didn't know started to appear among the weeds. Suddenly, Ōtsuki picked up the spare wheel of the coupé from behind a dried-out bush. The men remained silent, but their anxiety grew. Small lights criss-crossed over the mountain surface, and the only sound was of shoes crunching down. But then the lieutenant stopped in his tracks.

There was no doubt that it was the cream-coloured coupé which was lying in the hollow right beneath them, flipped over to show its dark abdomen.

The lieutenant and Ōtsuki exchanged not a word as they climbed down and forced the upside-down door of the coupé open.

'Oh!' the lieutenant cried out. The car was empty. But then Ōtsuki crouched down, and from the driver's seat he picked up several bloody, entangled strands of grey hair.

The coupé was in a terrible state. All the windows had been broken and the glass fragments scattered around. The rear axle had been bent into a twist, and the passenger door had been snapped off and lost somewhere.

Suddenly one of the men picked out a trail of blood leading from the broken door into the undergrowth. The murderer had miraculously survived the crash. They started to follow the trail.

'So this means it was a girl with grey hair. Hmm, I am curious as to the evidence you found. Show me that knife of yours.'

Though annoyed by Ōtsuki's comment, the lieutenant withdrew the knife he had wrapped in his handkerchief from his pocket.

Ōtsuki took the knife and examined the engravings on the ivory grip with the help of a light. His eyes gleamed and he called out to the lieutenant.

'Didn't you see the date on this? You must be blind. A person who celebrates their birthday on February 29th is of course born on February 29th. But there is only a February 29th in leap years. So this person only celebrates their birthday once every four years. How old do you think this person is who has celebrated their seventeenth birthday? They should be over sixty.'

'Now I see!'

The lieutenant started to run forward, but Ōtsuki stopped him.

In the thickets of large bushes in front of them, they could hear the noise of leaves being disturbed. The men crept silently closer. Making his way to the dark side of the thicket, the lieutenant switched on his flashlight.

A small, dark human form was trying desperately to crawl back into the thicket, despite a broken leg. On seeing the light, it turned to face its pursuers.

'It's Evans!'

It was indeed the small face of the grey-haired Evans. It was the face of Evans, torn between her dignity to protect the purity of her beloved Tomiko and her regret for the crime she had committed.

First published in *Shinseinen*, August Issue, Shōwa 11 (1936).

---

[i] Traditional Asian age-reckoning practices had the newly born start at the age of one, so at the next birthday they celebrated, they became two years old. The traditional age system was abolished by law in 1902 in Japan, but remained widely in use until after World War II.

THE COLD NIGHT'S CLEARING

The season of snow has arrived once again. And snow reminds me of that tragic figure, Sanshirō Asami. At the time, I was working as a simple Japanese language teacher at an academy for girls in a prefecture far up in the north: let's call it H Town. Sanshirō Asami was an English language teacher at the same school, and also my best friend at the time.

Sanshirō's parental home was in Tōkyō. His family had made a fortune as trade merchants, but, as the second son, he wouldn't inherit and trade didn't really suit him anyway. So, after graduating from W University, he became a teacher, moving all around the country. He originally wanted to write literature, but he'd had little success, and by the time we became acquainted in H Town, he was already in his thirties and had become the caring father of an eight-year-old child. Sanshirō could be a bit quick-tempered, but he was also a frank and lovable person, and we quickly became friends. And it wasn't just me: there wasn't a person around who didn't become friends with him. This might have been because of his wealthy family, but he was also very easy-going with his fellow teachers and likeable in his dealings with his fellow man, with nothing calculating behind his actions. So he wasn't really suited to walking the dark path of literature writing—which might explain his lack of success. I quickly noticed this as I became friends with him.

Sanshirō at home was a joy to see. His deep love for his beautiful wife and his only child was evident, as was the respect he enjoyed from his girl students, albeit tinged with envy. In fact, even though every teacher is destined to be given a nickname at a girls' academy, I have to admit I've never heard one for Sanshirō. That was almost a mystery in itself. Yet, in hindsight, what occurred may have happened precisely because of his beautiful nature.

At the time of the horrific event I was living in a house very close to the Asamis, in the outskirts of H Town, which is probably why I was one of the first to hear about it. Sanshirō himself was away at the time and I was unsure what I should do. He had been sent by the Ministry of Education to a newly-opened agricultural school in the mountains, as a temporary teacher for the last month of the semester.

The school vacation was supposed to start on December 25th, so Sanshirō was expected to return home that night, but the incident had occurred the night before, on the 24th.

The cousin of Sanshirō's wife Hiroko had been staying with her since the start of the month; his name was Oikawa, and he was a student at M University. I didn't know much about him except that he seemed to be a good, bright lad; that he belonged to his university's ski club; and that he had been in the habit of visiting his cousin here in the north every winter. (The snowfall here in December is so heavy, it's possible to ski from the rooftops.) Oikawa, Hiroko and her son Haruo, who had just entered elementary school that spring, kept watch over the house during Sanshirō's absence. So Oikawa was Sanshirō's hired guard, in a way, yet the bizarre and horrific incident had occurred despite his presence.

Clouds had started gathering on the morning of the 24th, and the grey skies finally gave away around the evening, so by nightfall snow had started to fall. At first it was just dancing down gently, but by six o'clock it was falling quite heavily. Yet at eight, as if the show's final curtain had fallen, the snow just stopped, and a bright, star-filled sky could be seen from between the breaking clouds. Such sudden meteorological changes are pretty common in these parts. During the coldest thirty days of winter, the weather behaves strangely: by day the sky becomes more and more overcast, and then at night, as if it had all been just a dream, the clouds part and the moon and stars shine coldly in the clear blue night sky. Local people call it *Kan no Yobare*: Cold Night's Clearing.

I had finished a late dinner around eight. Because vacation had already started at the girls' academy, I was preparing for a trip somewhere to the south. Suddenly Miki, a student in Sanshirō's refresher course A, arrived at my door, bringing me the bad news of what had happened at the Asami home. Despite feeling a shudder because of the cold weather, I immediately grabbed my skis and hurried there with Miki. As I was leaving, I could hear the Christmas Eve bells of the town church ringing, so it must have been around nine o'clock.

Miki was a tall and lively girl, one of the early-maturing ones you see in every girls' academy. She had already mastered the secrets of make-up, the length of her skirt was always changing, and she was always filling the corners of her class-books with the names of poets in very small print. Miki often went to visit Sanshirō at his home. 'Mr. Asami is teaching me literature,' she would say, but she also visited the home during Sanshirō's absence, so it might have been Oikawa, and not Sanshirō, who was "teaching her literature." Anyway, that night Miki had gone to Sanshirō's house, but it seemed as though nobody was home, even though the doors and windows weren't locked. Thinking this was a bit strange, she opened the front door and went to the back, as she always did when visiting. When she discovered the abnormal state inside the house, she hurried to my place, it being one of the closest.

I lived less than ten minutes away from the Asami residence by ski. Their house was stylish, like a timbered lodge. It was the right-most house in a block of three. The people of the house on the far left seemed to have gone to sleep already, as the curtains were drawn. The house in the middle was also dark; a notice said it was for rent. When we stopped in front of Sanshirō's house, Miki was trembling and seemed as if she didn't want to go inside, so I told her to go to the house of Tabei, a physics teacher at the academy, who also lived close by. Finally, I got a grip on myself and entered the house.

Haruo's room was near the front door. A child's crayon drawings of "a general" and "a soldier with tulips" were pinned to the wall. In the middle of the room stood a potted fir tree, with braids of golden wire and chains of coloured paper threaded between the branches, topped by snow made of white cotton. It was the Christmas tree Sanshirō had bought for his son just before he had left for his temporary assignment.

But the first thing I noticed as I entered the room was the empty bed of the little master of the Christmas tree standing in front of a small desk in one corner. The blankets had been thrown back and the child who should have been sleeping there was nowhere to be seen. The silver-paper stars of the Christmas tree that had lost its master sparkled as they started to turn and sway in the cold currents of air.

It was then that I found the other, temporary, inhabitant of the room. Oikawa was lying in the opening of the door leading to the living room in the back, face down towards me. I recoiled, but when I saw the chaotic state of the living room through the door, I pulled myself together, cautiously sneaked to the opening and looked at both the man lying at my feet and the occupant of the living room.

Sanshirō's wife Hiroko was lying with her head leaning on a stove which was standing on a galvanized plate. The awful stench of burnt hair hung in the room. I stood there for a while, trembling in shock, but finally pulled myself together, crouched and carefully touched Oikawa's body. It was not the body of a living person.

From the disorder around their fallen figures, it seemed as though both Oikawa and Hiroko had put up a struggle. They seemed to have been beaten, as I could see countless purple welts on their foreheads, faces, arms and necks. I quickly found the weapon: the stove's iron poker, slightly bent, had been thrown near Oikawa's feet. The room was in chaos. The chairs had been overturned, the table pushed away and a big cardboard toy box, which had probably been on top of the table, had been thrown in front of the sofa. It was wet and crushed. A toy train, a mascot figure, a beautiful big spinning top and more had been thrown out of the box, together with caramel, bonbon and chocolate animal candies. You could almost sense a childish purity from these toys which had lost their master.

If I'd been a witness to this kind of scene in the house of a total stranger, I probably wouldn't have stayed to take in so much detail of what I saw. I'd have been so shocked at finding dead bodies that I'd have run to the police immediately. But at the time I was less troubled by what I'd seen than by what I hadn't seen. It dawned on me that I hadn't seen the son ever since I'd entered the house. It might seem strange, but I felt more anxious about the missing child than about the dead people in front of me. Just like Oikawa and Hiroko, I, too had been responsible for his safety during Sanshirō's absence.

The house was divided into four rooms. I quickly searched the other two as I tried to keep my fearful heart in check, but even after going through the whole house, I couldn't find any sign of the child.

Then a thought suddenly occurred to me: the sliding window of the room where the tragedy had happened was open. That was strange: nobody would normally leave a window open on such a cold night. I imagined that the individual who had beaten two people to death and taken the child must have fled through the window, failing to shut it in his haste. And so, with some trepidation, I returned to the living room. Inching slowly round the wall, and ready to take on the invisible enemy if necessary, I peeked out of the window, which looked out on a garden and hedge at the back of the house.

I saw exactly what I'd expected to see, there in the snow below the window. The chaotic prints of someone putting on skis were clearly visible, even in the dark. From those prints, two long lines went through an opening in the hedge and disappeared into the darkness beyond. Beneath the star-filled sky, I could clearly hear the tolling of the Christmas bells. They sounded eerie, like the whisper of the devil.

Without hesitation I returned to the front door, strapped on my own skis, and went round to the back of the house, to the open window of the living room. There were two parallel lines there in the snow, so one person must have skied there. Making sure not to erase the tracks, I went through the opening in the hedge and followed them. I'd only just started my chase, when I found an important clue: even though he was skiing on a flat surface, the kidnapper hadn't used both of his ski poles. On the left side of the tracks, I could see the snow being scattered around by the ring at the end of the ski pole every three or four metres, but there were no such marks on the right side. I felt anxiety in my heart. I was right: the skier was using a pole in his left hand, but couldn't use one with his right hand. That meant he was holding something else in his right hand. In my mind's eye I could clearly see the image of the child struggling in the arms of his kidnapper. I grew more tense as I followed the tracks, which seemed to continue forever.

The tracks went through the hedge, across an open field, and towards a silent back road. This was a new residential area of H Town. The houses here were spread far apart and had a lot of green space, with snow-covered fields. I couldn't tell whether they were farm fields or just open ground.

The snow had fallen from dusk till eight and almost no ski tracks had touched the fair snow skin. Besides some footprints in front of people's houses, and dog prints, nothing had disturbed the tracks I was chasing. But I had to watch out for my prey. I shuddered and continued to glide carefully beneath the silent night sky.

The ski tracks turned right at the back street and entered a wide snowfield. On the other side of the field was the main road that passed in front of Sanshirō's house, going towards the town. The ski tracks crossed the field diagonally, going in the direction of the town and looked as if they might get back onto the main road at some point. If so, I might be able to ask for help from a policeman on the way. My spirits rose at the thought, and I hurried across the large field towards the road. But my hopes were dashed in the most surprising way.

It had been a mistake in the first place to assume the tracks would continue on the main road. When I reached a point halfway across the field, I suddenly realised I had lost sight of the ski tracks. Shocked, I looked about me. But there was nothing there except my own meandering tracks! Cursing myself for my inattention, I hurriedly retraced my own tracks, looking from side to side as I went. But no matter how much I went back and looked around, there was no sign of those tracks. I felt perplexed.

But near the entrance to the field, I did finally manage to find the tracks again in the pale snow. Relieved, I went near them and followed them carefully like following a piece of thread, making sure I would not lose them once again. Once again the tracks appeared to cross the field diagonally, heading towards the road on the other side. I wondered how I had managed to lose them the first time. I cursed myself again, and proceeded very cautiously with my eyes locked on the tracks. This time I noticed something truly unexpected.

The tracks became less deep near the centre of the field. They hadn't been deep in the first place, but they became shallower and shallower with every metre and every centimetre as I proceeded forward. Finally, to my utter surprise, when the tracks reached the middle of the field, they disappeared completely, as if the person who had been skiing here had flown right into the sky above.

Judging from the way he disappeared, the owner of the skis had to have grown a set of wings, or fresh snow had to have fallen on top of the tracks; there could be no other explanation for such a strange disappearance.

Still perplexed, I thought as hard I could. But, as I said before, the snow that had started at dusk had stopped completely by eight, and it had been the Cold Night's Clearing ever since; snow had not fallen since then. Even supposing it had, why would it only have erased the tracks here and not the tracks back at the house? Snow would have fallen everywhere, and all the tracks would have been erased. Well then, could a strange wind phenomenon have happened here on the field, with the snow carried by the wind erasing the tracks just at this spot? But no wind able to do that had been blowing that night. I stood still in the field, feeling like I had seen a ghost. The eerie bells had not stopped tolling and the sound carried across the field, seeming like the sneering of the devil himself.

But I couldn't afford just to stand there. The kidnapped child's safety was at stake. Two people had died in the house and I had to contact the police at once.

I went straight towards the town. Locating the closest police box, I reported the crime. But, even as I went back with a young policeman, I still couldn't fathom the disappearance in the field.

When we finally arrived back at Sanshirō's house, we found a couple of people from the neighbourhood there who had just learnt of the incident and were just about to go to the police. Amongst the people in front of the house was also a shocked Miki, who looked as if she would cry at any moment. Mr. Tabei, whom I had sent Miki to fetch, was in the house, loudly opening and closing the doors of the rooms in search of the child, just as I had done.

Entering the house and taking a look around, the policeman told us not to tamper with the crime scene until the detectives from the precinct arrived. Then he called us, Miki included, into the room Sanshirō used as his study, and started questioning us. Both Miki and I talked feverishly about how we had discovered the crime and about the inhabitants of the house, occasionally interrupting each other. Tabei, however, was very calm and talked little.

Finally a stout, apparently high-ranking policeman arrived, together with several of his subordinates and started investigating the crime scene. I could hear the sound of a shutter several times, as they took photographs. When they had finished with the room, the police officers went back outside the house and gathered by the open window. The stout official was listening to the young policeman's report and looking at the bodies, while the policemen outside the window started following the tracks through the opening in the hedge towards the open field. The stout officer couldn't stay still either and, leaving the rest to the young policeman, went outside as well.

I wrote a telegram to Sanshirō and asked Miki to take it to the post office. When I finally regained my composure, I turned to Tabei.

He had been calm while I was explaining the events to the policeman, but now he wasn't looking calm at all, more as though he was thinking very deeply. What was he thinking about? Had he discovered a clue?

'Mr. Tabei,' I began resolutely, 'what are your thoughts about this case?'

'My thoughts?' Tabei replied, raising his head and blinking.

'What I mean is,' I said as I turned towards the other room, 'you probably saw it too. The tracks of the man who committed those violent crimes and abducted a child just disappeared into thin air. It's a very strange case.'

'That's true. It's really strange. But then, everything about this case is strange.'

'I don't quite....'

'The toys and candy lying around here, do you think they had been here from the start, I mean, before any of this had happened?'

'Well, they had probably been there already, with the kid playing and eating, I think.'

'I don't think so. If he'd been eating here, there should also have been silver wrapping paper or paraffin paper here and there. I took a look before the police arrived, but there's nothing at all. And those toys lying there, they're all brand new. And the fact that the crushed cardboard toy box lying in front of the sofa is all wet, even though nothing—not even a drop of tea—has been spilt, is very strange, too... I think it might have been snow from the top of the cover, which melted because of the room temperature. But even without those trifling details,' Tabei continued, changing his tone and looking me straight in the eye, 'the ingredients for a mystery have been gathering here from the start. It's Christmas Eve... skis in the snow... going in and out of the window... and returning to the sky....'

Tabei suddenly stopped talking and, gazing into my eyes, asked:

'Who do you think it was...?'

'Hmm,' I groaned. 'Do you mean... are you suggesting it was Santa Claus?'

'Yes. To put it simply, Santa Claus appeared in this room.'

I was very surprised. 'It must have been a very violent Santa Claus.'

'Precisely. A Santa Claus such as you've never seen before... maybe the devil himself turned into Santa Claus and paid a visit here.' Tabei suddenly took a serious tone and stood up. '... But I'm starting to see through the masquerade... I've already solved more than half of the puzzle. Let's track this Santa Claus down.'

Tabei went to the door of the living room and told the policeman, who had eagerly been taking notes about the crime scene, that he was going outside. Giving me a meaningful look, he left through the front door. I didn't really understand what was going on, but, impressed by his confident attitude, I stood up too, rather uncertainly. As I went out after Tabei, the image of the tracks I was about to follow again, and the image of the stout officer probably looking up into the night sky with his arms folded, appeared in my mind's eye.

But Tabei didn't go to the window in the back. Instead, he went to the hedge at the front, looking at the road there. In the snow were the tracks of the people who had entered and left the house, and some of the people from the neighbourhood were standing there with pale faces. What was he doing?

'Mr. Tabei, the tracks are at the window in the back.'

'Oh, those tracks,' he said as he turned around. 'I don't care about them any more. I'm looking for another set of tracks.'

'Another set of tracks?' I repeated.

'Yes.' Tabei laughed grimly, and continued: 'There was just one set of tracks outside the window, if you recall? You can't come and then go again leaving just one set of tracks. If someone entered back there, there should be tracks leaving here.'

He looked at the roof of Sanshirō's house and grinned. 'Even if he was Santa Claus, he wouldn't have been able to enter through that small chimney... because this murder case isn't just a fairy-tale.'

I saw it now: there had to be tracks entering the house, too. Realising my own carelessness, I felt ashamed. But suddenly, a thought entered my mind.

'Mr. Tabei, I see what you mean. It was snowing before eight. Santa Claus came here before eight, and went out after the snow had stopped. That's why the tracks of him arriving have been erased, and why only the tracks of him leaving remain.'

But, to my surprise, Tabei silently shook his head.

'You're gravely mistaken there. True, that's one way to look at the case. When I first took a look at the tracks outside the window, I myself thought so too for a while. But when I heard about the disappearing tracks from you, I understood I was wrong. The problem lies in the tracks that suddenly disappear.'

'By which you mean...?'

'So you think snow had fallen on top of the tracks?'

'Yes.'

'Then why had the snow fallen in such an uneven, irregular way?'

Tabei placed his hand on my shoulder. 'The starting point of your deduction is wrong, you see. Inside, people have been murdered and a child has been abducted. The window has been opened, and in the snow outside are ski tracks with just one ski pole; indeed as if someone had been carrying a child. But as you were observing this, you deduced that the fiend had abducted the child and gone out through the window. That was your mistake.'

Tabei changed his tone and added hand movements.

'So let's think about this situation... Let's suppose a man is walking in the middle of a heavy snow fall... but during his walk, the snow tapers off and the sky clears. How would the man's footprints appear then? ... You see, while the snow was falling, the footprints would be obliterated by the snow immediately, but if the snow started to taper off, his footprints would gradually appear deeper and deeper as they were less and less filled by the snow. But if you now think about ski tracks and follow them in reverse—unlike footprints, you can't tell which direction ski tracks are pointing in—the tracks in the snow would become shallower and shallower until they were gone completely, just as if a man had disappeared... So the snow didn't fall after someone had arrived here, nor did someone leave here after the snow had stopped: the snow tapered off just as someone was skiing ... So now do you understand the mystery behind those disappearing tracks? The man who made them didn't go out through the window, he came in. Tonight, the snow stopped falling at eight, so Santa Claus must have come from the town and entered the house shortly after eight.'

'Now I get it.' I scratched my head and asked:

'But what do you make of the tracks of just one snow pole?'

'That's easy. It was just as you thought from the beginning. Santa Claus was carrying something in his arms. Not a child, but that big cardboard toy box that was wet from the snow. It was a present from Santa....'

Tabei then said seriously: 'So now most of the case is clear to you, too. The tracks outside the window were made when entering the house, and there are no tracks leaving the house from there. As there are no signs of either Santa Claus or the child inside the house, the two of them must have left through the front door... by the way, when you first arrived here, were there tracks like that at the front? ... They should have left here before you arrived.'

'That's a difficult one... don't forget, I was in a panic then....'

'It can't be helped. It might take a while, but let's search for tracks with one snow pole amongst all these here.'

Tabei crouched down and started to look for such tracks. I did the same, of course, and started the hunt in the pale snow light. The onlookers on the road looked puzzled, not sure what was going on.

The snow had become messy because of all the different tracks, including ours and those of the police, and we couldn't find any ski tracks with just one ski pole. The policemen who had gone to the end point of the disappearing ski tracks had returned, and it had become crowded inside the house.

It was then that Tabei suddenly asked:

'Miki of class A arrived before you, didn't she? Was she wearing adult skis?'

I nodded.

'That means it must've been the child's skis,' Tabei mumbled mysteriously and he led me to where the hedge followed the road, and pointed to two sets of tracks that were still visible there.

'Of course we couldn't find a set of tracks with one ski pole. Santa Claus wasn't carrying the child. The child was wearing his own skis as he was being led away by Santa.'

Indeed, there in the snow were the tracks of narrow skis, next to an adult's skis, going towards the main road.

'Let's hurry and follow these tracks before the police call us in for questioning.'

We set out immediately.

A lot of time had passed since the incident, so we had no idea how far the owners of those tracks could have gone. Or so I thought at first, but after having gone about fifty metres parallel to the hedge, the two tracks, as if to evade something coming from the opposite side, suddenly made a sharp turn to the right. I felt a shiver. It was the empty house in the nearby block. The two tracks went through the front side of the small hedge, turning away from the entrance, and going round the side to the back of the dark building. I held my breath.

'That was unexpectedly close by,' said Tabei with a pale face, as he followed the tracks. 'It seems likely there's a bad ending ahead... By the way, who do you think Santa Claus is? You probably already know, don't you?'

I shook my head vigorously as I scratched my head. As Tabei reached the rear of the empty house, he said: 'It's difficult to say it, even if you do know, isn't it? ... Who's the person who dressed like

Santa Claus and came through the window with presents? … And the child followed him on his skis, without any resistance… I believe there's a train which arrives at half past seven every day here in H Town… I think that Sanshirō Asami arrived by that train, one day earlier than expected.'

'What? Sanshirō!?' I cried. 'That's ridiculous… even if Sanshirō had come back, why would he have done such a dreadful thing? … No, someone who loved his family so much would never do something like that!'

But then Tabei discovered a large and a small set of skis beneath an open window, through which he too entered a pitch-dark room. I started to follow suit and it was then that I heard Tabei's quavering, painful cry.

'We're too late….'

When my eyes got used to the darkness, I could see the cold, dead figure of Sanshirō hanging from a curtain cord attached to the ceiling. At his feet was his child, strangled with a belt, lying there as if he were asleep. Some chocolate candies lay on the ground. A neatly folded piece of paper lay beside them. Tabei picked it up, looked briefly at it and then handed it to me. There were Sanshirō's last words, addressed to me. It seemed to have been written in a rush with nothing but the snow light, but as I stood trembling near the window, I could just make out the words.

Dear Hatano,

I have finally fallen down to hell. But I want you to be the only one to know the truth. Because of a snowslide, the agricultural school started vacation one day early. I arrived back in town by the seven-thirty train, when I remembered it was Christmas Eve and I bought some presents for Haruo and headed home. I think you know I am just a simple man, and how much I loved my wife, my child, my family. Thinking of how happy my wife and child would be with me coming back one day earlier, made me even happier and that's why I thought of Santa Claus. Bursting with joy, I went all the way to the back of the house, and silently sneaked up to the window. I removed my skis there and imagined the surprised look of my family as I went to the glass window and opened it.

But then I saw something I should never have witnessed. I entered the room to find Oikawa and my wife locked in an intimate embrace on the sofa. I threw the toy box, together with my happiness, at them.

But Hatano, do you think that would be enough to quell my overflowing rage? You probably know what I did with the poker I grabbed as I was crying with grief. Haruo, who had been sleeping in the room next door had woken up, so, making sure he wouldn't know what had happened, I lied to him and fled with him through the front door. But I have nowhere left to flee now. Even if I did, nothing can save my broken heart any more.

Hatano. I go with the joy that my beloved Haruo will be beside me as I leave on this dark voyage.

Farewell.

Sanshirō

Outside, snow blown by the night wind, which had just started, seemed like a funeral wreath. The church bells stopped ringing then, but their lingering sounds weighed heavily on my trembling heart.

First published in *Shinseinen*, December Issue, Shōwa 11 (1936).

THE THREE MADMEN

1

The private mental institution run by Doctor Akazawa stood on top of Akatsuchiyama, a small hill near the outskirts of M Town, amidst a thicket overlooking the road which led to the crematorium. It was an old fashioned one-storey building, resembling a large spider crawling on the ground.

Ill fortune never comes alone, they say, and indeed, even before the unbelievably atrocious incident occurred, a sinister miasma had already spread within the wooden walls of the Akazawa Mental Hospital. As the foundations of the institution were, by then, infested to the core, destruction was inevitable.

According to Doctor Akazawa, the care of the mentally ill was an incredibly complex problem. Many of the patients would—either with the most trivial of reasons or even completely unknown motives—resort to horrible deeds, like violence or setting fire to things. Others would run away, attempt suicide without any cause, refuse to eat because they did not feel like it, or decline to take their medicine. Understandably, patients like these frequently proved to be not only a danger to the nurses, but to society in general. In order to provide them with care and custody, as well as with mental peace, removed from the life of free society, it was necessary to confine such patients in a medical institution. But contrary to the ordinary sick and injured, most of these mental patients were not aware of their own illness. They did not fear the actions their bodies might take, and would remain extremely calm even in the face of any danger, so taking care of these people asked for caution and kindness. Studies showed that, as opposed to a large institution like a hospital, it was better to have a small number of patients at a homely place, where they could enjoy home nursing, with the first rule of nursing being that each patient would be attended to by their own personal nurse.

It was the grandfather on director Akazawa's father's side of the family who had first realised this. This was no wonder, as he came from Iwakura-mura in Kyōto, the first place in Japan to have home nursing. He managed to combine these two contradictory nursing styles, and opened what could be called the first small, homely hospital. But, since each patient had their own nurse, the expenses of this kind of hospital were very high. The first director had somehow managed to succeed with this concept. Financial problems only started to arise during the second director's tenure. And now the third and current director even had to put in his own private funds.

The hospital always had few patients, but with the arrival of a new era, and the opening of a new, municipal mental hospital, the number of patients started to dwindle even more. The decorated generals and great inventors who walked up and down the ward left one by one. The singing, which at one time had sounded cheerful to listening ears, had now turned into a strangely lonely tune, and it became especially eerie on nights when the wind howled. Two, three nurses basically fled as they quit their jobs. Only one nurse past his fifties remained, taking care of the last remaining three patients, who had no guardians. Besides the nurse, there was also a medical student there—who also worked as a maid—as well as the director's wife, so there were seven men and women in total residing in the hospital. But the small group was not enough to win against the silence of the desolate hill.

As this aura—which reminded Doctor Akazawa of closed windows covered by spiders' webs and stuffy *tatami* mats with mould—became stronger, the doctor no longer tried to hide the fact he that he'd already reached his limits. For example, he'd accidently pull out too many young shoots while taking care of his *bonsai* tree—a hobby he had started at some point. One day, during his rounds, the distressed doctor cried out irresponsibly to his patients: 'You're just imbeciles! There's no hope for you unless you get a new set of brains!' It was lucky the patients were having one of their moments at the time. The nurse and maid who were witnesses to the scene were more disturbed by the director than the patients, and both grimaced as they shot glances at each other. But the patients suddenly shut their mouths, shrank visibly as they looked up at the doctor, and retreated, as if they'd understood what the doctor had said after all.

All three patients were middle-aged men. They of course had names of their own, but in the hospital they were called by nicknames. The man in room 1 was "Knock Knock." He would spend every day standing near the window of his room. He had a tic where he would constantly kick the wainscoting with the toes on his right foot as he looked outside at the row of cars heading for the crematorium and the ravens sitting on the utility pole. This tic was very persistent, so the *tatami* mat beneath the window where Knock Knock always stood had been worn out completely as the sole of his foot was always rubbing there. The hairs of the mat were all standing up, resembling the insides of a pharmacist's mortar.

With the dwindling number of patients, these three had all been moved to rooms 1, 2 and 3, closest to the main building, for nursing convenience. The man in room 2 was called "Diva." He was a man with a bearded face, but day and night, he would sing outdated popular songs—which he probably remembered from the time his condition first started—dressed in a woman's kimono. He would then applaud himself and ask for an encore, but instead of giving one, he'd laugh without any reason.

The person in room 3 was called the "Injured." He was not actually injured, but he claimed he had great injuries. His whole face was wrapped in bandages and he lay the whole day on his back, saying he needed total rest. Whenever the nurse tried to approach him, he'd scream, and vehemently refuse to have other people lay their hand on his wounds. He was only obedient to the director, who would replace the bandages from time to time, to maintain hygiene.

The three patients were all mild-tempered, cheerful men and each of them went about his business each day within the cramped, walled space of the Akazawa Mental Hospital, without any worries about the future. But as time went by, their care would sometimes get neglected, and the quality of the meals also dropped, so a dark cloud started casting a shadow on both the spirits and the faces of even this cheerful bunch. With these patients clashing with the increasing business worries of the director, the atmosphere in the hospital became darker, curling around like the wind, reflecting precisely the mood of everyone inside. This wind became stronger and stronger, more violent until it finally rose up like a whirlwind, cruelly blowing the Akazawa Mental Hospital towards its end.

It happened on a stuffy, hot morning. For some reason, there had been a constant flow of cars heading towards the crematorium, kicking up an endless screen of dust on the hill.

The old nurse Ukichi Toriyama got up at six as he did every morning. He walked down the hallway towards the ward with a toothpick in his mouth, but he stopped in shock when he noticed that the back door of the wooden fence in the corner of the exercise yard was wide open.

Allow me to explain further. The grounds of the Akazawa Mental Hospital are spread over five hundred and fifty *tsubo*, and are enclosed by a high wooden fence. Within these grounds, there was a hundred and fifty *tsubo* wide exercise yard, which was flanked on three sides. On one side stood the main building, which housed a consultation room, a pharmacy, and the rooms for the director and his wife and the other employees. The V-shaped ward stood at another side of the yard. The last remaining side of the yard was flanked directly by the wooden fence. The wooden back door in the fence stood near the ward and led to the surrounding thicket. As it led directly to a playground of mental patients, this exit was of course not treated like one of the main building's back doors, or the main entrance, and was always kept locked tightly. The director would go out through that door to take a stroll in the thicket from time to time, so, as Nurse Ukichi Toriyama hurried to the door, he thought that the director might perhaps have gone out. But it was definitely unforgivable that the director had left that important door open during his stroll, even if he was out for only a moment, thought Ukichi Toriyama as he arrived at the door and looked anxiously outside the fence.

Not a soul.

The birds hiding in the treetops were singing their morning song. But Ukichi then realised something very curious, which made him remove the toothpick from his mouth.

He hadn't heard the soprano singing voice of Diva this morning yet, even though he'd always start early in the morning. No, it wasn't just the Diva's soprano voice. He also hadn't heard that persistent, loud Knock Knock either. The lonesome ward was completely silent. It appeared to be an eerie, lonely place now, as if the place had died beneath the morning sun. It was completely silent. From within this silence, the only noise you could hear was the low and slow, but gradually hastening, beating of Ukichi's heart.

'... This is... a disaster!' Ukichi Toriyama whispered. He became visibly pale. He hunched forward as he ran back to the ward.

Rattle rattle. Bam bam. For a while, the noise of doors being opened and closed continued, followed by a trembling voice. '... Do-doctor... this is terrible....' Ukichi started with room 4 and made his way to room 1, ran out to the hallway and loudly made his way to the main building, where everybody was still asleep.

'... We've got a problem. It's terrible. All the patients are gone....'

The people inside the main building were shocked by the news and commotion suddenly started there.

'Where is the doctor, where is he?'

'In his bedroom. Wake him up now.'

'He wasn't in his bedroom.'

'He wasn't there?'

'Anyway, all the patients ran away.'

'And the empty rooms?'

'They weren't in any of them.'

'Wake the doctor....'

'But I can't find the doctor.'

Eventually, Nurse Ukichi Toriyama, Mrs. Akazawa and the maid ran out to the exercise yard, the women carelessly dressed.

They had a situation at hand now. They couldn't do nothing.

Ukichi immediately led the group outside, inside the thicket, and with bloodshot eyes, they split up and started searching for the patients. But they found no mental patients. Not long afterwards, the group reassembled again in front of the back wooden door, all almost in tears.

'...But where is the doctor?' the maid asked anxiously.

Surprised by the noise, ravens started to raise their ill-omened cries from among the treetops. Ukichi's knees were trembling, and he had no idea of what to do next. But then he crouched down.

'Oh. What's that...?' he exclaimed, and he leant forward. On the hospital side of the door in the fence, something like a beer bottle had been smashed into pieces. A closer look revealed that it was one of the glass bottles with deodoriser for the toilets in the ward. Dried-up spots of dark red fluid were spread here and there around the location of the bottle fragments. The maid shrieked.

'Toriyama. Aren't those marks made by something being dragged along the ground?'

Mrs. Akazawa had pointed towards a part of the ground with vague tracks that continued towards the ward, as if something had been dragged there. Those tracks were accompanied by dark red drops....

The three gasped and followed the tracks. They followed the wooden fence and arrived at the outside toilet of the ward. Inside was a cement dirt floor, without panelling. The moment the three peered inside, they cried out in fear and stood frozen to the spot.

The whole dirt floor was covered by a sea of blood. The person lying near the centre of this blood puddle was the gruesome figure of director Akazawa, still dressed in the pyjamas he'd had on the previous night. Blood had flown out from the horrible scratches across his face and head—probably made with the glass fragment that was shining coldly in the sea of blood—and what made this sight truly impossible to watch, was the fact that a large hole had been opened in his head, starting from his face, across his forehead to the skull, and his brains had been removed, leaving the inside of his head completely empty. The brains had been taken somewhere else, as there was no sign of them anywhere close by....

2

It was twenty minutes later by the time the senior police detective sent from the police station in M Town, which had received the urgent message, arrived with his team of police officers.

The detective's name was Lieutenant Yoshioka and, after he'd listened to a simple explanation of the events by an agitated Ukichi Toriyama, the lieutenant sent out his subordinates in all directions with orders to find and detain the three madmen who had escaped.

Not long after that, the people from the prosecutor's office arrived, and promptly an investigation of the surroundings and the questioning by the preliminary judge started. Ukichi, Mrs. Akazawa and the maid were all three very confused. At first, the officers had trouble with their incoherent testimonies, but as they slowly calmed down, they managed—with some detours—to get their questions answered about the sinister mood caused by the current financial situation of the Akazawa Mental Hospital, on how the director had become aggressive lately, and about the peculiarities of the three madmen.

Meanwhile, the medical examiner had placed the death of the director around four o'clock in the morning. At that time everyone was still sleeping and nobody had heard anything. The police learned that the director always got up early, and would often do exercises or go out on a stroll in his pyjamas.

After the preliminary investigation had been concluded, the prosecutor said to the lieutenant:

'Anyway, we know what the motive behind this crime is. The question is whether these three madmen committed the crime together, or whether one of them did it and they all escaped the hospital separately after discovering the door was left open. By the way, how many police officers did you send out to arrest them?'

'I've got five men out there at the moment.'

'Five?' The prosecutor grimaced. 'And did they bring you any news?'

'Not yet.'

'Of course they haven't. Five men are too few. We've three escaped lunatics here. They might be hiding…,' said the prosecutor, but he then thought of something horrible. His face visibly tensed up. He then continued speaking:

'Yes, this isn't just a matter of whether we can catch them or not. This could be terrible. Listen, the murderers are crazies. Three of them. And they're not just mad, but they have grown violent now, so who knows what they'll do?'

'Precisely.' The preliminary judge joined the discussion looking ashen.

'… If those men reach town, with all the women and girls there, who knows what will happen?'

'This is horrible,' said the prosecutor in a trembling voice and he turned to the police detective. 'We can't waste time. Call quickly for more assistance. Yes, we need to inform all the police boxes in town….'

Lieutenant Yoshioka's eyes changed colour and he ran to the telephone room in the main building.

The news went from the crime scene to the police station, and from the police station to each and every police box in town. A painfully tense atmosphere was suddenly spread across the telephone lines. The temporary investigation headquarters set up at the Akazawa Mental Hospital grew anxious.

The reinforcement police troops which arrived shortly were split into two groups. One group was sent into town, while the other group was sent to search the outskirts surrounding the hill of the mental hospital.

However, good tidings did not come. The senior police detective's teeth were chattering in irritation. The only relief was there had been no follow-up on the violent incident yet.

But this was not the time to dilly-dally. They needed to arrest these men as soon as possible to prevent any more tragedies from happening. But if these three madmen were hiding somewhere out of fear of other people, it could become a very troublesome problem.

Once the lieutenant arrived at this point in his mind, he couldn't sit still any more.

Would a mad person in a situation like this hide? And, if so, where? He would need to ask the opinion of an expert.

When no good news had arrived by noon, the lieutenant made up his mind and stood up. Investigation headquarters was moved to the police station in town and, having left care of that to the department chief, he headed for the municipal mental hospital in the outskirts on the opposite side of town to where Akazawa Mental Hospital was located. Doctor Matsunaga answered his call and immediately agreed to a meeting.

'They did a horrible thing, didn't they?' ruddy-faced Doctor Matsunaga said as he offered the lieutenant a seat. He had already learned the news somehow.

'Actually, to get down to business right away, I'm here to ask you a question about that.'

'You haven't caught those three men yet?'

'Not yet,' the lieutenant put his cards on the table and frowned. 'Doctor, where do insane people like these hide in a situation like this? Or would they....'

'Well... I guess they would hide in a place where they won't be found, if they happened to come across one.'

'And in what manner would they hide themselves? They are a dangerous lot, so we need to act quickly....'

The doctor answered with a wry smile. 'That's a difficult question to answer. You see, I really can't say without observing each of them in detail. In general, people like them demonstrate limited thinking and few emotions, but even so, there are still different levels to their conditions and each has his unique kind of logic. And, if you permit me to state my own opinion on the matter, in this case, I think that, rather than looking at how they might have hidden themselves, it's more urgent to determine whether they committed the murder together, or whether it was committed by just one of them. In the latter case, the murderer might be difficult to apprehend, but at least the remaining two should be quite over their initial excitement by now and have grown hungry. And once they're not agitated any more, they represent little danger. However, if they worked together....'

The doctor squirmed in his seat and suddenly started speaking in an agitated manner.

'... If they were working together, this could turn into something very troublesome.'

'By which you mean?' The lieutenant couldn't help but lean forward.

'If this was the crime of one person, it is unlikely that person will be found unharmed, but for that same reason, if this crime was committed by the three of them, I fear for the lives of all three.'

'... I don't get what you're saying. What do you mean...?'

The lieutenant had a troubled expression on his face.

'You see,' the doctor said with a grin, '... I picked this rumour up at the pharmacy, but it appears that Doctor Akazawa had been worn out lately, and that he had started yelling things to his patients like "Get a replacement for your brains."'

'Yes, that's correct. That's their motive.'

'Please listen. I heard this rumour only once or twice, but without a doubt they were told to "get a replacement for their brains," not "get a brain." You do understand there is a very big difference between replacement and procurement.'

'... Yes....'

The lieutenant gave a vague answer, as he had not understood the implications completely. The doctor continued.

'You see, you might call them imbeciles, but even imbeciles have some powers of comprehension and reasoning. If someone is told to get a replacement for his brain, and they manage to take out the brains out of an intelligent man, what do you think they'll do next?'

Silence.

The lieutenant uttered not a word as he stood up in shock. He grabbed his hat with trembling hands and bowed deeply before Doctor Matsunaga.

'Thank you. I see what you mean.'

The doctor laughed jovially.

'That's quite alright. Please capture those poor men before they smash their own heads in and die.' As he stood up, the doctor added: 'There's much to be learned from this incident. Everyone has to be careful....'

3

After leaving the mental hospital, Lieutenant Yoshioka felt relieved for some reason. The fear of the escaped patients attacking the general public had been alleviated tremendously due to Doctor Matsunaga's explanation. Rather than assaulting other people, the three madmen—or one of them—were more likely to be absorbed in replacing their own brain with the brain they took Doctor Akazawa. Nevertheless, it still remained an utterly mad and terrifying matter.

Lieutenant Yoshioka broke out in a cold sweat as one worry was replaced by another. On returning to headquarters, he resumed the baton of command again to lead the investigation.

The expert's view was soon proved to have been correct, and so the lieutenant's efforts had paid off.

It was in the evening of that day that they captured the first of the three madmen, Diva, near the crematorium. As Doctor Matsunaga had suggested, Diva had calmed down and when the western sky started to glow red, that sorrowful soprano voice started to sing from his hiding place in the thicket behind the crematorium. A bright plain-clothes constable heard him, and carefully approached him while being careful to applaud. Diva stopped singing for a moment and silence reigned, but—seemingly relieved—he resumed his seductive song. The constable clapped his hands once again. This time, an encore followed immediately. Once again applause. And another encore. Eventually, Diva even started to laugh. The distance between the two slowly shrank, and the fugitive was caught surprisingly easily.

Diva, wearing a woman's kimono, was taken by car to the police station, where the elated lieutenant started to question him immediately. But it soon became obvious that the lieutenant was in no way capable of dealing with the person in front of him, so he made a telephone call to Doctor Matsunaga.

Having left his hospital, the doctor was visiting the Akazawa Mental Hospital, but once he got the telephone call from the lieutenant, he immediately headed for the police station. Once the situation had been explained to him, he first praised the quick thinking of the police officer who had made the arrest.

'That was a fantastic idea. The one thing you must never do when dealing with such people is to agitate them. You need to handle them softly, like softly strangling them with silk floss. Get down to their level, and go along with their infantile feelings and way of thinking.'

The doctor then proceeded to ask Diva some curious questions, while observing his body closely. He turned to the lieutenant and said: 'This man is not the murderer. There is no blood on him anywhere. The madman responsible for that tragedy could not be this clean. So it appears they did not work together. The murderer is one of the remaining two men. Anyway, let's get this one back to his home.'

Diva was thus safely returned to the Akazawa Mental Hospital as per the doctor's orders.

The lieutenant then poured all his energy into finding Knock Knock and the Injured.

Not even an hour had passed, when a report came in that told them that Doctor Matsunaga's gruesome prediction had finally come true.

The hostess of Azuma, a brothel for workers near the outskirts of M Town, was pulling back the rope curtain in front of her shop prior to leaving for the public bath, when a middle-aged man came staggering towards her from the dark street up ahead. She cried out as he approached her, for his clothes had not been buttoned up and his face was covered in blood, with an eerie glimmer in his eyes. Like a *jizō* statue, the man held one hand out in front of him—palm upwards—and in it he held something which looked like broken tofu. With unsteady steps, he disappeared in the direction of the nearby railway tracks.

After receiving the report, the lieutenant jumped up, his face pale. He asked Doctor Matsunaga to accompany him, and had a car take them to the brothel.

There he confirmed once again the contents of the report, and immediately started an investigation of the area that led in the direction of the railway.

At around the same time, the last remaining madman was captured near M River, which ran right through town. It was precisely as if he had calmed down now and was getting hungry, as Doctor Matsunaga had predicted he would.

It was the Injured, whose face was wrapped completely in bandages. He'd suddenly appeared on a bridge, peering down at the dark water surface with a strange look. Having received a report from a passerby, a police officer managed to capture the patient in the same way you'd capture a cicada. Unlike Diva, the Injured did resist capture slightly. But he soon calmed down and was brought to the police station.

When the lieutenant had been informed of the capture, he'd been at a booth next to a railway crossing. He asked the police officer who'd brought the report: 'Did that lunatic have any blood on his clothes?'

'No, not at all. But it did appear he'd been sleeping somewhere, as there was a lot of straw clinging to the bandages on his head.'

The lieutenant shot a glance at Doctor Matsunaga and smiled.

'Okay. Bring that loony back to the Akazawa Mental Hospital. But handle him gently.'

'Yes.'

The police officer departed and the lieutenant walked side by side with the doctor along the dark railway tracks.

'I think we finally know what happened,' said the doctor.

'Yes,' the lieutenant nodded energetically. 'But where could he be hiding?'

The beams from the police officers' flashlights appeared and disappeared in the surrounding darkness. The sight reminded them of fireflies.

They'd hardly been walking for ten minutes, when in the darkness of the railways in front of them, a flashlight suddenly made a large sweep.

'Heeeey,' a voice called out.

'What is it?' the lieutenant yelled back.

A voice answered: 'Lieutenant? He's here! He's dead!'

The lieutenant and the doctor immediately ran forward.

They soon arrived at the spot where the police officer was standing, and the lieutenant took in the terrible scene.

Knock Knock was lying sideways on the railway tracks, his head resting on the rails as if they were a pillow. It had already been cruelly run over and crushed into pieces, which lay scattered over the surrounding pebbles.

They moved Knock Knock's remains to the side of the railway tracks for the moment, and the lieutenant and the doctor began to examine the body. Soon the lieutenant appeared to have seen enough, however, and muttered to nobody in particular: 'What an absolutely terrifying end....'

The doctor was still crouching in front of the body, carefully examining the soles of the man's feet. He raised his head with an expression of dissatisfaction.

'The end?'

The words were spoken reproachfully as the doctor stood up wearily. For some reason his demeanour had changed completely. His face was completely pale, and his face showed signs of intense suspicion and anguish.

'Please wait,' the doctor finally grunted. He turned his angry face away and, as if he was still in doubt, kept glancing at the body of

Knock Knock. But then he raised his head again with a determined look.

'Yes. Please wait. You just said this was the end? No. I might have been under a horrible misunderstanding. Lieutenant, I fear this is not the end.'

'Wha-what?'

The lieutenant approached the doctor as if he'd had enough. But the latter took no notice of the lieutenant's menacing look, and said something curious as he glanced at the body of Knock Knock:

'By the way, is Director Akazawa's body still at his mental hospital?'

4

Approximately twenty minutes later, Doctor Matsunaga had succeeded in dragging the reluctant lieutenant to the Akazawa Mental Hospital.

The treetops on the hill in the night were rustling in the wind, and an owl cried from some hidden place.

The doctor found the nurse Ukichi Toriyama in the main building and explained that he wanted to see the body of the director.

'Very well. We haven't had permission to bury him yet, so we haven't held a wake for him,' said Ukichi, as he led the two to the ward, guided by candle light.

They passed by room 2. From inside the room, they could hear Diva's soprano voice. Tonight, he was singing in a faint, docile voice, almost as if he were simply muttering. The party then passed by room 3. Inside the illuminated room, the Injured had set the glass sliding window ajar, and he watched the group pass by with a suspicious look as he cast a large shadow on the window. There was no electric light from room 4 onwards, so the hallway was pitch-dark.

Ukichi's shadow danced by the candle light, as he led the group to room 5.

'We don't have a coffin yet, so we laid him out like this,' Ukichi explained as he held the candle in front of him.

The director's body had been laid on top of oil paper in the corner of the room, and was covered by a white cloth. Without uttering a word, the doctor walked over to the body, crouched down and removed the cloth. He raised the body's right foot and said to Ukichi: 'Light, please.'

Ukichi held the candle in front of him with trembling hand, and the doctor started rubbing the sole of the deceased's foot with both thumbs. Despite his rubbing, the sole wouldn't give and remained extremely stiff. It appeared to be covered with large calluses. The doctor raised the leg, and moved the tip of the large toe closer to the candle light. In the light of the flame, the toe looked swollen and dried up, resembling a pumice stone.

Ukichi dropped the candle.

Suddenly it became pitch-dark inside the room. And from within came that crying, wailing, that terrifying voice of Ukichi.

'... Aaah... but that's... Knock Knock's foot...!'

But Ukichi's shriek had not even tailed off when it was followed by another, sharper one from Doctor Matsunaga, who had fallen over noisily in the dark as he darted for the door.

'Lieutenant! Follow me!'

From the hallway came the noise of frantic footsteps, something hitting a door, and the sound of glass breaking.

The perplexed lieutenant rushed into the hallway as well. Two figures were fighting in front of room 3, rolling over on the floor. The lieutenant ran over to them. He hesitated for a moment, but then the twenty *kan* heavy body of the lieutenant lunged for the figure whose head was wrapped in white bandages.

The Injured was quickly caught. Handcuffed, the man sat angrily down on the floor, and his eyes blinked with a grave look, as if he was having a bad dream.

Doctor Matsunaga rubbed his waist as he got up and brushed the dust off his pants with his other hand.

'This is the first time I've ever been in a fight.'

The lieutenant could not contain his curiosity anymore.

'But, what does this all mean?'

The doctor looked at the Injured.

'Heh. Still playing dumb? Let's have an experiment to see if you are really dumb or just pretending.'

He crouched down to the Injured and stared right into the man's eyes, the only things visible from behind the bandages. The Injured tried to struggle again.

'Lieutenant. Hold him down tightly.'

With that, the doctor extended both his hands to the face of the Injured. The figure still tried to struggle with all its might. The lieutenant became angry and tried to pin him down. Eventually, the doctor managed to begin removing the bandages around the face. Despite the struggle, the long, white fabric was slowly removed, and from beneath appeared…a chin, a nose, cheeks, eyes! Ukichi, who had been standing behind Doctor Matsunaga, cried out in utter astonishment.

'But…that's the doctor!'

Yes. There in front of everyone was the pale face of Doctor Akazawa, who had been presumed dead.

Inside the car the police had sent, Doctor Matsunaga explained the case.

'Never before have I heard of such a crafty crime. A patient, who was always being yelled at that he should get a replacement for his brain, obediently did exactly what he had been told…. This was how the case appeared to us, but in reality, the mad patient was the one who was murdered, and it was the doctor himself who pretended to be dead. Yes, if you perform a savage operation like taking the brains out, then obviously there's little of the face left to identify the person with. So if you then exchange your clothes, you're all set. But it was a really big mistake for the director to mistake the bodies of Knock Knock and the Injured. The man the hostess of that brothel saw was not Knock Knock, but the director. He performed that scene in front of a witness and fled to the railway tracks. He had murdered the Injured in advance, and then placed his head on the rails and had a train run over it, to make it appear Knock Knock had done it himself to replace his brains. He expertly used the psychology of these patients, as you would expect from someone in this field. After killing the Injured however, he wanted to bring this case to an end as soon as possible, so he dressed up as the Injured himself and allowed himself to be caught. That was a mistake. He thought we would automatically assume that the man who died on the railway tracks was Knock Knock. He would have been safe if I hadn't noticed that there were no calluses on the soles of the foot of that fake Knock Knock, even though the real one wore *tatami* mats down with his tic. If he'd murdered the Injured first at the hospital, and then murdered Knock Knock on the railway tracks, then his crime would have succeeded. Then in two or three days, some person would arrive at the hospital to take the fake Injured away from the Akazawa Mental Hospital. Akazawa's widow would then proceed to take care of the remaining business and sell the hospital for money. Oh yes, the life of that director was probably insured for a fortune. The widow would then meet up again with her husband who was supposed to be dead. That was probably the gist of their plans. That director must have felt quite cornered in his life, but I cannot approve of such a cruel deed, making use of those innocent people as his scapegoats.'

The doctor looked at the lieutenant after he had finished. Then he remembered something, and with a grimace, added one last comment.

'Yes, there's much we can learn from this incident. Everyone has to be careful....'

First published in *Shinseinen*, July Issue, Shōwa 11 (1936).

THE GUARDIAN OF THE LIGHTHOUSE

...Yes, they all ask me that. Why remain on this lonely small island, all alone at this age, without a wife, without a son, just keeping watch on a lighthouse while listening to the never-ending noise of the waves....

Depending on how you look at it, this might appear like a monotonous way of living, but to an old man like me, this is a joyful duty, one I will never abandon as long as my body is willing to move and my eyesight remains intact.

Mind you, ever since I lost my wife several years ago through disease, I too have realised that this task is a sad one. I had even considered having my son succeed to my job, with me moving to the town on the other side of the sea and enjoying my retirement.... I was having those sweet dreams when that incident happened with my only son Masayoshi. Everyone, please listen to this.... Allow this old man to explain clearly to you all what a noble work, what a noble task all lighthouse keepers perform, even a lighthouse on a small island forgotten by all.

...This might sound like bragging, coming from his own father, but my son Masayoshi was a well-raised, reliable and outstanding son of a lighthouse keeper. Every time I think of the noble teaching Masayoshi left me, my heart hurts, and it really makes me feel lonely. Let me explain to you what happened ....

...Oh, an awful wind has starting blowing now.... Yes, yes, there was a storm the night it happened, with a wind as strong as the one now blowing over the rough sea.

These days, even lighthouses on an island like this one have some facilities, with several lighthouse keepers staying there. But back then, we only had a small household here, consisting of myself and my son, and lighthouse keeper Tonomura and the wife whom he had recently married. We lived in the old living quarters over there and, well, we lived a peaceful life. But you can't fight fate, so one day, lighthouse keeper Tonomura, who was usually all energy, unexpectedly contracted appendicitis. So he was immediately taken across the sea to the hospital in town. His wife naturally also went to stay by his side. And while it was not ideal, my son Masayoshi and I worked in shifts to watch the lighthouse at night.

Because Tonomura had been taken immediately to the hospital, his recovery had been rapid, and he was released quite quickly. Once I heard the news, I couldn't wait anymore and went right away to prepare the boat to pick the Tonomuras up. We had a small motorboat which belonged to the lighthouse, so I loaded it with some extra oil, spread a straw mat out on the seat and went out on the refreshing June sea to the town on the other side, leaving the lighthouse in Masayoshi's care.

...Now I think about it, that was the last time I said farewell to my son. The sea was strangely calm that day, so I decided to try and return by evening and increased the power, speeding across the sea as if I were coasting downhill. But you know, you can't trust the seas around here at all from the summer to autumn. I was careless. I hadn't thought about that at all, and there's nothing I can do about it now, but after I had arrived in town, I picked the Tonomuras up and we headed straight back to the lighthouse. Just at that moment, a thunderhead cloud was raising its grey head in the southern sky like a mallet, and I could see how the head was growing larger in size.... It was too late by then. The waves started to roll higher and higher, the colour of the sea had changed in an instant and large drops of rain falling from the pitch-black sky were hitting us from the side. We had quite a lot of experience at sea, and we realised there was nothing for it but to turn back to town right away. As you know, there's a customs office there and we'd always been friendly with the folks there, so they offered us a place to sleep. There was nothing we could do but wait for the calm.

But, as they say, bad luck never comes alone. The sea became rougher and rougher and it wouldn't calm down one bit. We started to become very worried. I had told Masayoshi to watch the lighthouse, but he was all alone and who knows what his duty would bring him? Back in those days, the old building had not been renovated yet, and every time we had a storm like this, we'd have some damage. Even if the lighthouse came out of the storm unscathed, just imagining my son all alone on top of a creaking tower swinging in the wind.... Oh, you didn't know that? On stormy nights, the top of the lighthouse sways around. Just a little, of course, but when a strong gust of wind hits it right... But as long as the building swings, it means the iron reinforcements are still resilient, so that's a relief in a way. Anyway, I was sure it wouldn't be pleasant up there. I couldn't stay put any more, so I went around trying to arrange for a large boat, but while there were boats coming in the harbour to find shelter, none of them would go out again to this island here with these heavy currents and reefs and rocks hiding beneath the sea surface. Amidst all this anxiety and impatience, night eventually fell. It was a stormy night. I tried to calm the pounding in my chest, so I went up to the first floor of the living quarters of the branch office and looked through the windows which were being lashed by the rain. I could have cried out in relief when I saw that, faraway, the light Masayoshi had lit was piercing through the dim, raging darkness at exactly the rate of once every ten seconds. It was like the sight of a firefly making its way through the rain. I could only pray the light would continue like that and, after we had finished our dinner, the people at the branch office were kind enough to offer us beds. But with the start of the night, the storm started to get more violent too. Tonomura and I didn't manage to get any sleep at all. We'd wake up, go to the front window on the first floor, see if our prayers were being heard and check to see if the light from the lighthouse was continuing its flicker faraway across the sea, and then go to bed again.

Yes, yes, Masayoshi was twenty-one back then. Younger than any of you. He had a florid complexion, which would shine during tide, but he looked a bit like his father too, and he had a courageous personality. He would never give up... No, I can't complain about my son. Anyway, I hardly got a wink of sleep that night, as I'd wake up and keep watch from the window over the light from the island out there in the storm. My Masayoshi held on until the morning.

The morning made it seem as if the night before had been nothing but a lie. The storm had disappeared completely, leaving nothing but a calm wind. Only the waves still had something left of yesterday, as the large waves come rolling here slowly. We thanked the people at the branch office warmly, and quickly left in our boat. It didn't even take two hours for us to reach the island. But as we approached it, with that familiar sight of the lighthouse standing tall, I felt an undeniable anxiety well up from within me.

Our return had been delayed for one night because of the storm, so Masayoshi must have been eagerly awaiting us, and I had imagined that by now, he'd have appeared from behind the lighthouse and be standing at the cliff in front of us, energetically jumping up and waving his hands and calling out to us to welcome us back. But as we neared the shore, my rising expectations were revealed to be nothing but mere delusions. I couldn't restrain myself any more and I yelled out towards the island, but there was no answer. There was only the echo of my voice hitting the cliff walls, and disappearing in the rumbling of the waves at the shore.

It was then that anxiety really began to take hold of me. With a pounding heart, I landed the boat at the simple pier in the bay and we quickly set out on the cliff path. As you can see for yourselves, once you climb this path, you end up at that open space where the living quarters are. There we started to cry out for Masayoshi, but no matter where we searched, in and outside the living quarters and all over the open space, there was no sign of my son anywhere. I first had the Tonomuras rest a bit, and I headed for the lighthouse on top of those large boulders over there. As I climbed the spiral staircase of the lighthouse, I called out Masayoshi's name, but my trembling voice would only reverberate everywhere, and there was no answer from my son. I finally reached the top of the lighthouse: the lantern room which also served as the room for the lighthouse keeper on night watch. My son wasn't here either, of course. But instead of my son, I did find something extraordinary.

What I found was... You've all participated in the tour, so you know this lighthouse has a revolving lamp which emits a ray of light every ten seconds. The large lamp with the Fresnel lens at the centre of the lantern room is hooked up through a mechanism of gears to a large weight suspended inside the shaft—the large tube placed right in the centre of the tower, encircled by the staircase. It's this mechanism that makes the lamp revolve so it only sends out a beam of light every ten seconds. At the time I jumped inside the lantern room, this lamp was still turning around. The pale fire running on acetylene gas was still burning, even though it was already day. This meant that Masayoshi had gone off somewhere before it was time to extinguish the light this morning. I trembled as I considered this, and I quickly extinguished the light, stopped the revolution of the lamp and went down the tower again. Down below, the tool storage at the foot of the lighthouse caught my eye and I entered it. But my son wasn't inside the dimly lit storage either. I turned pale, and almost cried as I ran back to the Tonomuras.

I've seen quite some things in my life, but even I was out of my wits by that time. My son had disappeared while leaving the lighthouse running. But I needed to clarify what had happened to my son, so even though Tonomura had not been able to rest much, the two of us went around the island searching every corner.

The circumference of this island is about ten *chō,* so it's not large enough to have real hiding places, but there are some bushes and grass fields and there are the uneven cliffs at the shore that go up and down, so it still took some time to search all the places. Considering we'd had to search this desperately, I knew that even when we did manage to find my son, he wouldn't be all right. The thought of it made me cry. I climbed on top of a boulder near the shore and looked down at the sea, anxious he might have been drifting off shore.

But listen, everyone. We searched the whole island, but we didn't find him, and eventually it became night. Like the creeping darkness, my mind was slowly filled with suspicion, distress and frustration.

Tonomura had already recovered sufficiently from his hospital visit, so he was kind enough to watch the lighthouse that night instead of me. The light went on in the lighthouse. And as always, the lighthouse performed its task. But even as the night passed by, my son Masayoshi did not return. Tonomura's wife hardly slept, as she came several times to my living quarters to cheer me up. We were all exhausted by the time it became morning.

I had regained some of my spirit in the morning, and while it was just a fleeting hope, I headed out in the boat to search the surrounding sea. But this, needless to say, turned out to be a futile effort. And then another night of despair fell. But I still had not given up and, the following day, joined by the Tonomuras, we searched every corner again both in and outside the lighthouse. My son had disappeared during his work, so it was unlikely he had committed suicide. Something had to have happened on the island that night, and Masayoshi must have left his post because of that, and then through some accident, he must have fallen into the sea. I could not think of any other reason. The Tonomuras then said to me that we should give up and notify the police and my family. But I'm a father, and you don't give up on your own child so easily. Masayoshi had been so full of energy and knew no equal when it came to swimming. I could not believe he would drown in the sea without leaving some clue to what had happened. Overcome with all these events, I spent the following day and the day after that wandering in a daze all over the island in search of Masayoshi, while the Tonomuras watched me with pity. Desperate to find my son, I started to have delusions and looked beneath the floors, and tapped on the concrete walls of the lighthouse, just to see if he wasn't hiding there. But while my mind was completely off the rails, the lighthouse would do its work every night without any mishaps.

My madness however did not stop there, and once it had reared its head, it started to get worse and worse. One night, I was climbing the spiral staircase in the lighthouse, when I imagined I heard my son yelling, sometimes from strangely far away, sometimes from very close by. I stopped in my steps and stared at the large concrete wall of the inner shaft, which was like a large cylindrical chimney encircling the spiral staircase. As I explained earlier, a weight of forty *kan* hooked up to the timing mechanism rotating the lamp of the lighthouse was suspended from a rope inside the shaft. The weight would be lowered down the shaft very slowly. As it was a very narrow shaft, anyone who would fall inside would definitely get caught by the weight, and the extra weight would make the lamp upstairs turn faster than it was supposed to. There was however nothing wrong with the lamp. When I realised that, I became scared of my own mind, and when I caught the pitiful eyes of Tonomura, who was just coming down from the lantern room, I ran back to my own living quarters.

But I guess this is what they call a sixth sense. For, no matter how terrible they may have seemed, my crazy delusions turned out to be right. It was a small incident that led us to find Masayoshi, in a state that was too horrible to look at.

It happened on the afternoon of the fifth day after my son's disappearance. Tonomura discovered that the wiring to the signal post opposite the lighthouse had been heavily damaged by the storm earlier, so he went out to the tool storage to get the instruments to make the repairs. But no matter where he looked, he could not find the tool set he needed, so he hurried to the garden of the living quarters, where I was sitting absentmindedly. The tool set contained all kinds of instruments and materials. Tools like a saw, a plane, a chisel and a hammer were of course part of the set, but also a sledgehammer, an axe, Western nails, a spanner and nuts and bolts. All of that had been thrown together in two long and sturdy canvas bags. But indeed, when I went to the storage to take a look myself, both of the bags were gone, even though nobody had used them lately. We searched high and low but did not find them. This was an odd incident. I had considered that Masayoshi might have taken them, but why would he have the need for so many tools? And furthermore, the two bags together would easily weigh over twenty *kan* together. I was more than a little baffled by this.

Tonomura had been searching all the corners of the storage at the time, and he suddenly walked over to one corner. There was an old platform scale there, which we used to weigh the oil we have. Tonomura crouched down in front of the scales, cocked his head and while looking intently at it, moved his fingers over the platform. He immediately called me over.

'I think Masayoshi has been here. There are traces in the dust here which indicate he placed two bags on the scales,' he said with a pale face. And indeed, as Tonomura said, there were clear markings on the scales. I started to understand less and less of all of it. Tonomura then looked up at me, smiled and pointed at the weights hanging from the balance beam and the smaller scale on the balance beam. The weights hanging from the balance beam indicated forty *kan*, while the smaller scale was set at five-hundred *monme*.

That meant that a total of forty *kan* and five-hundred *monme* had been placed on top of the platform scales. But those two tool bags together would only weigh over twenty *kan*, nowhere near forty *kan*. How strange! But as I looked at the strangely frozen face of Tonomura, a puzzling sign flashed through my mind.

Forty *kan* and five-hundred *monme*! But that was the exact amount of the weight which made the lighthouse lamp revolve! Tonomura had of course also realised this. We almost tumbled over each other as we stormed inside the lighthouse. We opened the cover of the shaft at the bottom of the spiral staircase.

How can I ever describe what we found inside? The worn-down rope holding the large weight had snapped, and the weight had come down with immense force, smashing the concrete floor at the bottom of the shaft and sinking deep into the ground. When had the weight fallen? Even the two of us could not move the weight one bit. Tonomura peered up inside the dark, narrow shaft, but suddenly turned around to me and grabbed me by the shoulders.

'How many *kan* does Masayoshi weigh?'

'About eighteen *kan*…,' I answered trembling.

'That's it!' cried Tonomura and he opened his eyes wide. 'That night, this old rope broke, and the weight fell down here, which stopped the turning of the lamp in the lantern room. Shocked by this, Masayoshi ran down here and tried to make emergency repairs. But this weight had come falling down from high up and had dug itself deep in the floor, so he could not even move it. But even so, the lighthouse had stopped working. And there was a storm raging outside. He simply had to work out something fast. But there weren't even any other people here he could send out to get help. Masayoshi however was resourceful, so he ran to the storage to find something that could serve as a temporary weight. His eyes fell on the two heavy tool bags. But unfortunately, those two bags were only a bit over twenty *kan*. There was nothing else he could do. So Masayoshi started looking for something—anything—eighteen *kan* heavy that could fit inside the shaft so it could serve as the remaining necessary weight….'

As I listened to Tonomura's explanation, I finally started to understand what had happened.

Yes, everyone, what happened here was an absolute tragedy. My son Masayoshi did find something eighteen *kan* heavy. He found *his own body*.

We of course hurried up to the lantern room at the top of the lighthouse and quickly headed for the winch of the revolving machinery to raise the weight that was hanging down from the central shaft. Tonomura turned the winch, while I stood on the staircase right below the lantern room, looking at the open top of the shaft which ended there. Anxiously, I watched the opening and finally it appeared. The horrible body of my son Masayoshi, who had died of starvation and had slimmed incredibly down in just five days. He was wrapped around in rope. The two bags appeared after my son, and had also been tied to the rope.

I couldn't believe it. My poor Masayoshi had tied himself to the rope and jumped down the shaft from this side opening, so his own body could serve as the weight. Thanks to him, the lighthouse could return to its task immediately, and as we ourselves had seen from the windows on the second floor of the customs office, the lighthouse performed its duty perfectly. But as time passed by, Masayoshi's body was lowered further and further down the shaft. Inside this narrow, dark, and hot shaft, surrounded by concrete walls, Masayoshi must have cried out for help, not knowing when we'd return, and he was eventually dropped into a hell of fatigue and starvation. You can't hear anyone yelling from inside that shaft. And by the time we returned, he must have been tired and his voice must have been worn down. Even if we'd heard his voice then, we'd just have thought it was like some ghost story. A voice from the walls. And on this island, you hear, there's always the noise of the wind and the rumbling of the waves.

...Everyone, you all realise what it is now, right? The lesson Masayoshi taught me using his own life?

As long as my body will hold, as long as they will keep me here, I will honour this teaching of Masayoshi, and work humbly on this small island. But I do feel sad at times....

First published in *Teishin Kyōkai Zasshi*, July Issue, Shōwa 11 (1936).

THE DEMON IN THE MINE

1

The Takiguchi Mine, owned by the Chūetsu Coal Mine Company—located amidst the desolate grey mountains on the edge of Cape Murou—had been in business for a very long time, but activity had significantly increased over the last few years. Long, dark tentacle-like tunnels had spread out underground to a depth of five-hundred *shaku*, and at one point had gone down to a point within half a mile of the sea bottom. Most of the company's business depended on this mine, with its estimated coal reserves of six million tons. Men and machines were all pumped into that tense atmosphere, and the heavy work continued day and night without a break. But a mine so close to the bottom of the sea was always in danger and only one step away from becoming a living hell. The better business went, the bigger the underground caverns became, making the danger more and more likely. The people working in the mines were chipping away at a thin barrier which separated them from hell.

It was still cold in early April when the strange incident happened: a violent incident, fitting for such a mad underground world. Above ground, snow had been reluctant to leave its place on the mountains, and a chilling sea wind from the north blew darkly throughout the whole day, but five-hundred *shaku* underground, the fierce heat of the earth was suffocating. It was a naked world down there, with scarcely a piece of clothing. Men carrying pickaxes on their shoulders and muddy up to their navels would pass by with a gleam in their eyes, while naked women with only a cloth around their waist would show themselves, twisting and turning their bodies while pushing coal trolleys.

O-Shina and Minekichi were a married couple who had found each other in this fierce, dark world. Just as at all mining spots, the two of them formed a pair, with the man acting as the digger and the woman as the transporter. The two young people had their own mining spot. And in the dark, where the sub-foreman couldn't see them, the two would always be in each other's arms. But their world had no room for exceptions, and their happiness would not continue for long.

It happened on a morning when the cold wind brought a mist from the underground currents, blowing all the way down into the mine shaft.

After receiving her second slip, O-Shina took the dirty coal trolley which had been emptied and started on her way back through the mine to Minekichi's mining spot. A coal mine is, in a way, similar to a dark underground city. There is an open brick-walled space, connected to the world above through two mine shafts. This main hall, where the never-ending groan of pumps and ventilation machinery, the sounds of the engineers' T-squares and the laughter of the foreman could be heard, was the heart of the dark city. The wide, level tunnel starting from the main hall could be described as its main street. The side passages opening on both sides of the main street were, in turn, like side streets running from east to west. And the mining spots connected to each of these streets, like teeth on a comb, were the branch streets which run from north to south. O-Shina's feet quickly brought her along the trail from the main street to the side passage, until she reached Minekichi's own mining spot.

On the way, O-Shina passed by a foreman and an engineer, who appeared to be making inspections of the side passage, but saw no one else from the company before she made a sharp turn to enter her husband's mining spot.

Minekichi had been waiting for her in the dark mine tunnel, as always. O-Shina gave the coal trolley a push to get it out of the way, and threw her young body into the arms of the man standing in front of her. While being embraced, she looked in a dreamy state at the dim, swaying safety lamp hanging from the back of the trolley, which was proceeding on its way into the darkness.

It was indeed like a dream. Although she would later be questioned about it several times, and she herself would go over it in her mind until what happened became as clear as day, it would nevertheless also be as fleeting as the memory of a dream.

O-Shina's swaying safety lamp had retreated far away, only faintly illuminating the sides of the trolley now, as if it was being considerate enough to give the embracing couple some privacy. But, just before the trolley reached the end of the mine, it appeared to hit a pickaxe or something similar lying on the rails, because it made a shrill sound and started to sway. The shock threw the lamp from its nail, and it fell on the track.

The safety lamps distributed to the workers at the Takiguchi mine were Wolf safety lamps, just as at all other mines. To avoid the dangers of a naked flame in a mine, Wolf safety lamps could only be opened with a magnet held by a watchman at the guard post at the entrance to the mine shafts. But if workers weren't careful with them and placed them on uneven surfaces or broke them, there was nothing safe about them.

Sometimes when things go wrong, they go terribly wrong. O-Shina's safety lamp had been hanging from the back of the trolley, and the trolley had been running faster and faster on the rails, so there was a kind of wind current near the end of the line. The highly inflammable coal dust, which until then had been settled on the floor, was swept up by that wind. It was really just an unfortunate accident, but all the conditions for a disaster came together in a single moment, and the safety lamp, which had been a symbol of the happiness of the young couple, caused an unexpected tragedy.

The scene which unfolded before the girl's eyes was like a hundred magnesium sticks being ignited at the same time. Faster than the sound was the violent wind pressure, which hit her ears, her face and her whole body. She staggered back and could faintly feel countless tiny pebbles hitting her in the face. At the same time, she saw how the flame jumped onto all four walls of the mining spot, and she desperately turned round to run back to the side passage. She turned her head as she thought of Minekichi and saw the man running behind her, with the blazing flame behind him. The flame became more intense, as it spread via the loose clumps of coal and extended itself quickly through the clouds of coal dust. While O-Shina was running for her life, she did feel somewhat relieved to hear the footsteps of the man behind her and see their two shadows cast vividly on the ground in front of her. Then the figure behind her suddenly fell down, as if it had tripped over the rails. In front of her, she saw the electric lights of the side passage.

But the real tragedy happened when O-Shina stumbled beneath the electric lights. She had reached the side passage when she tripped over the complex rail network laid there and fell over. By the time she recovered, the foreman, who had come running there as soon as he heard the explosion, was busy closing the sturdy iron fire door at the entrance to the tunnel from which O-Shina had appeared. She felt relieved for a second because she had managed to avoid being caught inside, but when she looked around she realised the horrible truth.

Her beloved husband Minekichi had not come out of the tunnel. O-Shina grabbed the foreman, who was jamming the door shut with a bar, by the arm. But a violent slap rendered her cheek numb and burning with pain.

'You fool! The fire will spread!' roared the foreman. The image of Minekichi locked in and suffering on the other side of the iron door increased O-Shina's determination and she once again went for the foreman.

But she was again thrown to the floor, this time by an engineer who had also come running. Another workman arrived as well and the foreman ran off to get some clay to fully seal the iron door. It is a long-standing tradition of mines, both past and present, that the lives of one or two individuals do not weigh against the risk of the fire spreading to the rest of the mine. Men and women started to gather in front of the mine on fire, bumping their naked bodies against each other. The engineer was the only person wearing corduroy pants. When they saw how the engineer and the workman were holding the upset O-Shina down, and when they noticed that Minekichi was nowhere to be seen, all those present realised what had happened and turned pale.

An elderly couple stepped forward. They were Minekichi's parents, who worked in the mining spot next to their son's. The father was pushed violently away by the engineer, and remained on the floor without uttering a word. The mother lost control of herself and started laughing madly. One miner stepped out to help the crushed O-Shina up from the rails she had been pinned against. It was her older brother Iwatarō. As she had lost both her parents, he was her only remaining family.

Iwatarō helped his sister up, cast a hate-filled glance at the engineer and the workman, and disappeared into the crowd of the people who had started making more noise.

The foreman returned with a bamboo screen which he had spread over with clay. He was followed by two miners carrying similar heavy bamboo screens. The workman picked up a trowel and started sealing up all the gaps around the iron door.

The sub-foremen of other sections of the mine arrived, together with the mine supervisor, who had been notified of the emergency. The engineer and foreman gave orders to the workman sealing up the door and told the noisy crowd to disperse.

'Return to your places! Go back to work!'

Following orders, the people reluctantly pulled back, pushing their coal trolleys out again and picking up their pickaxes. Once the commotion had subsided, the men who remained in front of the iron door finally showed signs of relief.

The damage had been confined to one mining tunnel. And because they had sealed it shut, the fire would eventually die out on its own through lack of oxygen. A mining tunnel is basically like a well opened into the coal bed, so with the iron door closed, not even an ant could make an escape.

A few minutes later, at exactly ten-thirty in the morning, the sealing of the door was complete, so the fire had probably started at ten o'clock. The iron door, a sensitive conductor to heat, had been warming up silently, glowing in an alarming way, so it appeared that the fire must have spread through the entire tunnel of that mining spot. Where the clay had only been applied sparsely between the gaps, it had begun to dry out and change colour, and countless cracks had appeared, reminding people of geckos on the wall.

The engineer, workman and foreman all grimaced at the sight. An office clerk arrived at the scene, together with the hired police constable, who had caught wind of the incident[i]. The supervisor spat on the ground angrily, and took the constable with him to the office back in the main hall. Minekichi's father had remained seated on the floor all the time, but a sub-foreman helped him stand up and they too left the scene.

The foreman gave orders to the workman and started cleaning the place up. There was nothing else to do until the fire died out.

It was an engineer's job to verify whether or not the fire had died out. Each mining tunnel was equipped with an iron pipe for ventilation, which in this case stuck out from the clay in the gaps above the door, and was connected to a larger iron pipe in the side passage. The engineer remained on the spot and cut the pipe where it joined the larger one in order to analyse the blazing smoke being pumped out from the pipe under high pressure.

From time to time a row of transporters pushing coal trolleys would pass by on the rails. The air in the side passage trembled in silence, compared to the earlier commotion, except that the mad laughing of Minekichi's mother could occasionally be heard.

The usual silence had also returned to the main hall at the entrance to the mine. The Takiguchi Mine had to produce a hundred thousand tons of coal before the summer. A minor incident could not be allowed to delay the whole operation for even a minute. The coal trolleys and the cages, the pumps and the ventilation machinery, everything continued with business as usual under the watchful eyes of the sub-foremen. But inside the office, the supervisor was in a bad mood.

He had immediately started calculating how many trolleys had stopped in the side passage and how many miners had laid down their pickaxes in the twenty minutes after the fire broke out. And then there was the question of how many tons of coal had been lost because of the fire, but that he could not calculate yet. He also had to pinpoint the cause of the fire and who was directly responsible for all the losses. The supervisor ordered another clerk to bring him the woman who had made it out alive. Then he turned to the hired police constable who had been standing next to him. The officer behaved as if he were an observer sent directly from the Bureau of Mines.

'It appears it wasn't that big a deal.'

Perhaps it hadn't been a big deal to him at the time, as only one miner had been sealed up. But the real big deal happened shortly after the conversation. It was when the clerk who had just been sent to check up on the condition of the fire returned with the report that someone had murdered engineer Maruyama.

2

The engineer's body lay in a corner of the side passage, not far from the iron door. It appeared he had been murdered while conducting an analysis of the smoke. At a nearby wall, the ventilation pipe which had been cut loose was hanging from iron wires from the pit props on the ceiling. Analysis tools had been scattered on a stand.

The victim's body was lying face down, and the dark liquid which dripped from his head glistened on the dirt floor. The big wound on the back of his head had ruffled his wet hair, in a manner reminiscent of a chestnut burr. His mouth was open. The murder weapon was discovered right away. A large round clump of coal, as big as a stone weight, was lying not far away from the victim's feet, bathed in blood and glistening black. The moment the supervisor saw it, his eyes went straight up to the ceiling. The ceiling was still intact. But you didn't need a cave-in to make a wound like that.

The pressure at five hundred *shaku* below the ground was high. Above ground, a person could jump to their death from a thousand *shaku*, and most of the time, the body would still be largely intact. But if you fell five hundred *shaku* into a mine underground, there'd be nothing left of you. That's why a cave-in was so frightening. Even the smallest fragment falling down could crack a person's finger like a twig. Therefore it should come as no surprise that a clump of coal could serve as a murder weapon. The supervisor, who had picked the murder weapon up, threw it away and turned his pale face to the foreman.

The workman, who had remained frozen on the spot until then, was the first to speak up.

'After we got things under control, Mr. Asakawa went to do his rounds, while I went to return the trowel to the storage. It happened while we were gone.'

Mr. Asakawa was the name of the foreman. The workman's name was Furui. The two hadn't fully recovered from the commotion of the fire when they had come across the murder, so they were quite agitated. But they weren't the only ones to have lost their composure. The usually easygoing supervisor himself was also quite distressed.

The fire had indeed been contained to one spot. But they didn't yet know how much damage it had caused, and now one of their more precious resources, an engineer, had been killed by someone. The supervisor, who had been earning his living in mines for a long time now, was probably the first person to be truly alarmed by this murder, not just of anyone, but of an engineer.

Eventually the supervisor made up his mind.

'Who could have killed him? Do you have any idea?' asked the hired police constable casually.

'An idea? Of course I have!' said the supervisor, in a tone of displeasure as he turned to the constable.

'It was that fire. One of the miners was too late and was sealed inside the tunnel, which was on fire. A terrible tragedy of course, but we couldn't open the door to save him. It was engineer Maruyama who led the group who sealed up the door. And now Maruyama has been killed, so of course I have an idea as to the murderer. Even if I don't know who exactly, we only have a limited pool of suspects.'

'That has to be it,' agreed the foreman.

The foreman had actually been secretly assigned to this function directly by the mining company, and was a faithful dog in search of profits. While he ostensibly worked under the supervisor, who was the boss of the whole mine, the foreman secretly held as much power as the supervisor, who had worked his way up from an engineer. The constable nodded. The foreman continued:

'Nobody would do something as horrible as this for someone they didn't know. I think his name was Minekichi? The miner who worked here.'

The office clerk nodded and now the supervisor took over.

'Bring his parents and the woman who made it out alive to my office. And that woman's brother is also here, right? Bring him along too.'

'The first thing we need to do is to investigate the people close to Minekichi,' said the foreman.

The constable and the clerk disappeared into the darkness immediately. The supervisor walked over to the closed iron door and stood still right in front of it.

It appeared that sealing off the tunnel had been effective, and that the fire inside had almost died out now, as the glow from the iron door had almost gone. But if they were suddenly to open the door now, there was no doubt that the new supply of oxygen would give new life to the dying fire. The supervisor clicked his tongue and turned to the foreman.

'Call engineer Kikuchi from the Tachiyama Mine and get him here. And come to my office as well, once you're done with your rounds.'

The Tachiyama Mine was a sister mine of the same company, located on the other side of the mountain, at the centre of Murou Cape. The mines each had their own engineers, but engineer Kikuchi, who had been at the Tachiyama Mine for a few days now, was basically a chief-level engineer who worked on both mines. The foreman jumped on a passing coal trolley and disappeared into the darkness.

With the people gone, silence reclaimed its place. From beyond the darkness further down the level main tunnel, the supervisor thought he could hear the laughing of Minekichi's mother. From between the screeching of coal trolleys, he could also hear some clamour. The sub-foreman of the left-wing side passage had arrived with a straw mat and, following the orders of the supervisor, he placed it over the body of the engineer and left again. The workman stood in front of the cut-off ventilation pipe and began the task left by the murdered engineer. But he suddenly turned to the supervisor.

'Supervisor. It appears there's some dangerous smoke build-up here.'

'You know what you're talking about?' the supervisor smiled at the workman.

'I don't know about any difficult stuff, but you can tell from the smell. It seems like most of the fire is out now, but the smouldering has resulted in some bad smoke.'

The supervisor walked over to the iron pipe and immediately grimaced.

'Ugh, we'd better connect this pipe back to the main pipe of the side street and get all that smoke out of there. You're right, the smell tells us enough. Okay, you come here from time to time to check up on the smoke. I'll have to go question the miners now, but engineer Kikuchi should be here soon.'

The workman started connecting the pipes again. The supervisor left the workman to his work.

The four suspects were sitting inside the office in the main hall, watched by the constable and three sub-foremen.

O-Shina had changed into her night dress and her hair was dishevelled. She was hiding her face against the wainscoting, her shoulders heaving up and down. Her brother Iwatarō, his face and chest still muddy, was breathing heavily like a pair of bellows. He glanced at the supervisor when the latter entered the office.

Minekichi's father did not move his eyes, but stared blankly in front of him like a dead fish. The mother was held by a sub-foreman, as she could not remain still and would at times laugh out in a terrifying manner.

The supervisor stood in front of the four and silently took a look at all of the suspects in turn.

'So these are all of the people close to Minekichi.'

'Yes, the others have nothing to do with him,' answered one of the foremen.

The office held several rooms. The supervisor told the four foremen to bring the suspects one by one. The supervisor and the constable went in another room, and took their places in the chairs there.

Iwatarō was the first to be called.

The supervisor shot a glance at the constable, and leant towards Iwatarō. At first it appeared he would yell at him, but he bit his tongue and changed his approach, starting with a relatively friendly tone.

'Where did you take your sister just now?'

Silence.

'Where did you go?'

On the other side of the table, Iwatarō's lips remained sealed.

'Why ask him? This man and the woman were brought here from the shed....'

The constable was talking about the shed in the miner's village outside the mine. The supervisor did not react to the constable and said to Iwatarō:

'What I'm asking is whether you went straight to the shed.'

Iwatarō finally raised his head.

'Went straight to the shed,' he answered bluntly.

'You're sure?' There was tension in the supervisor's voice. Iwatarō nodded gently without saying anything else.

'All right.' The supervisor turned to the sub-foreman next to him. 'Take this man back to the other room. Then ask the guards precisely when this man left the mine with his sister.'

The sub-foreman quickly directed Iwatarō out.

O-Shina was next to be called. When she was seated, the constable said to the supervisor: 'We need to ask this woman about how the fire started.'

The supervisor nodded in silence and turned to the woman.

'Was it a safety lamp that caused the fire?'

Silence.

'The cause of the fire was a lamp, was it not?'

O-Shina nodded lifelessly.

'Which was it? Your safety lamp, or your husband's?'

'It was mine.'

'How did it cause the fire? Tell us exactly what happened.'

O-Shina hesitated about answering the question. But after a while, tears started to fall, and with her eyes cast down, she started to talk in a subdued voice. Her testimony was exactly the same as was recorded at the beginning of this tale.

When the woman had finished her confession, the supervisor repositioned himself on his seat and said:

'We will have to investigate to see if what you said about the fire in that tunnel is true. But I have another question. It appears you were taken by your brother to the shed, but is that true?'

The question, however, was quite futile. Pure despair had put O-Shina out of her mind at the time, and while she knew she had been carried out by Iwatarō, she herself could not remember whether they had gone straight to the shed or not. But in the eyes of the supervisor, both O-Shina and Iwatarō remained viable suspects, so he tried pressing the matter.

But at that moment the door of the office opened and the sub-foreman brought a guard into the office.

The guard studied both Iwatarō and O-Shina and turned to the supervisor.

'These two people? Yes, I am sure. They took the cage lift and left the mine between twenty-five and half past ten.'

'What! They were outside before half past ten?'

'Yes, I am sure of it. They were the only two miners to leave at that time, so I remember them well.'

'I see. And until they were brought here just now, they had not once returned to the mine?'

'No, they did not come back. The other guard will also confirm that.'

'Okay. That's enough.'

After the guard had left, the supervisor and the constable looked at each other.

The tunnel that was on fire had been sealed off at exactly half past ten. At that time, engineer Maruyama was still alive and well, so how could Iwatarō and O-Shina, who had left the mine before half past ten, have killed the engineer? With this, two of the four suspects were eliminated. Only two remained.

The supervisor had Iwatarō and O-Shina moved to the waiting room, and then called for Minekichi's father.

'The sub-foreman of the left-wing side passage took you away somewhere. Where did you go?'

Every time the old miner spoke—his eyes like that of a dead fish—large folds formed on his stomach.

'Please ask the sub-foreman,' he said.

The sub-foreman of the left-wing side passage was eating his lunch in the food hall, where he was called back per orders of the supervisor.

'You led this man away from the tunnel, didn't you? Where did you take him?'

'This old man?' The sub-foreman laughed as he answered the question. 'He couldn't stand on his own legs any more. So I brought him to the aid station. When I went to the aid station to pick up the straw mat we used right now, he had just started getting up again. The nurse had his hands full with the man.'

'I see,' the constable commented. 'But you don't know where he went after he was able to stand up again, or do you?'

The constable then turned to the supervisor. 'There's something fishy about this. I found the man, together with his mad wife, wandering around near the entrance of the side passage. What could he have been doing after he left the aid station?'

The supervisor had remained silent until then, but then said, surprisingly: 'I think you might be under some misunderstanding. It's true we don't know where he went in the period after he could stand again.'

The supervisor turned to the sub-foreman. 'But he couldn't even stand until you went to the aid station to get the straw mat to put over Maruyama's body, isn't that correct?'

'Yes.'

The supervisor turned back to the constable. 'Engineer Maruyama was murdered while this man was still unable to stand. He collapsed in front of the tunnel on fire, and was brought to the aid station. The engineer was killed after that, and the sub-foreman went to get a straw mat to cover the body with. It was only then that this old man managed to stand up again at the aid station. So at the time engineer Maruyama was killed, this man was still under the care of the nurse. If he couldn't stand up, he most certainly couldn't have gone out to the side passage and killed someone. Do you see? But now we know who the murderer is. Tie that crazy old woman up.'

The hired police constable jumped up and went to the room next door. Under the eyes of Iwatarō and O-Shina, he started tying up Minekichi's mother.

Then an unexpected interruption occurred which completely invalidated the supervisor's assumption.

But first it must be mentioned that the murdered engineer Maruyama had always been a very disciplined worker. Because of that, the miners feared him, and the managers respected him but tried to keep him at a distance. But he was not normally the kind of person who would become the target of such bitterness that somebody would want to kill him. The incident where he sealed up the miner Minekichi was the first time he had done anything to incite such feelings. After questioning all the people who would have a reason to hate Maruyama for sealing in Minekichi, the supervisor believed he had identified the culprit and so finally achieved his goal. But, from the time the questioning had begun until the moment the interruption occurred, not one of the suspects had been allowed to leave, whether they had been cleared of suspicion or not. Thus they were all still in the office when it happened.

The hired police constable was about to restrain the mother of Minekichi. Suddenly the sound of an agitated person could be heard approaching the office. The glass door burst open and foreman Asakawa rushed in. He took no notice of the happenings inside the room, but turned breathlessly to the supervisor.

'Workman Furui has been murdered.'

3

Even men who do rough and tough work, like sailors and miners, have a frightened and overly worried side deep within them, unimaginable to the average person. Just as sailors have all kinds of strange beliefs about the sea, and it's almost hilarious to see how they consider the sea a mystic place, miners too have their own curious stories to tell, such as how, if you whistle in a mine, the mountain gods will get angry and cause a cave-in. Or how the spirits of people who died inside a mine will linger at the spot and cause more calamities. Frequently, places inside a mine which had been tainted by blood would be sealed off by a *shimenawa* rope to purify the place[ii]. Even though there was no evidence as to whether such bizarre actions were effective or not, they had become widespread customs to calm the miners' lingering fears.

A *shimenawa* rope had been stretched across the side passage of the Takiguchi Mine. But even though it was supposed to purify the area in front of the iron door, fresh blood had been spilled there not once, but twice. Illuminated by the dim electric lights, the miners who worked on this side of the mine gave the fire door of the sealed-off tunnel, where two bodies were lying, a wide berth. Unlike earlier, an eerie silence now reigned there.

Next to engineer Maruyama's body, which was covered by a straw mat, lay the workman's body, bent double. It appeared he had been pushed to the ground while he was standing on tiptoe to check up on the smoke. The stand had been thrown over and next to it lay a bloody clump of coal, larger than the one used on the engineer. The clump had probably been thrown with a lot of force as the workman lay down with his face to the floor. A large wound had cracked the back of his head down to the neck, and there was almost nothing left of his left ear. The murder had happened between the time that the supervisor had left the workman alone in front of the tunnel to return to his office, and the time the foreman, after making a phone call to engineer Kikuchi at the Tachiyama Mine and had his lunch, had gone on his rounds. Just as in the attack on engineer Maruyama, the murderer had waited until no coal trolleys were passing and had approached the victim in the dark.

The supervisor, as pale as a sheet, looked around and chased the miners away in an irritated manner.

The workman had been killed with a weapon similar to the one used on the engineer. But the similarities didn't stop there. Both the workman and the engineer had something in common which might have been the reason for their murder. While it had been on the orders of engineer Maruyama and the foreman, the one who actually sealed up Minekichi behind the iron door by smearing clay on it, had been none other than workman Furui. The murderer of both men was obviously the same person, motivated by hatred for the death of Minekichi.

But then the supervisor hit upon an iron door of his own within the depths of his thoughts.

With the murder of the engineer, the supervisor had quickly caught on the truth and had immediately started to investigate all those who might wish to take revenge for Minekichi. However, workman Furui had been killed in the same manner as the engineer while the four suspects were still in the middle of being questioned. Furthermore, the four suspects were all being held in the office at the time the workman was murdered, and had not set foot outside. Did that mean the murderer was someone other than these four people? But it was unlikely that among the simple-minded miners here, anyone would do something as dramatic and crazy as going around killing the men of the company on behalf of total strangers.

The supervisor had thought he had the whole thing wrapped up, but now he'd hit upon this iron door of his own he felt completely clueless.

Finally a ray of light hit the supervisor in his search in the dark. But it was also an indescribable ray of light and it pushed the supervisor deeper into the terrifying pit of fear.

It was the custom at the Takiguchi Mine to perform the superficial examination of the dead, so typical of such places, at the aid station.

While electric light was available throughout the mine tunnels, those lights were covered by coal dust, and were only set to guide the movement of the coal trolleys inside the mine, so it was all rather cramped there. The examinations were therefore held elsewhere so as not to obstruct the movement of the trolleys and endanger the coal output of the mine.

When the supervisor got the message that the medical staff was standing by at the aid station, he ordered the two bodies to be moved there. A straw mat was placed in a coal trolley which had been brought over for the purpose, and the bodies were moved onto it.

Just as the supervisor, the foreman and the constable were about to jump on the next trolley, a young miner came running from the back of the side passage carrying his own safety lamp, as well as another safety lamp without a flame. When the miner spotted the supervisor he stopped in his tracks, stood up straight and said: 'Sir, I picked this safety lamp up at the drinking spot.'

'You found a safety lamp?'

The supervisor turned around with a scowl on his face.

Inside a mine, a safety lamp meant life and never left a miner's side. It was not just used to illuminate one's surroundings, but the movement of the flame inside also served as a vital tool to determine whether there was any inflammable gas around. But, as mentioned earlier, these lamps could also be very dangerous depending on how they were used, so at this mine, each lamp had its own unique number and they were checked carefully at the guard station at the entrance to the mine whenever a lamp was brought in. It was the fact that a lamp like that was just lying around that caused the sour expression on the supervisor's face.

'What's the number?'

'C-121.'

'C-121?'

The foreman cocked his head. The supervisor stepped out of the trolley and pointed with his chin to instruct the transporter behind the trolley.

'Go to the guard station now and ask which miner C-121 belongs to.'

'And at a time like this,' the foreman sighed, 'we can't have people around who are careless.'

He turned to the miner. 'Where did you find this?'

'Right beside the drinking spot. It was lying there, as if somebody had forgotten it.'

A drinking spot was simply a place where natural underground water was caught in a reservoir. The one in this side passage was located at the end of the tunnel. There was a little open space there, with some smaller caves and also a crude toilet. Whenever miners got thirsty, they'd go there to drink water.

'Someone leaving his lamp behind? Once I know who it is, he'll be suitably punished,' bellowed the foreman angrily. The supervisor looked around to see if the transporters standing there were all carrying their safety lamps. But of course nobody had forgotten their light in this world of darkness. Forgetting the light was impossible. It had probably not been forgotten, but left behind on purpose. If it had been left on purpose, it meant that the miner didn't need it, or that it was actually in his way, for some reason. As the supervisor thought about this, the female transporter he had sent away came running without a trolley, looking very pale.

'C-121 belongs to the deceased, Minekichi....'

'What?'

'Yes, this is Minekichi's safety lamp....'

A surprised expression appeared on the supervisor's face.

'But how... how could Minekichi's lamp...?'

Who could have expected Minekichi's lamp to appear now? There was no way to punish him now. But this wasn't about punishment. How could the safety lamp of Minekichi, who had been working inside his tunnel and had died inside, appear here now?

The supervisor scowled as he thought about these events. He lifted the safety lamp up and turned to foreman Asakawa, who was also visibly shocked. The supervisor said in a trembling voice: 'Anyway, let's go now. We need to think carefully about this. It's just not making any sense any more.'

4

Engineer Kikuchi from the Tachiyama Mine was not yet forty and still in the prime of his life. He had been a brilliant student when he graduated from Tōkyō University's Engineering Faculty, but despite that, he hated sitting still behind a desk in a dark room. It was said he went around chasing bears with a rifle in his free time. He had a suntanned face and a voice which could send all the plans on his desk flying whenever he laughed, shaking his broad shoulders.

By the time engineer Kikuchi had received the notification and arrived at the Takiguchi Mine, the hired police constable had left for the district's police station to get back-up. Meanwhile, the supervisor had forgotten all about the examination of the dead bodies and the smoke after the discovery of Minekichi's safety lamp. He had been cooped up in his office, racking his brains about the extraordinary events ocurring.

Once the supervisor saw engineer Kikuchi though, he brightened up again. He immediately started explaining the situation at the sealed-off tunnel, but as he related the details, he went into a digression, and the fire incident changed into a murder incident. Engineer Kikuchi too had come here expecting to deal with the aftermath of a fire, but as he listened to the supervisor's desperate story, he got more interested in the murders. The supervisor explained everything in detail, starting with the murder of engineer Maruyama and the four suspects, to the murder of the workman and the mysterious appearance of Minekichi's safety lamp. However, he did not address in so many words the great contradiction he was facing at that moment, nor the eerie suspicion that had risen from that contradiction, but simply laid the problem in front of the engineer.

'This sounds as interesting as hunting for bears.'

After the supervisor had finished with his story, Kikuchi grinned, even though it appeared he hadn't fully grasped the situation yet. He remained silent and appeared to be thinking hard about the difficult problem.

'I'm afraid even I can't answer your questions if you ask me so suddenly about such strange murders out of the blue,' the engineer began. 'But, supervisor, you're being a bit unfair. Why don't you say clearly what's on your mind right now? What's the problem you're facing? Of course I know what it is. I also understand how utterly childish, stupid, no, how utterly illogical the whole thing is. I see why you don't dare name it. But you don't even have the courage to laugh at this ridiculous situation. Please don't get angry. Let me show you one way to help clear away your worries. It's very simple. Just open up the sealed mining tunnel. Yes. I don't know how hot it was in that tunnel during the fire, but there's no way the fire would've been so hot as to incinerate the bones of a human being completely.'

'You're right,' said the supervisor. 'It didn't take long to get the fire under control. But there's smoke there.'

'But you had the tunnel vented, didn't you? The smoke won't stay inside forever. And we can put on some masks. Oh, but before we do that, supervisor....' The engineer seemed to have had a new idea. His eyes sparkled and he looked about him.

'Where is Mr. Asakawa?'

'Asakawa?' The supervisor turned around. The office clerk standing next to him responded: 'He went out because he had a phone call from the main office in Sapporo.'

There had only been a short wait before foreman Asakawa returned. After a simple greeting, engineer Kikuchi quickly started talking again.

'Mr. Asakawa, this might sound strange, but I believe there were at least three men involved in sealing up that miner in the tunnel. And you were one of them, correct?'

The foreman turned pale. The engineer shot him a brief glance and quietly continued:

'These murders might not be over yet. I fear you may be next.' Here the engineer raised his head again and started speaking faster.

'But you don't have to worry. Listen, Mr. Maruyama and Mr. Furui were both killed using lumps of coal. That means the murderer is not in possession of a murder weapon. But you, you can carry a weapon with you. So if we're lucky, we can catch the murderer. Exactly. No, this is not just a possibility. As you are being targeted by the murderer, you are in the best position to catch the murderer. He might hide from us, but he will definitely appear in front of you.'

'I see,' said the supervisor. 'What a clever idea, as you might expect from a bear hunter.'

But engineer Kikuchi continued in a serious tone: 'I have a plan I wish to propose to the two of you. We'll have Mr. Asakawa here carry a weapon, and have him go alone to the murder scene. We of course, will be right behind you. I don't think we need to worry, if you're carrying a gun on you. How about it? I think this is the quickest way to catch the murderer.'

The supervisor agreed to it immediately.

The foreman thought for a while and then stood up. He produced a dagger from somewhere which he had bought during the heydays of strikes. He tapped the floor with the tip of the sheath.

'The rear is yours,' he said as he boldly stepped forward.

The supervisor and engineer Kikuchi waited for a while and then followed the foreman. After they had passed the main mine street and stood at the entrance of the side passage which led to the sealed-off tunnel, the engineer stopped and said to the supervisor:

'How much is the production of coal held up if you forbid everybody to enter or leave this side passage for one hour?'

'What, you want to seal off this part of the mine?' The supervisor's eyes opened wide.

'Yes.'

'Don't make jokes about that. I can't stop production....'

'But what if the murderer slips by us and escapes through here?' the engineer insisted. 'How about it? This part of the mine is probably good for about thirty tons, I reckon? You'd only be losing out on that amount. Please stop the work. It's an emergency.'

'It appears you're more interested in hunting after prey than profit.'

The supervisor gave a wry smile. The engineer immediately stepped over to the large fire door at the entrance to the side street and explained the situation to the miners and the sub-foreman who had been watching them in suspense. He had the sub-foreman close the fire door from the outside and bolt it after he and the supervisor had entered the side passage. A row of trolleys coming from the left wing of the mine quickly ran into the obstruction, and, given that the sealing-up of Minekichi had just happened not long ago, everybody was on edge and started to cry out. But once everybody saw that the supervisor and engineer were inside too, they quickly realised they had not been sealed up because of some crisis, but there had been some reason to close the fire door, and the commotion slowly died down.

The supervisor and engineer Kikuchi proceeded into the depths of the side passage as they explained the situation to the transporters they met on the way, but they had to face an unexpected situation when they arrived at the entrance of the tunnel where Minekichi had been sealed up.

The decoy—foreman Asakawa—was stronger than the average man, had been carrying a weapon with him and had been on his guard. Also, the murderer did not have a weapon and had to have been hiding. Which meant there should have been no danger, but despite that, by the time the supervisor and engineer arrived at their destination, the foreman was already lying dead on the ground.

He was lying face up, his arms and legs spread out and with a flat lump of coal, bigger than the previous ones and reminiscent of a stepping stone, covering most of his upper body. It didn't appear as if the lump of coal had been brought here from elsewhere. It seemed to have been cut from the irregular surface of a nearby wall, leaving a spot that resembled a cave-in. Smaller bits of coal were lying around the body on the floor. Foreman Asakawa had first been sent sprawling on the floor, and then the cruel murderer had struck him with a weapon torn from the wall, dropping it on top of the foreman's body.

The supervisor didn't say a word as he picked up the foreman's dagger. Together with the engineer, they moved the clump of coal from the body. The head and chest of the body had been smashed to pieces, and it was such a hideous sight they could not bear looking at it.

Because they had been just a fraction too late, their precious decoy had been taken from them, without them even catching a glimpse of the murderer. While this had been an unexpected turn of events by any standard, they could not have guessed their mistake would turn out to be so fatal. A furious feeling of guilt descended upon the two, but their minds were also relieved by what this incident also clearly indicated. Revenge had now been completed. But who was the man who could accomplish a task like this without even a weapon? Was it one of the miners in the side passage, or perhaps...? The supervisor stole a glance at the iron door of the sealed-off tunnel. He approached it and placed his hand on it. The door had cooled off completely. Engineer Kikuchi checked the ventilation pipe. The smoke level had reduced considerably and no longer posed any danger. The two clicked their tongues, and together, they started scraping away the dry clay from between the gaps around the door.

After a while they had removed all the clay. The engineer lifted the bar and pulled the door open with all his strength. An unreal, warm breeze came blowing out from the darkness. The two held their dim safety lights in front of them and took their first steps in the now open tunnel which had been on fire. Once they were inside, they pointed their safety lamps to the floor and started searching for the remains of Minekichi. But eventually an indescribable fear caught hold of them.

Minekichi's bones weren't there!

No matter how much they searched, they couldn't find them. The walls of both sides of this tunnel had been burned, leaving an irregular surface reminiscent of old cotton smeared with ink. The pit props, which supported the tunnel like a *tori'i* archway, had been heavily burned. The liquid that dripped here and there from the walls like coal tar was the source of a horrible smell. But no matter how much they proceeded inside the tunnel, they couldn't find the remains of Minekichi, not even one little bone. The two kept searching the tunnel, as if they were possessed. The rails on the ground would sometimes make turns and go up and down, and ended in a distortion. There was a burnt pickaxe and a coal trolley that had been turned over. Here, where the air was still eerily warm, was where the centre of the fire had been. But at this spot, at the end of the mining tunnel, they still could not find any signs of Minekichi. They remained frozen on the spot when they finally realised the impossibility of the situation.

This was the worst possible scenario. As mentioned earlier, a mining tunnel is basically like a well opened into a coal bed, so with the iron fire door closed, not even an ant could make an escape. Therefore, the body of Minekichi should have been sealed off inside this tunnel and been burned. Even if they couldn't find his body, it was impossible that even his bones would have disappeared. Yet that is what had happened. The supervisor realised that his suspicion had turned out to be the horrible truth and his whole body froze at the thought.

It happened at that moment.

Suddenly, without any warning, the walls above them, faraway, close by, all around them, started shaking, breaking the silence around them.

...Boom....

...Boom....

They heard an ominous noise.

The two held their breath and listened carefully. But before the noise became louder, it stopped and silence was upon them once again.

But people who have spent a long time in mines knew exactly what that noise meant.

That was the terrifying sound you would hear whenever the support pillars are removed after a coal mine has been exhausted. Once the support pillars are gone, the unstable walls collapse on each other and the pressure would bring the ceilings of the tunnels down. The earth settling down like that happened slowly, but once the pit props broke and cracks appeared in the ceiling, that's when the spine-chilling rumbling would be heard. The sound was a sign of imminent cave-in, and in their fear, miners had dubbed the sound the cry of the mountain.

And the sound they had heard now was exactly that cry. The pit props had been burnt by the fire in the tunnel, and because of the fire the pressure inside the tunnel had increased. This had caused weaknesses in the walls of the tunnel, and little by little, the ceiling was preparing for a cave-in.

The supervisor turned pale and pointed his safety lamp at the ceiling. An even worse truth had been awaiting him.

Large, dark fissures as big as crocodiles had appeared on the ceiling, which was slowly coming down towards their heads. Inside those fissures were smaller, burnt cracks from which water drops came falling one after another. They had hit water. The moment the supervisor saw the water, he put his hand out, caught a drop in his hand and gingerly brought it to his mouth. He jumped back aghast.

Ceilings coming down, cave-ins, fires and hitting ground water are, in a way, all part of mining work. Just as at mines everywhere, the Takiguchi Mine was always prepared, lest something like that should happen. But there was one thing they feared even more than any of those things, and that one drop resting on the supervisor's tongue meant that the fate of the whole Takiguchi Mine had now been sealed. They had no way of stopping that water anymore. For it was not ground water, nor was it condensation.

It was seawater.

'Oh My God!' The supervisor's voice trembled as he tasted the first arrival of the sea in the mine. 'This is no time to be concerned about a murder. We've hit the sea!'

But despite the crisis, engineer Kikuchi had been acting in a strange way. He appeared to be lost in thought, and remained frozen to the spot, as if he was sleeping while standing. He was still calm, his audaciously brilliant mind busy with something.

'There's no way we can fight the sea,' the engineer said finally, in a calm voice. 'Supervisor, we have to give up here. We still have time, so we need to prepare the evacuation calmly. By the way, you just said this was not the time to be concerned about a murder. You might be right, but this seawater and the murder are not unrelated. Look carefully at those big burnt cracks inside the fissures. I think I'm starting to see the truth behind this case.'

5

A few minutes later, a sense of alarm began to spread within the dark underground city, with the sealed-off side passage at its centre.

After the supervisor had closed the heavy iron doors of the mining spot on the verge of collapsing, he ran to the telephone room and informed the Tachiyama Mine field office and the head office in Sapporo that the sea had compromised the mine. He then prepared a controlled evacuation plan to ensure they wouldn't have miners crush each other to death in front of the narrow entrance of the mine shafts.

Meanwhile engineer Kikuchi showed off the daredevil courage he had built up during all of his bear hunting. After he had exited the iron door of the side passage in question, he closed it off again and called for the sub-foremen of the main street. Together they worked on how to watch the entrance closely. The cruel murderer was still hiding somewhere inside this part of the mine. They couldn't allow any miner to exit the side passage until they had caught their man. After he had prepared his tight surveillance team, Kikuchi headed for the office inside the main hall.

The miners from the tunnels closest by had already gathered in the main hall, questioning and complaining about the sudden order to stop work. The supervisor was giving instructions to several sub-foremen when he spotted Kikuchi and went over to him.

'Now we have to deal with that left-side passage. Let's go.'

'Please wait,' urged Kikuchi. 'There are a couple of things I'd like to investigate first.'

'What?' The supervisor seemed both surprised and annoyed. 'Do you have any idea of what you're saying at a time like this? We have the murderer captured inside that part of the mine. We need to find him and then get the miners out of there.'

But Kikuchi did not budge. Eventually the supervisor said he'd go to the side passage alone first, but that he would not let any of the miners leave until Kikuchi had come back.

After the supervisor had disappeared into the darkness of the main street, engineer Kikuchi quickly slipped into the office, where O-Shina was still being held. She calmly gave him the same explanation she'd given the supervisor about how the fire had first started. Once she'd finished her story, Kikuchi pressed her on a couple of matters.

'This is important, so please answer carefully. You'd barely escaped the tunnel that was on fire when the foreman, the engineer and the workman closed the iron fire door. You're sure that, at that moment, Minekichi wasn't there?'

'Yes. I'm absolutely sure.' O-Shina answered with conviction, as she looked straight at him through swollen eyelids.

Kikuchi closed his eyes for a second, as if he was sorting his thoughts out in his mind. Then he walked over to the telephone room, returning after ten minutes. It was probably a long-distance phone call. There was a look of determination on his face as he took O-Shina with him to the main street.

The supervisor looked pale and was holding a dagger in his hands as he stood in front of the sealed-off side passage, together with a couple of the sub-foremen. As soon as he saw Kikuchi, he approached and announced: 'Kikuchi, we have a problem.'

'What's wrong?'

'It's just unbelievable. The murderer wasn't inside the side passage. We searched everywhere, the tunnels, all of the mining spots, the open spaces, the smaller caves, but he isn't here.'

Kikuchi's calm response took him by surprise.

'But who were you looking for in that part of the mine?'

'What? Who I was looking for? The murderer of course,' replied the supervisor.

'That's what I was asking. You keep saying murderer this, murderer that, but who are you talking about?'

'What?' The supervisor became even more confused. 'The miner Minekichi of course.'

'Minekichi?' repeated Kikuchi. He said nothing, but a complex expression appeared on his face. After a short pause he began again calmly.

'You see, when I entered this side passage with you, I had no idea as to the identity of the murderer. Obviously, he had to be sealed inside this part of the mine, but with only an abstract concept of the murderer in my mind, I had no idea who I'd be looking for and who I needed to catch. But now I believe I know the truth.

'And I believe you are gravely mistaken about this whole case. You have been too entranced by the superficial facts, and by an ostensibly plausible theory that combines all those facts. But you have ignored logic. One miner is sealed up, and the men who were responsible for that are murdered one after another. The murderer, however, is not among the suspects: the family of said miner. And then the miner's safety lamp is discovered outside the sealed-off tunnel, even though the miner is supposed to have died inside. Then it turns out that there aren't any remains of the miner inside the tunnel after all. Combining those facts, you concocted a theory that the miner had somehow escaped the tunnel alive and had started exacting revenge on those who had sealed him inside. But there's no logic to your theory: it can't explain the impossible contradiction of a person escaping a tunnel from which there is no possible means of escape.'

'What do you suggest then?' The supervisor frowned. The engineer continued his explanation.

'I started to get a new idea in my head when we didn't find the miner's remains inside the tunnel. Not even his bones were inside, so Minekichi had definitely left the tunnel. Now, the fire had died soon after the iron door had been sealed, meaning you had deprived it of oxygen, which in turn meant that there was no other way to leave the tunnel except through the door. Therefore Minekichi could *only* have exited the tunnel that way. The door, however, had been shut and bolted with a bar from outside, and sealed off by covering it up with clay. The clay had dried, and there were no signs of the door having been opened. So that means that after the door was shut, it couldn't have been opened until we unsealed it just now. Doesn't that tell you that Minekichi had already left the tunnel before the fire door was shut? With that thought in mind, let's review the other facts. This poor O-Shina woman had heard the footsteps of a man walking behind her as she fled the tunnel which was on fire. When she finally got out and turned back to look, she saw foreman Asakawa busy closing the iron fire door, having apparently come running there at the sound of the explosion. After the door was closed, the engineer arrived, followed by the workman, and they started sealing it off completely. This is the crux of the problem. Listen carefully. Minekichi must have exited the tunnel before the fire door was closed. That would appear to mean that he must have exited the door after the woman had got out of the tunnel, but before foreman Asakawa started closing the door. In that case Minekichi should have been in the empty space between the woman and the foreman closing the door....'

'Wait, wait. I think I get what you're saying, and then I don't think I get what you're saying.' The supervisor interrupted as he scowled at Kikuchi. The engineer, however, was not bothered and continued.

'It's not surprising that you don't understand it. I only started to understand it myself after thinking it all through thoroughly. It was a really odd incident that had occurred there. It was as if Fate was playing a trick.'

The engineer then turned to O-Shina, who was standing beside him.

'There's something I have to ask you. You said you'd emptied your trolley and returned, and after you'd gone inside the side passage to your own mining spot, you'd jumped into the arms of Minekichi, who'd been waiting for you in the dark. Are you sure the man was Minekichi?'

O-Shina gasped and opened her eyes wide at Kikuchi's unexpected query.

'…Yes….'

'Then I've another question for you. Did Minekichi have his safety lamp with him at that moment?'

'No, he didn't have it with him.'

'And where was your lamp?'

'Hanging from the rear of the coal trolley.'

'That means the light from your lamp was blocked by the trolley and couldn't illuminate anything in front of the trolley, and only the ground at rear of the trolley. You said you'd pushed the trolley forward and jumped in Minekichi's arms, but that means the light of the safety lamp could not have illuminated Minekichi's face when he was standing in front of the trolley, and after the trolley had gone past Minekichi and the light of the safety lamp could finally shine on him, the light would've been coming from behind Minekichi's body. How then can you be sure that you saw Minekichi?'

Silence.

O-Shina didn't appear to understand the problem, and looked down at her feet. But you could clearly read her uneasiness from her face. Kikuchi turned back to the supervisor.

'I think you already understand what my conclusion—no, the only possible conclusion—is: Minekichi was not even inside the tunnel at the time the fire first broke out.'

'Hold on,' said the supervisor. 'You mean that the man this woman embraced in the dark was not Minekichi?'

'Precisely. Minekichi was not seen outside the tunnel at the time, nor was he inside, so that's the only conclusion we can come to.'

'Then who was he?'

'The man who left the tunnel after O-Shina and was standing in front of the fire door when she turned round.'

The supervisor couldn't utter a word because of the shock. But it didn't take long for him to continue his questions.

'If what you say is true, then the whole case has turned into an unbelievable mess. For example, where was Minekichi if he wasn't inside the tunnel when the fire broke out?'

'That's the next problem,' sighed the engineer. 'Let's look at another fact with our new set of eyes. Remember the safety lamp left at the drinking spot? You interpreted that fact as proof that Minekichi had escaped from the sealed-up tunnel and that he had left it there because it would get in the way during the murders. But to me, it simply tells us where Minekichi was when the fire broke out. He had left his tunnel for the drinking spot.'

'I see. So you say he wasn't involved with the fire. And he had nothing to do with sealing up the tunnel. But if he hadn't been sealed up there, why would he go taking his revenge and killing all the people who sealed the tunnel up?'

'It appears you're still the prisoner of a mistaken preconception.'

A wry smile appeared on Kikuchi's face, and he started walking around. He had clasped his hands together and looked slightly annoyed as he talked.

'I'm sure I haven't addressed the question of the murderer's identity until now. Let's take a look at another fact first. One that has to do with the murders. Consider this: the three murders were committed separately, but there are some interesting points that connect them. First there is the murder weapon. All three of them were hit by a lump of coal. That might seem a meaningless fact, but it certainly is not. Supervisor, do you know what statistics say is the murder weapon most often used in assault and murder incidents among miners? The answer is hammers and pickaxes. Are there any weapons closer by or more effective to any miner? Like a safety lamp, any miner will always have one of these crucial tools of the trade with them. But strangely enough, the murderer in our case has only used lumps of coal to kill his victims, suggesting the murders were committed by someone who only had easy access to lumps of coal at the time of the murder: these were murders committed on a whim by someone who was not a miner. You are under the impression that the victims were all murdered in the same way because someone was taking revenge for sealing a man up. However, we now know that no man was sealed up in that tunnel, so your theory has proven to be wrong. The three men were hated by Minekichi's family, but since we know the murderer cannot be one of his family, that matter is of no consequence. So was there no other common motive for the murder of those three men? Well, yes there was! I noticed it just a while ago: all the victims were murdered while they were checking whether the fire had died out and how the smoke was inside that tunnel, in the hopes of opening it up again as soon as possible. So if we look at the murders from a different angle, we can say their work was being obstructed. Someone was interfering with your order to re-open the tunnel again and investigate how the fire started. To put it another way, the murderer was trying to prevent you from seeing the inside of the tunnel until a certain moment. That's why they tried to delay opening the tunnel for as long as possible.'

'Wait,' the supervisor interrupted again. 'Why was the murderer so desperate I wouldn't see the tunnel? The two of us searched it together, but there was nothing there that had anything to do with the murders.'

'But there was. Supervisor, think carefully. Didn't we discover something very serious there? I don't mean the fact that Minekichi wasn't there, even though we thought he had been sealed up inside. We made an even more important discovery: the fissures in the ceiling and the seawater!'

Those words set off a grim commotion among the miners around them. The mine had been compromised by seawater! To these miners, this revelation was many times more shocking than any murder. The gleam in Kikuchi's eye intensified, and he said to the supervisor as he pushed the people around him away:

'Open up the side passage now. Let's get everyone out together with their coal trolleys.'

Moments later, several sub-foremen pulled the heavy iron doors wide open with trembling hands. From inside the side passage, the cries of the miners could be heard. The tanned, naked female transporters—their bodies shining because of their perspiration—started pushing the coal trolleys out, but Kikuchi stepped forward and yelled at them: 'Dump all of your coal out of your trolleys! Leave without the coal!'

The women all looked at each other at Kikuchi's odd order. When they saw the supervisor standing beside him and nodding in silence, they started acting on the engineer's curious instructions.

The coal trolleys of the Takiguchi Mine were all dump cars, which allowed them to tip over the containers once the catch was released.

The transporters followed Kikuchi's orders and came out of the side passage one by one, turning their containers around and emptying their coal outside. Before their eyes, a small mountain of coal was created.

But when the twelfth trolley emptied its contents, it brought out something unexpected.

From among the coal that came rolling out of the large container appeared the naked body of a man, painted black by the coal. The man stood up and looked warily around him.

The supervisor exclaimed. 'It—it's foreman Asakawa!'

That was indeed foreman Asakawa, who was supposed to have been crushed by a lump of coal. The man tried to attack them, but Kikuchi snatched the dagger from the supervisor and hit Asakawa hard with the back of the blade.

After putting the foreman down, Kikuchi took the surprised supervisor and O-Shina with him as they side-stepped the trolley and headed inside the now-open entrance to the side passage, leaving the other miners, who were still in a commotion, behind. Once they arrived at the tunnel where the fire had been, Kikuchi pointed to "Asakawa's body" with his chin and told O-Shina: 'Take a good look. He's wearing the foreman's clothes, but it should be the body of someone you know.'

At first, the frightened woman stood still in front of the body, but then she hesitantly leant forward and looked intently at the face which had been crushed almost beyond recognition. She crouched down and cried out in a hoarse voice as she embraced the body: 'This is my husband, Minekichi.'

6

Meanwhile, the revelation made earlier by Kikuchi had caused great shock. The news that seawater had entered the mine had quickly spread among the miners still below ground. Everyone left their trolleys, threw away their pickaxes and ran to the entrance to the mine shaft in waves. The telephone in the main office kept ringing and the rescue teams which had been sent from the field office which controlled both the Takigawa and Tachiyama Mines started getting into fights with the miners who wanted to get out.

The supervisor had jumped on a coal trolley and was hurrying to the mine entrance, but he still had questions for Kikuchi.

'So it was foreman Asakawa who killed engineer Maruyama, the workman and finally Minekichi?'

Kikuchi nodded in silence.

'But if Minekichi was killed last, where had he been all that time?'

'Minekichi was killed first.'

'First?'

'Yes. He was probably killed at the drinking spot. The foreman then hid Minekichi's body in one of the caves nearby and headed for the mining spot to start the fire.'

'What? He set the fire?' The supervisor asked, surprised.

'Yes. You're gravely mistaken if you think it was just an accident. He put Minekichi's pickaxe on the rails on purpose. He embraced the woman in the dark and, by exploiting the couple's love and her safety lamp, set fire to the coal dust. It put him in a very dangerous situation, but by so doing, he himself, as the foreman, would not be blamed for the fire even if there were an investigation from above.'

'But why did he want to set fire to that mining spot?'

'That's exactly the question you should ask.' Kikuchi spoke louder as he continued. 'As I mentioned before, there was something in that tunnel that he absolutely did not want people to see until a specific moment in time. That's why he set a fire, so people couldn't enter the tunnel. And that's also why he got rid of engineer Maruyama and the workman, who were working on opening the door again and checking on the smoke inside. Now, you may well ask, why did he allow the two of us to enter the tunnel when we did? That was because, by then the critical moment had already passed. Also, by that time everyone had already fallen for the foreman's trap, but then I arrived and suggested that if these murders were committed out of revenge, that it would be the foreman's turn next. Thus pushed into a corner, Asakawa pulled out Minekichi's body from the cave where he had hidden it and made it appear as if he himself had been killed. He hid himself inside a coal trolley to avoid being caught, hoping to escape from the mine, which had outlived its usefulness.'

'Hold on,' the supervisor interrupted. 'You just said that the foreman did not want others to discover the fissures in the ceiling and the seawater which had infiltrated the mine. But that has nothing to do with the murders. Also, at the time the fire was set in that tunnel, there was nothing wrong with the ceiling yet, isn't that so?'

'You can't be serious! The seawater entering the mine and the murders are inextricably connected. And while the fissures in the ceiling were made worse by the fire, they were already there before it started. The crust there was probably weaker than we'd thought. Didn't you notice it? Think back. The fissures were all burnt on the inside. That means the crust didn't crack because of the fire: it had already cracked before the fire started. And there you have it. The foreman knew before anyone else about the fissures and the seawater dripping inside the mine.'

'I see. But if he knew about that so early already, why did he try to hide it from us? And what is that critical moment you said he was waiting for?'

'That's the entire motive behind all that's happened. The foreman was the first to discover that seawater had entered the mine and reported this to a certain party. He was probably offered a very handsome reward if he could prevent the horrible truth from coming out until a certain moment. And that certain moment was, well, you yourself already know. When I arrived in the mine, there was a phone call from Sapporo for the foreman, remember? He was waiting for exactly that. To confirm my own suspicions, I made a telephone call to the stock exchange in Otaru. Do you know what I found out? The stocks of Chūetsu Mining have been quite active since eleven o'clock this morning. Since eleven o'clock. An executive in the company already knew of the fate of the Takiguchi Mine hours before even we, the people on the scene, knew.'

Less than ten minutes later, an unearthly rumbling made all the people who were running around at the entrance to the mine freeze to the spot. A rumbling roar went through the whole Takiguchi Mine. Soon after, muddy water came flowing out from the mine drains, covering the four overheating multistage turbine engines. And the water level rose and rose....

First published in *Kaizō*, May Issue, Shōwa 12 (1937).

---

[i] It was possible for local governments, private organisations and persons to hire police constables in Japan between 1881 and 1938. They were for example hired by mining companies to ensure safety among the miners or by the wealthy for protection.

[ii] In folklore, a *shimenawa* rope is used to seal off consecrated areas, and as a talisman to ward off evil.

THE HUNGRY LETTER-BOX

Toki's Great Mistake

'I-I'm terribly sorry. My hand… just slipped like that....'

A flustered Toki adjusted his grip on the razor as he bowed his head towards the mirror, where the furious face of a customer with a crookedly shaven moustache was reflected.

Toki's apprentice Minkō grinned to himself as he washed the face of his own customer.

'Man, the boss has really been distracted lately. It's his third mistake in a row. The first one was yesterday, when he mistook the scissors for the clipper. And this morning, he applied pomade to a customer's face instead of shaving cream. And tonight, he's just ruined that man's moustache. I'm getting really worried about him….'

Minkō was still chuckling as he went over in his mind what had happened lately, but then he frowned.

Toki, young master of the barber's shop Cotton Rose, was still single. After finishing his five-year apprenticeship last autumn, he had opened his own shop there on Benten Street. Since then, several people had suggested he get married. Toki was by nature a very introverted man, however, and even a simple mention of the topic was enough to make him withdraw into his shell, to the point that he was risking the opportunity to find a partner. But, of late, longings had begun to stir within him.

The object of his affections was O-Sumi, his female counterpart over at Tachibana Hairdressing. She had wide, bright eyes and an alluring mouth. Toki had fallen in love with her just two months earlier, on a two-day group tour to Narita-San Temple organised by the Tōkyō Metropolis Barber's Union.

She was the reason why Toki's actions had been erratic of late. Being such reserved person, two months had already passed without him expressing his feelings to her, although he'd been agonizing about it all that time. Finally, two or three days ago, he'd made up his mind and started to write a letter.

It was by no means a long letter, but it had taken him so long because it was the first time in his life he'd written anything of the kind. That being so, it wasn't surprising that Toki would occasionally slip up during his work, as his mind was preoccupied.

He'd stayed up almost the entire night before and had finally completed the letter. He'd kept it in the pocket of his barber's uniform throughout the day as he anxiously weighed his options, and it was all that worrying which had eventually led to his latest mistake that evening.

But that was not what was uppermost in Toki's mind. There came a point when there were no customers in the shop, and he decided to seize the opportunity to send his letter to O-Sumi.

'Minkō, I've got to go out for a second. Watch the shop.'

Yelling those words to his apprentice, Toki rushed out into the street.

At the end of Benten Street was a major thoroughfare with a tram line down the middle. To the east the pavement was packed with the night stalls of street vendors with their backs to the tram line. The street was always bustling with pedestrians passing by.

At the end of the line of night stalls, adjacent to the stall of a second-hand book dealer, stood a letter-box, partially hidden in the shadow of a tree in the adjacent side street. Toki had been lost in thought until he arrived in front of it. With a pounding heart, he inserted his letter and quickly pulled his hand back, as if his fingers had been burnt.

When he thought the letter must have hit the bottom, Toki blushed and, in a strangely agitated manner, hurried back to Benten Street. As he was passing a tobacconist's shop, however, he stopped suddenly in his tracks and cried out.

He'd forgotten to put a stamp on his precious letter.

Toki's Shock

What a stupid mistake.

Toki hadn't reacted strongly when he'd accidently cut part of the customer's moustache off, but now he turned pale at the realisation of what had just happened.

He'd really done something unbelievably stupid. The letter would be delivered to O-Sumi, and she'd have to pay double the amount of the unpaid postage: ten *sen*! He'd been nervous, no doubt about it, but how could he have forgotten to put a stamp on the first letter he'd ever written to a girl?

'Well, there's no sense in moping about it.'

He started back towards the letter-box when a thought suddenly struck him. It would be locked up tightly, of course!

The only thing he could do was to wait for the postman to arrive, explain what had happened and have him put a stamp on the letter. He didn't know when the man would come, but he'd just have to wait around until then!

Having made his grand resolution, Toki started to pace conspicuously up and down near the letter-box, like a sentry in the Chinese army.

The book dealer, whose stall was barely two *shaku* from the letter-box, and who didn't seem to have many customers, kept staring at Toki's suspicious behaviour. But the postman still hadn't appeared.

It seemed as though the only people who used the letter-box were the waitresses working on Benten Street and the young men living in the boarding house for the recently built military factory. A thought struck Toki.

'Of course, instead of waiting here I should ask someone what time the post is collected.'

He ran to the nearest public telephone.

'Hello, is that the post office? I'd like to know the next collection time for the letter-box at the entrance to Benten Street, please.'

'Please hold.' For a while there was silence on the other end of the line, but then the voice returned. 'Hello. The mail won't be collected again until tomorrow morning, at eight.'

'Tomorrow at eight? The letter-box won't be opened before then?'

'Absolutely not!'

Toki stepped back out onto the pavement.

Even though he could hardly contain his impatience, he really had no choice but wait until eight o'clock the following morning. Crestfallen, he turned to Benten Street.

The next day, Toki arrived in front of the letter-box at half past seven.

He waited until the clocks in the nearby shops struck eight, and sure enough that was the exact moment he saw the postman arriving on his red bicycle. The Japanese post office is very precise with time.

'Excuse me, I wonder if you could be of assistance?'

'What kind of assistance?'

'Last night, I posted a letter here....'

'Yes?'

'And I forgot to put a stamp on it....'

'Oh, so you want me to put a stamp on it now? To whom is it addressed?'

'Eh? To whom? Errr, she's, I mean, her name is Sumiko Koiso. Hahaha.'

'Sumiko Koiso....'

The postman smiled humourlessly, opened the letter-box and withdrew a bundle of envelopes. He quickly scanned the names of the addressees, then turned back to Toki with a suspicious expression.

'There's no such letter here.'

'Eh? Wha-what did you say?'

'There is no letter addressed to Sumiko Koiso here.'

'Tha-that's not possible! I definitely posted it here last night at eight o'clock, addressed to Sumiko Koiso of Tachibana Hairdressing of XXX Ward, XXX-Chō. Please check again. Could it have got stuck somewhere inside the letter-box? It was a square, brown envelope.'

The postman looked visibly displeased, but checked the bundle of letters again carefully, this time in front of Toki.

'Look for yourself. There's no such letter here.'

And indeed, there were only a few letters in the bundle, and the important letter Toki had posted last night was not among them!

He crouched down and peered inside the letter-box through the square opening. But there was nothing there!

Toki was absolutely dumbfounded.

Toki's Prolonged Battle

The more he thought about it, the more mysterious the incident seemed. That Toki had posted his important letter to Sumiko in that very same letter-box was an undeniable fact. However, that the letter he had posted had seemingly disappeared before it had been collected was also an undeniable fact. That meant that Toki's important letter had disappeared while it was still inside the letter-box. Almost as if the box had become jealous of Toki and eaten his letter....

A hungry letter-box. That's the sort of thing you'd expect to see in a detective story.

Toki put on a *hachimaki* headband and concentrated furiously on the problem. But he was unable to solve the mystery.

He thought hard about it until the evening, and then decided that he would write a replacement letter, so he'd at least accomplish his original goal. This time, he would hang around the letter-box until the postman came, no matter how long it took.

Toki decided to execute his plan immediately. After he'd finished supper at around eight, he left the shop in Minkō's care.

This time, he didn't forget to buy a stamp at the tobacconist's shop. He returned to the same place as the night before and posted his letter in all innocence. As it would look strange if he stayed standing next to the letter-box all the time, he decided to walk around the area, still keeping his eyes fixed on the letter-box.

He was prepared for a prolonged vigil.

As always, the street was lively with night stalls. The unsuccessful book dealer who had put up his stall right next door mistook Toki for a customer, as he kept walking up and down in front. In the beginning the dealer had called out to Toki two or three times, but when each time Toki would appear to be surprised and pay no attention, now the dealer just shot him the occasional distrustful glance.

Toki, too, would cast sidelong glances at the letter-box from time to time as he walked up and down.

But nobody suspicious passed by. The only people who came were the waitresses working on Benten Street. At one point an attractive waitress at one of the cafés finished saying goodbye to a group of people working with the military and discreetly posted a pink envelope.

Ding…Dong…Ding…Dong…

A nearby clock struck ten.

Toki had not noticed until that moment that the number of people on the street had dwindled. Loudly, the nearby shops started to close up. The book dealer kept glaring at him.

'I must be getting on his nerves. I'm probably standing outside his stall too much.'

Toki decided to change his strategy and headed for the dimly-lit entrance of Benten Street, where he started walking up and down.

The street was almost empty. By that time it was easy to count the number of pedestrians easily, and the night stall vendors started to pack up there too.

But not the book dealer adjacent to the letter-box, strangely enough. He started to glare even more intensely at Toki.

Toki didn't like being scrutinised, so he tried not to look in the man's direction. As it happened, he'd been feeling something in his bowels for some time, so it was a convenient moment to go into a dark alley and answer the call of nature.

While he was busy breaking the law, Toki turned back to take a look at the letter-box, and what he saw took his breath away.

Toki's Great Adventure

Once all the onlookers had departed, the book dealer suddenly began to dismantle his stall. He swiftly packed all his books together and, in a trice, the stall became a cart for carrying the books.

Having cleared away his wares, the man removed the tent sheet from the bamboo poles and folded it up two or three times, like a mosquito net, and placed it nonchalantly over the letter-box Toki had been watching. The sheet covered the box completely. Next, the man started taking the bamboo poles apart.

And, surprise, surprise! Right beside the letter-box being covered by the white tent sheet, and to the rear of where the stall had stood, appeared *another* red letter-box.

There were two of them.

Needless to say, Toki could not believe his eyes.

'Am I imagining things?'

Toki rubbed his eyes and opened them again. Even though there were indeed two letter-boxes in his line of vision, the first one was now covered by the tent sheet, so it appeared simply like some part of the night stall, under the cover of a sheet.

'No, no, but I'm sure I didn't imagine it....'

But, as Toki was thinking the incident over, something even more curious happened.

The dealer had finished taking the bamboo poles apart and had placed them in the cart. He walked over to the first letter-box, with the apparent aim of collecting the sheet. But instead, the man picked up the sheet together with the letter-box inside, as if it weighed nothing. By the time Toki had realised what had happened, the man had already put the whole package on his cart and departed in the direction of the tram line, pulling his cart behind him. Toki was left behind in surprise.

'Oh no!'

Toki finally regained his senses.

Desperately, he ran noisily after the man, who seemed to have noticed his pursuer, and had started to accelerate.

'You there! Over there! Wait!'

The man started to pick up speed but, since he was dragging a heavy cart behind him, there was no way he was going to win the race. Toki finally managed to grab the back of the cart near the foot of a bridge.

'Yo-you, why are you stealing this letter-box?'

The other man said nothing but kept tugging on the cart. In his excitement, Toki clutched at the letter-box wrapped in the tent sheet.

'Ma-mail thief!'

'Shut up!'

The man finally turned around and hissed at him. At that moment, Toki slipped and fell.

The letter-box flew out of Toki's hands and landed on the road. It rolled over, making a noise like a large bucket. Finally, a policeman wielding his sabre arrived at the scene.

Toki started to feel giddy because of his fall....

Toki's Exploit

'Oh, that was a fantastic feat.'

Two or three days later, inside the barber's shop Cotton Rose, a student customer was listening to Toki's story.

'So the letter-box was made of tin plate....'

'Precisely. It was a fake made of tin, painted to look like the real thing. It had stood there in a shadowy spot next to the night stall, and because people posting letters don't touch the box at all, only the metal lid needed to be made with special care.'

'I see,' continued the customer, 'but why did that book dealer place the fake letter-box there at all?'

'That's precisely what makes this a big deal...,' replied Toki. 'The man was a complete fake. The police investigated him, and while he looked and talked exactly like a Japanese, he was actually a secret agent sent here from China a long time ago. He needed an occupation to cover his activities here, so he became a second-hand book dealer, working mostly at night. He was a pretty nasty piece of work, involved in all kinds of spying activities. As it said in the newspapers, he'd set up his night stall there, and noticed how the waitresses of Benten Street and the young men living in the boarding house of the military factory all posted their letters there. He thought it would be a great opportunity for spying, so he made use of the darkness and boldly placed a fake letter-box right next to his stall. And so he began retrieving important intelligence from the letters those people posted, who of course suspected nothing. He'd take the fake box back to his lair and open all the letters posted that night. While laughing at his own brilliance, he'd copy all the information he needed. When he was done, instead of destroying the letters, he'd return each one to its proper envelope, reseal it, and then post it in the real letter-box.'

It was vexing to think that hateful man had also read Toki's important letter. The customer nodded with wide-open eyes and observed: 'What a terrifying guy. Awful thing he did there. Makes you scared of writing letters.'

'You've said it. We need to be careful even when we're just chatting like this in the open.'

'Yes. But you were pretty amazing, seeing right through that guy's schemes. You should get a medal for distinguished service for that. I bet the authorities will reward you.'

'I really didn't do much, hahahaha.'

Toki laughed cheerfully. He left the earpick inside his customer's ear and brought his hand up to the pocket of his barber's uniform. Inside was the biggest reward Toki could ever receive.

It was O-Sumi's answer.

First published in *Kitan*, November Issue, Shōwa 14 (1939) with the title *Love's Exploit* (*Koi no Otegara*).

THE GINZA GHOST

1

Shops of different colours lined up to form a rainbow on each side of a narrow street a mere three *ken* wide, creating a bright neighbourhood in the backstreets of Ginza. There was a place there—large for those backstreets—with a blue neon sign bearing the words "Café Blue Orchid," and opposite it stood a neat little tobacco shop called Tsunekawa. It was a two-storey building, the front not even two *ken* wide. The shop was brightly lit, with beautiful, detailed decoration. For this reason, it managed to attract customers from all over the neighbourhood and make a comfortable living for the owner, as if it had found a way to capture all the jazz music emanating from the surrounding shops.

The owner of the shop was a woman well into her forties. A sign written in a woman's hand said "Fusae Tsunekawa." Rumour had it that she was the widow of a retired government official, with a daughter about to graduate from the local girls' school. She was a fair-skinned, full-bodied woman. While she did dress simply, befitting her age, she nevertheless projected an aura of youthfulness. At some point in time, a featureless young man—somewhere in his thirties—had moved in with her, but he was very reserved in his contact with the people from the neighbourhood. But this intoxicating period of happiness didn't last for long. The tobacco shop thrived, and eventually a young girl was hired as both a shop assistant and maid. It did not take long for the peaceful harmony which had existed between the couple up until then to visibly break down. Sumiko, the shop assistant, was a young girl in her twenties with a beautiful tan complexion, and a body as bouncy as a ball.

The waitresses of the Blue Orchid were the first ones to learn of the couple's fights. From the Blue Orchid's first floor box seats, one could see through the windows into the front of the first floor of the tobacco shop opposite. As the street was only three *ken* wide, they could also from time to time hear Fusae Tsunekawa's desperate cries. Occasionally, one could even see her dishevelled shadow projected on the glass windows. At such times, the waitresses of the Blue

Orchid would secretly look at each other and sigh, while entertaining their guests each at their own tables. But the disturbing atmosphere at the tobacco shop came to a head faster than anyone had expected, reaching a truly horrific conclusion. And it was the waitresses working on the first floor of the Blue Orchid at that time who became the witnesses of a baffling, inexplicable tragedy.

Even the weather seemed to have contributed, as it was a night with an uneasy feeling to it. A cool wind had starting blowing from the west early on in the evening, but had suddenly stopped around ten o'clock, causing the air to become heavy with a peculiar stuffy heat, not at all to be expected from an autumn night. One of the waitresses, who had been entertaining a guest in a corner seat at the first floor, stood up and walked over to the window, fanning her neck with a handkerchief. She opened the sliding glass window, and absentmindedly looked at the house in front of her, but she suddenly turned her face away as if she had seen something awful and returned to her seat without saying a word, giving her colleagues a sign with her eyes.

On the first floor of the tobacco shop, beyond the half-open window, the fair-coloured owner Fusae could be seen wearing a plain pattern-less, blackish kimono. Her man was not there, but the assistant Sumiko was sitting in front of her and appeared to be pleading with her about something. Sumiko in turn did not react to Fusae, but remained silent, with a sullen look on her face which she turned away from Fusae. The kimono she was wearing—with a gaudy crimson well curb pattern[i] on a black background—made her look even more beautiful. But Fusae had quickly noticed the eyes staring at them from the Blue Orchid's first floor. She turned a hostile face to the café, got up hastily and banged the window shut. Despite all the clamour of the jazz music, the noise of the window had been so loud that it was almost as if Fusae had shut the Blue Orchid's own windows.

The waitresses gasped and looked at each other. They started to send meaningful glances to each other.

Tonight's different from usual.

Sumiko is really going to get it, finally.

Tonight was indeed different from usual. Fusae was not screaming at whim, but slowly and surely applying pressure. Even if she had raised her voice, it would immediately have been drowned out in the din of the neighbourhood. At precisely eleven o'clock, schoolgirl Kimiko shut up shop, as per her mother's instructions. But there was a little hole, like a small window, open in the glass door of the counter, and late customers could buy their tobacco there. Tatsujirō—that was the name of Fusae's young man—had not shown his face at the shop that night, for some reason.

Tonight's really serious.

She's probably found proof of Tatsujirō and Sumiko's relations.

The waitresses once again whispered to each other with their eyes. But eventually all became silent, and by the time they could hear the rumbling of the train passing the Fourth Avenue crossing, the girls had already started thinking about closing time and had forgotten about the tobacco shop. They were trying to work out how to get rid of the group of three who had arrived early in the evening and were dead drunk by now. It was at that precise moment that tragedy reared its head.

First a low, muffled scream—it was difficult to tell whether it was wailing or yelling—came from the lighted room on the first floor of the tobacco shop. The windows were still closed shut like a clam.

The girls of the Blue Orchid looked at each other again in surprise. But then they heard a heavy thud from the same direction, like that of a person falling over. Surprised by this, the girls turned pale and, leaning forward over the window frame, they tried to peer into the building opposite.

They caught a glimpse of a swaying figure, but it almost immediately collided with the light, and the room instantly became pitch-black. But the swaying figure then appeared again, having staggered to the front window. With a loud crash, the figure broke the window in the middle, and its back became visible.

It was a woman, the nape of her neck pale, and dressed in a blackish, plain kimono. Her right hand was sticking out of the window, and in it she held a sharp instrument—it appeared to be a razor covered in blood. Her shoulders were heaving because of her heavy breathing—her back still leaning against the window—and she appeared to be looking back into the dark room in a dazed manner. The figure seemed instinctively to sense the eyes watching from the windows of the Blue Orchid, and as she turned around, she staggered back into the darkness. It was a ghastly bluish face, glaring and with distorted features.

The waitresses of the Blue Orchid screamed. The three remaining customers, who had also witnessed the tragedy from behind the waitresses, quickly ran down the staircase and shouted out to the women and customers who were still having a good time on the ground floor:

'Something horrible happened over there!'

'Murder!'

The men ran out in front of the café and one of them ran to the police box. The remaining two had awakened from their drunkenness and were walking up and down in the street, but then they heard a loud noise from inside the tobacco shop. They heard a violent crash as the door swung wildly open, and out stumbled the daughter Kimiko, dressed in a pink terrycloth nightdress.

When she saw all the men and women who had come out on the street and were milling up and down, she cried out to nobody in particular:

'Sumi was killed!'

It didn't take long for the police to arrive.

It was indeed Sumiko who had been killed. She was lying with her face up in the pitch-black first floor room where the light bulb had been broken, wearing the dishevelled kimono with the gaudy crimson well curb pattern the waitresses of the Blue Orchid had seen earlier. A police officer with a flashlight, who had reached the room first, could hear heavy breathing escaping from Sumiko's throat. But when he went to help her up, all she could manage was to gasp out:

'Fu-Fusae…'

After that, she went limp.

It appeared her throat had been cut, and the sharp blade had left two clear lines on her neck. There was a pool of blood around her. At the edge of that bloody pond, near the window, was a blood-covered Japanese razor which appeared to have been thrown away.

As for Fusae, she was nowhere to be found inside the house. She was not the only one missing: Tatsujirō was absent as well. Fusae's daughter Kimiko didn't go up to the first floor, but remained in front of the shop, pale and trembling.

The girls of the Blue Orchid told the police in a brief but agitated manner all they had seen. The three men also confirmed their story. With the testimony of these witnesses, as well as the dying words of the victim, the police quickly grasped the situation and started an investigation into Fusae's whereabouts.

There were two more rooms on the first floor of the tobacco shop besides the room where the murder had taken place: a room that faced the back of the building, and one in between. But Fusae was not to be found in either room. Downstairs was the shop, and two more rooms. Needless to say, Fusae wasn't to be found there either. The front had been locked at eleven o'clock and she couldn't have left the building after the police had barged inside. The police headed for the kitchen, where there was a back exit leading on to an alley—only three *shaku* wide—which went past the three neighbouring buildings and ended up in another street. At the end of this alley stood a friendly-looking *yakitori* vendor, who had his street stall there at night. The man was adamant that nobody had appeared from the alley in the last three hours. The police returned to the shop and started a rigorous search of the house. They went through every nook and cranny, from the toilet to the built-in closets, and on the first floor—inside the built-in closet of the room where the murder had taken place, they finally found Fusae.

When the police officer opened the paper sliding door of the closet, he cried out: 'This can't be!'

Fusae was already dead inside.

She was lying there, still dressed in the pattern-less blackish plain kimono the girls of the Blue Orchid had seen earlier. A towel had been twisted around her neck. Had she strangled herself, or had someone else strangled her? Her pale, colourless face was already slightly swollen, but there was no doubt that it was Fusae. Her daughter Kimiko was comforted by a police officer as she cried loudly in front of the lifeless figure of her mother.

One of the three drunken men, who had been staring intently at the corpse, said in a shrill voice: 'She's the one. She's the one who killed the woman in that gaudy kimono with the razor.'

One police officer—apparently a senior officer—stepped forward, nodded intently and said: 'That means that after Fusae murdered the girl Sumiko, she stood here in a daze, but then she noticed that you had seen her from the windows of the Blue Orchid, which brought her to her senses. It was too dangerous to go downstairs, so she staggered around and hid herself inside the closet. Eventually she became overcome by remorse and, unable to take it any more, she took her own life.... That's probably what happened.' He crouched down by the sobbing Kimiko, still dressed in her pink nightdress, and took out his pocket notebook.

The investigating magistrate and the medical examiner arrived at the crime scene soon afterwards and the investigation started in earnest. It wasn't long before a truly baffling, horrific truth was revealed through the autopsy of Fusae's body.

Fusae had murdered Sumiko, so naturally, Fusae should have died after, and not before Sumiko. But despite that apparently self-evident truth, it was Sumiko's body which was still warm and showing some signs of life, while the appearance of after-death signs had already progressed quite a lot on Fusae's body. Based on a scientific and coolheaded observation of all the signs, such as cooling, stiffness and death spots, the medical examiner determined that at least one hour had passed since Fusae's death.

'But that's crazy...,' said the police officer, who was completely overwhelmed by this fact. 'That means...no, that's impossible. It's been twenty minutes since Sumiko was killed, but you say it's been an hour since Fusae died, so that means that forty minutes before Sumiko was killed, the murderer had already died, before her victim.... In other words, the Fusae Sumiko mentioned with her dying words, the Fusae wielding a razor seen by a number of witnesses, that was not the real Fusae, but a Fusae who was dead already.... Unbelievable. That means it was Fusae's ghost. A murder committed by a ghost.... A ghost appearing right here in Ginza, in the middle of the jazz neighbourhood. The newspapers will have a field day....'

2

The case had been thrown into confusion. The police officers felt as if they had run into a brick wall. The problem had been split into two. They had two victims. One of them was killed by a ghost. The other had first died and then turned into a ghost and committed a murder. What a strange story.

However, they couldn't allow the setback to impede their investigation. They quickly regained their spirit and were determined to move on. For the time being they set aside the problem of Sumiko, who had apparently been killed last, and started investigating the death of Fusae.

Had Fusae committed suicide? Or had she been murdered?

The medical examiner's answer to the problem was that, unlike death by drowning, it was very difficult to strangle oneself with a towel, and he was therefore of the opinion it was murder. The investigating magistrate and the police officer in charge both agreed broadly with that opinion. Investigation headquarters was set up in the shop downstairs and the formal questioning of the witnesses began.

Kimiko, the daughter, was the first to be called. Having lost her mother, the girl was naturally extremely upset and made her statement between sobs.

That night, mother Fusae had ordered her daughter to watch the shop, and taken Sumiko up to the first floor. That was around ten o'clock. Kimiko had noticed that her mother was in a very bad mood, but that was not a rare thing, so she thought nothing special of it and she watched the shop while reading some magazines. Because she goes to school, she has to get up early every morning, so she was quite sleepy at eleven and, as always, she closed up the shop, went to her room—at the back of the first floor—and went to sleep. She had not heard any voices from the front room when she came up the staircase. However, Kimiko said that she did not consider that suspicious; it was rather the cause for some strangely embarrassed feeling. She had fallen asleep but had been wakened by a scream and the noise of someone falling coming from the room at the front. She had remained in her bed for a while, thinking about what to do, but eventually she could bear it no more and slid out of bed. She went to the room at the front, but the light was out. With fear in her heart, she switched the light on in the middle room, and opened the sliding door to get a look inside the room in front. There, she saw Sumiko lying in the middle of the room. She then ran down the stairs, opened the front door and cried for help. That was the extent of her testimony.

'When you looked inside the front room, did you see your mother standing near the window?'

Kimiko shook her head at the police officer's question.

'No, she wasn't there at that time.'

'Didn't you think it was odd your mother wasn't anywhere around when you hurried downstairs in shock?'

'...Mum sometimes goes out late at night drinking with an uncle, so I thought she was gone....'

'Uncle? Your uncle, eh? Who might that be?'

The police officer had seized on her words. Kimiko hesitantly explained that she meant Tatsujirō. Nervously, she added: '...Uncle Tatsujirō went out before Mum did, while I was still watching the shop. But the back door is left open, so he might have returned later. I was asleep, so I can't say.'

'Where did he go for a drink?'

'I don't know.'

The police officer immediately sent out a subordinate with the order to look for Tatsujirō. It then became the turn of the waitresses of the Blue Orchid and the three men to be questioned. The witnesses repeated the story they had told the police earlier. They weren't able to offer any new information besides that. However, their statements did correspond with that of Kimiko, particularly in regard to Tatsujirō.

After the questioning was over, the conclusions about the estimated time of Fusae's death became available. It had happened between the time that the waitresses of the Blue Orchid had seen Fusae sitting opposite Sumiko and then slamming the window, and eleven o'clock. That meant that if Kimiko's testimony was correct, Tatsujirō hadn't been present in the building then. But couldn't he have easily sneaked inside through the back entrance while Kimiko was watching the front, gone up to the first floor, killed Fusae and then fled again? In any case, it was imperative to investigate this Tatsujirō.

Shortly thereafter, however, Tatsujirō came strolling back home on his own, without the company of a police officer. He looked as though he had no idea what had happened, and answered the police's questions haltingly.

According to Tatsujirō, he had been drinking at an *oden*[ii] stall called Takohachi in Shimbashi from ten o'clock until just now, and had only just learned of the murder. The proprietor of Takohachi was sent for, and as soon as he saw Tatsujirō, he said: 'Yes, this customer was with me from ten until just now. My wife and the other customers will also confirm this....'

Disappointed, the officer in charge indicated the exit with his chin.

Tatsujirō had been provided with an alibi. At that, the investigation began to feel desperate. Kimiko had been on watch at the front, and the *yakitori* vendor was adamant that nobody had left by the back alley. The windows on the first floor had been under observation from the Blue Orchid's first floor and the window in Kimiko's room at the back of the first floor had been locked from the inside. Even if that window had not been locked, you could only walk out into the two *tsubo* wide space to dry clothes located on top of the kitchen roof, which was closely surrounded by barbed wire. To make absolutely sure, they also checked the three houses facing the alley that connected the back of the house to the street where the *yakitori* stand was, but the back doors of all three houses had been locked since the evening, and there didn't seem to be anything suspicious about them. That meant that at the time Fusae was murdered, the only people inside that tobacco shop, which had basically turned into a locked room, were Sumiko, who was later murdered herself, and Kimiko, who had been watching the shop.

At this point, all the police could do was suspect these two persons. Kimiko was the first to be put under the spotlight. But here it appeared the scope of the investigation had become too limited. Their initial approach had been to find the murderer of Fusae, but this line of investigation overlapped with the mysterious murder of Sumiko, and the result was bewildering. It might be too farfetched, but suppose Kimiko had first killed her mother Fusae? In that case, Fusae could not have killed Sumiko later. Now suppose it was Sumiko who had killed Fusae. But this would lead to the odd conclusion that a dead Fusae could later kill Sumiko. In the end, the conundrum always came back to the mysterious murder of Sumiko. The officers in charge had no choice left but to tackle the ghostly murder case head on. Everyone tried their best to think the problem through.

First of all, at the time Sumiko was murdered, the only persons present in the tobacco shop—which was basically a locked room on its own—were Fusae, who had been killed before Sumiko, and Kimiko, who said she was sleeping in her room at the back of the first floor. The police officers of course could not simply go believe in the existence of ghosts. The witnesses who saw Fusae kill Sumiko from the windows of the Blue Orchid only caught a glimpse of her. Nobody had clearly seen Fusae's face, and the testimonies only agreed on the fact the murderer was wearing a blackish pattern-less kimono. What if it had not been Fusae who had murdered Sumiko, but Kimiko—wearing her mother Fusae's kimono—who had killed Sumiko and later changed into her pink nightdress?

But this idea was quickly shot down. It had only been about three minutes between the time when the figure who resembled Fusae had staggered away from the window at the crime scene after the murder, and when the group from the Blue Orchid had come out on the street and run into Kimiko, who was wearing her night dress. It would have been impossible for Kimiko to take off her mother's kimono and put it on her mother again in that short amount of time.

Well then, what if she had not been wearing her mother's kimono, but had fooled everyone by wearing a similarly blackish kimono, which would have appeared to be a plain kimono seen from three, four *ken* away? That seemed plausible, so the police officers started a rigorous house search of the tobacco shop. It did not take long for them to find two or three of Fusae's kimonos that seemed to fit the description from her chest of drawers. But these kimonos had all been prepared with moth repellent and been neatly wrapped in kimono wrapping paper. One could not do this in a mere three or four minutes. No, even if Kimiko had been the murderer, it would not explain why Sumiko had uttered Fusae's name as she was dying. No matter how they thought about it, it was impossible for Kimiko to be Sumiko's murderer.

The police finally gave up on the investigation for the night.

The following day, the newspapers all had big headlines on the appearance of the ghost. The irritated police started repeating the things they had done yesterday. The only new discoveries were that after they had sent the murder weapon—the razor—to forensics, they got confirmation that no clear fingerprints had been left on the grip because it was too narrow, and that after further questioning of Tatsujirō, they found out that he and Sumiko had become intimate at some point in time, and there had been quarrels about that in the house.

And as the police were wandering aimlessly about in this thick fog of mystery, a call came in from an amateur detective, asking to speak to the police officer in charge. It was the bartender of the Blue Orchid, a young man called Nishimura.

'...Hello, am I speaking to the chief inspector? This is the bartender of the Blue Orchid speaking. I know who the ghost is. I know the true identity of the ghost who killed Sumiko. Could you come over here tonight? Yes, I will explain everything then. You'll see a ghost....'

3

By the time the chief inspector arrived at the Blue Orchid together with one of his subordinates, it was already growing dark outside. The side street was lively and overflowing with jazz music, as if the events of the previous night had already been forgotten, except for a few curiosity seekers gathered in front of the tobacco shop. It was quite busy both up and downstairs at the Blue Orchid, and everyone was sharing stories about the ghost of the tobacco shop.

Bartender Nishimura, dressed in a white jacket and wearing a bow tie, warmly welcomed the police officers, led them up to the first floor to a seat near the front windows and had a waitress bring them a drink. The chief inspector, however, appeared irritated from the beginning. He hardly said anything, but watched the suspicious bartender's actions closely.

The room on the first floor of the tobacco shop was right across the street from them. The bodies had already been removed from the room for autopsies. Through the windows, fitted with sliding doors, they could see the electric light was switched on, as it usually was.

The bartender finally started to speak. 'You see, I thought that rather than clumsily explaining it to you over the phone, you'd understand better if I showed it to you in person.'

'What are you planning to show us?' The chief inspector asked suspiciously.

'Well, the ghost, actually.'

The chief inspector interrupted him. 'So you mean to say you know who killed Sumiko?'

'Yes, more or less....'

'Who is it? Did you perhaps witness the crime scene?'

'No, I didn't see it. But seeing as Fusae was already dead at the time, there were only two persons left....'

'So you believe the murderer's Kimiko?' The inspector laughed at him.

'No, not at all.' The bartender shook his head fervently. 'You already ruled her out as a suspect, didn't you?'

'Well, then, we're all out of suspects.' The inspector leant back, as if he had given up on the whole problem.

'But you do have one,' said young Nishimura with a smile. 'You still have Sumiko.'

'What, Sumiko?'

'Yes. It was Sumiko who killed Sumiko.'

'You mean it was suicide?'

'Precisely.' A serious expression appeared on Nishimura's face. 'Everyone has been under a ridiculous misapprehension right from the beginning. If Sumiko had been discovered after she'd died, the misunderstanding probably wouldn't have occurred. But she was seen squirming around in agony after she'd cut her own throat and was writhing in her final moments. That is why everyone mistook her suicide scene to be a murder scene. I believe it was Sumiko who killed Fusae. Last night, Fusae's scolding led to a quarrel between the rivals in love, and eventually, Sumiko strangled Fusae. When Sumiko came to her senses, she realised what a horrible crime she'd committed, one she could never get away with, and the first thing she did was to hide Fusae's body inside the closet. She probably did that because she knew it was dangerous to leave her out there, because Kimiko would come up at eleven. And after grappling with her conscience over what she'd done, she finally committed suicide. So what happened was the exact opposite of what you thought when you discovered Fusae's body. Sumiko's dying words—Fusae's name—were not uttered to accuse the person who'd killed her. She called out the name of the person she'd killed, out of remorse. Anyway, that's just how I see it.'

'Don't joke around!' bellowed the inspector. 'Do you mean to say that the woman all the waitresses here saw, the woman who was leaning against the window wearing a plain kimono and holding a razor was not Fusae, but Sumiko? Impossible. You're the one who is under a misapprehension here. Listen to me. Most importantly, you should consider the kimono. Fusae was wearing her plain kimono, and Sumiko was wearing that gaudy kimono....'

'Wait a minute.' This time it was the bartender who interrupted. 'That's exactly the point I want to make. You see, that ghost appeared because... Oh, I think preparations are completed now, so now I'll have you witness the appearance of your ghost.'

He continued as he got up: '...You still don't see who it was? The true identity of the ghost who appeared right in the middle of Ginza? I'd think that anyone would realise it if they reflected closely on what actually happened during the incident, and the position of that building....'

Having said that, a cocky smile appeared on the bartender's face and he went downstairs, leaving the perplexed police officers behind. But he soon returned with a large National bicycle lamp, and said to the chief inspector as he walked over to the windows: 'The ghost will now appear before you, so please stand here.'

The inspector grimaced, but walked over to the windows as instructed. The waitresses and customers, who had all been watching them discreetly from a distance, now stumbled over each other as they made their way to the windows. Nishimura said: 'Look at the window opposite.'

The electric light was still shining in serene silence in the first floor window of the tobacco shop only three *ken* away, but then they caught the glimpse of a figure inside the room, and a shadow was cast on the windows.

Expecting something unusual to happen, the people in the Blue Orchid all leaned forward and stared at the window. The shadow on the window swayed and stuck a hand out. Suddenly the light went off.

'Listen carefully. At the time of the incident, the person behind that shadow staggered around and hit the light and the room became dark, just as it has now.'

The bartender had barely finished speaking when the window opposite was opened noisily from the inside, and out of the darkness emerged the back of a woman wearing a blackish, plain kimono, pale in the nape of her neck, precisely like the figure the people had seen last night. But then the bartender aimed the light of the National lamp he was holding at the woman's back. The figure of an older woman wearing a blackish, plain kimono promptly changed into the figure of a young girl wearing a kimono with a gaudy, crimson well curb pattern on a black background.

'Kimiko, thanks,' yelled the bartender to the figure opposite. The woman in the window turned silently around and smiled sadly at him. It was Kimiko.

'Now you've all seen it. I had to borrow Kimiko and that kimono for the experiment,' said the bartender as he smiled mischievously at the chief inspector, who still remained baffled.

Nishimura continued. 'You still don't understand what's happened? All right, let me explain. Think of it like this. Suppose you have something written in red ink. If you looked at the text through normal, plain glass, it will be red, precisely as if you looked at it without the glass, correct? But suppose you look at something written in red ink through a red glass. You won't see any writing. Just as when you develop a photograph. That's a hobby of mine, by the way. Sometimes when I'm developing a film beneath a red light I get confused when my package of printing paper wrapped in red paper disappears, even though I'm sure I placed it right next to me. I fumble around and suddenly my hands feel something, even though my eyes can't see it. This is the same phenomenon. But if you use blue glass instead of red glass to look at the writing, it will appear to be black.'

'Aha,' said the chief inspector, 'I think I get what you're saying. But still….'

'It's really just a minor point,' said bartender Nishimura. He smiled at the chief inspector, and then continued with his explanation. 'And now we replace the writing made in red ink with a kimono with a gaudy crimson, well curb pattern. In normal light, we'd all see a crimson-coloured well curb pattern, right? However, just as in the example of the red ink just now, when you shine blue light on that same kimono, the crimson well curb pattern turns into a dark, blackish well curb pattern. And, if the fabric beneath is black too, then you'd have black on black, and the pattern wouldn't be visible any more. It'd only appear to be a black, plain kimono.'

'But the light in that room was off at the time.'

'Yes, you're right. It's only because the normal light of that room was off that the phenomenon occurred.'

'Was there a blue light on, then?'

'Eh? There's a blue light on all the time. If the blue light had only been switched on at that very moment, everyone would've noticed, of course. But that's not what happened. It was only when the normal light inside the room disappeared, that the blue light, which had been on all the time, started to have a clear effect. That's why nobody standing here at the window noticed anything.'

'But where is that blue light then?'

'Come on, think about it!'

The chief inspector thought for a moment and then rushed to the window, without listening to the rest of what the bartender had to say. He grabbed the frame, swung his legs over it and leant outside, almost enough to fall down. As he looked up, he cried out: 'Of course, that's it!'

Above the windows of the Blue Orchid, a large neon sign with the words "Café Blue Orchid" was shining brightly.

'It's quite impressive, noticing a thing like that,' said the policeman to the bartender afterwards, as he bought him a beer. The young man appeared to be embarrassed by the praise and smiled.

'Not at all. You see, I'm always witnessing a smaller variant of the ghostly phenomenon every day.' He indicated the waitresses with his chin. 'The girls here may be wearing the same kimono both day and night, but they appear like different people at different times. You might call them a kind of Ginza ghost too....'

First published in *Shinseinen*, October Issue, Shōwa 11 (1936).

---

[i] An *igeta*, or "well curb" pattern is a common pattern used for kimonos. It resembles a cluster of number symbols (#).

[ii] *Oden* is a popular traditional winter dish consisting of various ingredients like eggs, daikon and fishcakes stewed in a soy-flavoured *dashi* broth. It is a popular street stall food.

CPSIA information can be obtained
at www.ICGtesting.com
Printed in the USA
LVOW03s2218100817
544523LV00012B/954/P

9 781543 057423